SUNBEAM

AND THE CURSE OF THE

G✦LDEN

KEY

OUIDA D.W.

info@barringerpublishing.com
Copyright © Ouida D.W.
All rights reserved.

Barringer Publishing, Naples, Florida
www.barringerpublishing.com

Cover Art by Sara Tarr
Interior Sketch Illustrations by Frances O. O'Neal

ISBN: 978-0-9989069-7-3

Library of Congress Cataloging-in-Publication Data

Printed in U.S.A.

Sunbeam and the Curse of the Golden Key/Ouida D.W.

Dedication

Dedicated to the memory of Aunt Teresa Fisher—
a real legend. The seeds you planted in my life
continue to bear fruit.

Acknowledgements

I would like to thank a few special people who stood by me during the development of the book: Kyle Dahl for reading the very first draft; you always encouraged my vision. My insightful editors, for pushing me to do better when I didn't feel like it and for being amazing coaches.

Amy O'Neal, my closest friend, for your friendship and support; you always understood. Jenny Thompson for your willingness to stop, listen, and add valuable feedback. And certainly, my mother, for always being there.

PROLOGUE

In the deep Depths of Cypress, the place where light and dark meet, where good and evil kiss, I saw it for the first time: THE GOLDEN KEY. It was at that moment Sunbeam's life would change forever.

You might be wondering what Golden Key I'm talking about. Well, let me warn you of its dangers. Because if you *do* happen to find it, you must know there are rewards, but there are also consequences. *Serious* consequences. And right at this moment, it's missing. But it won't be lost for long because the Golden Key was made to be found. And believe me, it *will* be found. It is only a matter of time. You could find it immediately after closing this book; trust me, it's happened before.

Or, you may have already spotted it, held it between your fingers, but didn't recognize its power. You know how that is, someone comes across a random key and says:

"Hey! Do you know what this key is for?"

"I have no idea," the other replies.

Then it gets tossed. Cast aside. Unrecognized. Thrown away.

But if you are one of the special ones who does find it, and recognizes it, well, that is when things change.

If you do find the Golden Key, and I could give you only one tip to survive its power, it would be this:

> *Do not get stuck in the initial intrigue of its entertaining powers of pleasure or pain, but seek and break into the mysteries beyond it, because it is there, you will unlock the truth.*

Your four-legged servant,

Whitewing

Table of Contents

CHAPTER 1

THE DEPTHS OF CYPRESS

"Whitewing! Here, Boy! Here!"

My mistress, Sunbeam, would shout for me routinely at three o' clock from The School of Thornridge. I always stood in the pasture on school grounds or outside the classroom window in case she needed me. So, I saw almost everything that went on during Sunbeam's school days. She was thirteen, my best friend, and I was her best horse.

Her blonde hair stood out against the other students at Thornridge. All of the other kids in the school had either dark hair and brown skin, or fire colored hair and bronzed faces, because most people on the island carried the gene of the dark Vikings. So it was very rare to see a golden-haired girl. Her olive-green eyes were deep and piercing, and light freckles dusted her rosy cheeks. Although small, she was the fastest runner in school. She moved swiftly. Her gait was light, agile, and she was fleet of foot.

My mistress clashed with school like fire against water. Every day, she could not wait to bolt from the children who taunted and teased her unmercifully. "Yellow hair speckle face! You can't sit with us," snickered a group of kids every day at lunch when

Sunbeam walked by their table. She did not fit in the new school. The kids were horrid as snakes and made it known she was not welcome there.

This was Sunbeam's third school in two years. She and her mother lived on the Island of Ozmandia, a cavernous, rocky island in the middle of the sea. Though school was tough, home was tense, too. Her mother was kind, but over-worried.

"I put your lunch in Whitewing's saddle bag," her mother would say before school.

"Thanks, Mother."

"Wait, Sunbeam?"

"Yes?"

"You come straight home after school. Straight home."

"Yes, Mother. But it won't happen to me. Don't worry."

"You don't know that Sunbeam. You're all I have left. First your father—then Gilda," her mother said. A tear trickled down her cheek as she stared out the windowpane.

"Don't talk about Gilda. Not now," Sunbeam said. Her heart winced.

"I'm sorry. I know how much you loved Gilda. We both did." Her mother's eyes looked defeated.

"Goodbye, Mother," said Sunbeam, trying to escape out the door.

"Wait, Sunbeam. Your father, you must not be angry with him."

"I never knew the man," Sunbeam snapped. "And maybe Gilda would still be here if he never left. He could have protected her."

"Don't say that. Your father had to leave. He had no choice."

"Why? Tell me one good reason," Sunbeam said.

"The darkness," said her mother, staring blankly at the sky. "You're too young to understand. You better get to school now." Her mother shrugged it off and started busying herself in the kitchen.

Sunbeam dismissed it and walked out the front door with the same unanswered questions. She never understood.

The only thing we did know of her father was that he bought me when I was a young foal. It was said that I came from a long line of warhorses, but I was rejected as too small and timid—so they ripped me away from my family and sold me for cheap. The only skill I had, which warhorses have, is the ability to know what their masters are thinking and feeling, so we could know what our masters needed and what the enemy might do. Warhorses have a much keener instinct than humans have with all their five senses put together. This is called the *second sight*. And because of that skill, I could see and retell stories accurately, as I am doing right now. But since I didn't have the strength or size of the other warhorse foals, the overseers sold me. So, Sunbeam's father bought me to take home for his daughters to ride. And that is all we knew of him.

Once at school, Sunbeam would sit in class and stare out the window, pondering over what her mother called "darkness." She thought about her life, recalling the years. Before every move, her mother would hurriedly jam their clothes into boxes. The memories were all the same:

"Again? Moving—again?" Sunbeam would complain. "But I finally met a friend here!"

"We have to. We have no other choice," her mother would always reply, with fear cloaked behind her tired eyes. "Leaving is the best thing for us to do; leave the darkness behind."

"Darkness? What darkness?" Sunbeam would question and prod. "Maybe Gilda will find us here."

"Listen—we must go—"

Her mother never answered her questions. She'd only reassure her it was best.

"Here, I brought your favorite candy today." Her mother would bring her favorite candy, rainbow snaps, on moving days. Then she'd say, "Things will be better after the move."

"Yeah, but what about the move after that? And the one after that? Will it then?"

"Let's hope," her mother would say.

Sunbeam never understood what her mother was hoping for. She was hoping in something, but Sunbeam just didn't know what. Hope was something the people of Ozmandia had not known in hundreds of years.

❧ ❧

Snapping back to reality. Here she was again: the NEW girl. The outsider.

Only a month into this wretched place, and she already hated it. The only one who spoke to her at school was Harmon, the awkward boy who sat beside her in music class. He wore big, round glasses and was very clumsy, always dropping his books and tripping over things.

"I heard you turned in a stolen paper to Professor Plume," said Harmon. He sat down in the seat next to her.

"Well you heard wrong," said Sunbeam. She rolled her eyes.

"Helga was telling everyone in English class it was hers. She called you a thief."

"Helga lies. You should know that by now," said Sunbeam.

"I kind of figured it. I see her and her friends giving you a hard time," he said. "Let's face it, you're different."

"What's that supposed to mean?" Sunbeam snapped.

Suddenly, Mr. Bard, the music teacher, began roll call. "Next!" he said. "Harmon, it's your turn."

When Mr. Bard called him to play his assigned song in front of the class, Harmon stood tall and took off his large, round glasses. He opened his case and took out his flute. Then he raised his slouched shoulders and lifted his chin confidently to face the class. Harmon stepped on the stage and started playing his song. As he played, his fingers slid over his flute, hitting every note perfectly. When he played, it was like Harmon transformed into another person. After a little while, the song was over, and his glasses went back over his nose, and his shoulders sank back into his clumsy posture. Then he bowed before the class in all his awkwardness.

"Very nice, Harmon," said Mr. Bard, applauding with the rest of the class. Harmon stumbled and bumbled back to his seat.

"How'd you like the bridge melody?" he asked Sunbeam. "I—I added that part myself."

"It was OK I guess," she said.

Although he pestered and annoyed her, she had to admit that he was brilliant with his music.

In the next moment, Fawn plopped down next to them. Fawn usually sat with Sunbeam at lunch. She had olive skin, dark curly hair and innocent, chestnut eyes who loved animals way too much.

"Next!" called Mr. Bard. As the next student made his way to the stage, Harmon looked at Fawn.

"Did you practice your song?" Harmon whispered. "Our songs are due today."

"No. I was too busy nursing this little one back to health last night," said Fawn. She pulled a ferret out of her bookbag. She was always sneaking one of her pets to school.

"You should put that away," warned Sunbeam. "Remember what happened last time you brought one to math class." Suddenly, Sunbeam looked down and saw Fawn's bag jostling on the ground. "How many animals do you have in there?" Sunbeam asked.

"Just a few more," said Fawn. She giggled as she opened the bag to show Sunbeam and Harmon more ferrets. As soon as she opened it, one of them squealed and leapt out of the bag, and the other ferrets followed.

"Ahhh! Something scratched me!" shouted one of the girls in the front row.

"Look! Ferrets!" laughed one of the boys next to her.

Thereafter, students began screaming and standing on desks as the ferrets ran all over the floor and on Mr. Bard's violins. Then one ran up a boy's pantleg—and another one scurried to the stage and bit the boy playing his brass tuba, which knocked his melody into a harsh screeching note, completely out of tune.

"Nonsense! Get this nonsense out of my studio!" Mr. Bard screamed.

"Yes sir," said Fawn, trying to round up the furry scoundrels into her bookbag.

"To the office! GO! GO!" Mr. Bard ordered.

After a moment, she finally had them zipped back in her bookbag. On her way out the door, whispers and murmurs were heard from the students: "Loner" and "Creepy" and "Weirdo." But no one would ever say that to Fawn's face because the students were a little afraid of her and her toothy animals. So, they kept their distance.

❧ ❦

At the end of the day, the school bell gonged and echoed into the misty air, which was my cue to pick up my mistress from the front of the steps. Dashing out of Thornridge, Sunbeam leapt on my back. And as I set off to sprint, Helga Hammerstone, leader of the KWG (Kid Wolf Gang) pelted me with a rock—right in my hind-leg! Helga, better known as "Gingerface" was daughter to the wealthiest parents on this side of the island. Whatever Helga wanted, Helga got. Even the teachers avoided Helga's wrath. The instructors would always cave under her demands, doing anything to avoid dealing with the vengeful *Mrs.* Hammerstone, Helga's mother, who paraded in and out like she owned the entire school. Because everyone knew if you messed with Helga, you messed with her haughty-eyed mother.

"Playing with your best friend today? Your *only* friend? Some stupid, lame horse!" shouted Helga from the steps of the dark brick school. If I hadn't been a noble horse, I'd kick her like a horse kicks. But horses are to keep self-control if they want to avoid permanent fencing. So I stood there like an obedient steed, silent and docile, but with more wits than most humans. Besides,

I had to keep it together. Sunbeam wielded a temper that was hot enough for the both of us.

"I'm going to punch Gingerface right in the nose. First, she lies that I stole her paper. Now this?" muttered Sunbeam in my ear. She clenched my reins.

Oh no, not again, I thought. *Let's go Sunbeam, let's go now before it happens again. Let's go now* . . . went the meditative mantra inside my head. I desperately tried to keep my well-born composure. After all, even when everyone said I didn't look like a warhorse, I still tried to act like one: a steed of royal blood. So I stood there—a loyal soldier to my mistress.

Helga's hefty legs ran steadily toward me, pelting me with one rock after another until she abruptly stopped, skidding a cloud of dust on my saddle. With her rust-colored eyes glaring straight into Sunbeam's like sharp arrows, she picked up a pile of dirt and slung it all over Sunbeam's only school uniform. Helga stopped, stood as still as a statue, and anticipated an explosion of anger from her victim. But Sunbeam didn't budge. After a silent moment, Helga kept it up:

"Stupid, lame horse for a lame girl. Look at your ugly, dirty clothes!" Then she raised one eyebrow and kicked my same hind leg she'd been bruising with rocks. Gingerface wanted nothing more than a direct challenge—a fight with Sunbeam in front of the whole school. She wanted to show the "new girl" who was boss at Thornridge.

A small crowd of kids had stopped to stare with wide eyes. They stood in front of the stone steps and snickered, for fear if they did not, they might be next on Helga's hit list. And yes, despite the fact I'd like to see Gingerface get the good whupping she deserved, I wished more that Sunbeam would turn the other way and control her temper. Another school suspension would look bad. Only a month here, Sunbeam wanted to avoid trouble. This was a new school—a new start. But somehow, she was already getting labeled a "trouble maker" among the teachers.

However, Sunbeam's fists were tightened, and all I could do was hope she would not unleash her fiery temper on Gingerface. Unfortunately, I could see she was not backing down.

"And what kind of a name is Sunbeam? You're a joke! SUN-BEAM! With your smelly, yellow hair!" Helga boasted, sputtering out particles of food from her mouth as her jiggly belly shook with laughter.

Then suddenly, like a flash of lightning, Sunbeam jumped off my saddle and—THWAP! In one second, Gingerface was laid down in the dirt, trying to shake off the blow Sunbeam had just delivered to her face. It was then the whole world and all things in it stopped moving. Everything stood still. There was nothing—except silence. All one heard was the wind, billowing through the grey, misty island.

"Don't you ever touch me, Gingerface! And don't ever—EVER—touch my horse! You've been warned," said Sunbeam. She lorded over Gingerface with one foot pinned on her chest. And as soon as Sunbeam said that, she realized what she had done. And she regretted it. She knew she had just made a big, *big* mistake hitting Helga.

Suddenly, the silence was broken with Helga's whiney, deep breathing from the dirt as she tried to rise, wiping dust from her face. Filled with regret and fear, Sunbeam turned and left Helga flat on the ground, and mounted my saddle. But just as she stepped in the stirrup, Gingerface raised her torso from the dirt. With two hands, she latched onto Sunbeam's ankle like a bear, and jerked her to the ground. THUD! Sunbeam landed on her side, and for a moment, thought she'd cracked a rib.

"You're not going anywhere! Ugly Sunbeam!" blubbered Helga. Her forehead was scrunched and creased while she hammered down her infamous death grip on Sunbeam's ribcage.

With pain searing through Sunbeam's ribs, she feared Helga might do her in for good. Gingerface had her locked in the infamous Hammerstone death grip! The grip everyone in the school feared. And once Helga locked someone in her death grip, no one escaped. It was like trying to pry an enraged, wild bear off its prey. However, Sunbeam squirmed and jostled, trying to unpin herself from Helga's deadly lock.

"Turn me loose, Gingerface!" panted Sunbeam. She was losing more and more breath. She knew for sure she was about to faint. Then all at once, a foreign, mysterious force, like lightning, bolted through Sunbeam's body. With her other free leg, she whirled over Helga, and they rolled in a fog of dust.

Sunbeam, now over Helga, knew for sure she could take her. A strong, supernatural force traveled down Sunbeam's arms, and Helga squirmed at Sunbeam's mercy. But Sunbeam didn't strike. She feared another school expulsion. And while Helga lay underneath her, squirming, she thought of her mother, and the moving boxes, and the stone-faced teachers scorning her like many times before. And her shoulders sank inward.

"Let me go, Sunbeam," Helga pleaded quietly, so the crowd wouldn't hear her beg.

And when the cloud of flailing arms and kicking legs cleared, Sunbeam gave way. Helga, an opportunist, saw Sunbeam's eyes soften and felt her grip weaken. And seizing the moment, pinned her; then stammered and roared from the ground like a bear and stood over Sunbeam, who now lay flat on her back, sputtering dirt from her mouth in a cloud of humiliation.

"IT'S OVER, SMELLY SUNBEAM!" roared Helga.

Sunbeam lay in the dirt, defeated.

The whole school stared, awestruck. In all of school history, no one had *ever* fought Helga Hammerstone. Much less muster up the courage to back-talk her. But now, what would happen to Sunbeam's already tainted reputation? Even more, how would Mrs. Hammerstone inflict her wrath on the one who had put a hand on her precious, little girl?

But Sunbeam did not care to worry herself with any more questions that day. Slowly, with everyone looking, she staggered sorely toward me. Her lips quivered. I could tell she held back tears. But she would never let the whole school see her cry.

She climbed my stirrups, jerked my reins, and off we sped into the open plain. As we stormed off into the rocky grey mist—my animal instinct, which all wise horses should trust—drew my keen eye back to notice Professor Plume, staring intently from the window of his dark, shadowed loft on the third story of Thornridge—leaving only his black cloak silhouetted behind the curtain, which he'd slowly drawn to a close.

Professor Plume was a peculiar man: tall, with wavy, long hair as black as a crow. He had a sharp, pointy nose and beady little eyes that were small, but penetrating. Although everyone knew he was the best teacher at Thornridge, they also knew he was definitely the strangest. Every day, he would leave his dark loft only to teach class. If he wasn't teaching, he was locked behind his dark iron doors—the doors no one had entered. Ever.

He did not socialize like the other instructors did in the dining hall or stop to chat with students. Instead, after the last class, he would briskly step with determination to his cave, with his long, black coattail trailing behind him while he ascended the stairs like a fading ghost. But this ghost, I noticed, had his eye upon Sunbeam. For the entire month she'd been at Thornridge, he'd stop to study her through the window after school. My instinctive eye had not missed his haunting silhouette.

After a long run from the chaos and crowd of stunned kids we left behind at Thornridge, I wanted to go home. There'd been enough excitement for the day. But Sunbeam, she wanted to hide again: hide from the world, from her mother and the moving boxes that still needed unpacking. Sunbeam yearned to explore the Dark Depths of Cypress. Now, the Depths of Cypress was *not* just any place. It was off limits.

She'd been exploring the dark depths for more than a week since she'd heard some of the kids at school talking about it at lunch. When the kids said "no one ever returned" she felt a pit in her stomach and she thought of Gilda—her twin, her other half—whom hadn't returned in five years. And after lunch that day, she asked Harmon about it.

"Stay away from there, Sunbeam," said Harmon. "It's true. A couple of fourteen-year-olds went too deep in there a couple years ago and haven't been seen since."

For some reason, this sparked strange curiosities in Sunbeam, and she felt drawn to explore it.

Not one person in all of Ozmandia dared enter the misty-mazed forest in hundreds of years, because it was well known among the people of the island, that the few who did enter, never came back out. This superstition about the Depths of Cypress had been passed down from grandfather to grandfather, and to the sons and daughters of Ozmandia for centuries. But Sunbeam, well, she just laughed, chalked it up to silly myths and legends.

"Let's go, Boy!" Sunbeam smiled. "We both know about those tall tales, don't we, *Whitewing*?" She winked.

See, before being ripped from my family as a small foal, the stablemen named me Whitewing, after the tale of the flying warhorses. It was said that long ago some of the ancient warhorses grew shimmering wingspans and were spotted flying across the sky in battle. But they didn't fly for earthly battles to appease old kings' greed for more countries, but for more serious battles in the high places, ordained by the gods—who our breed called—the god of the four-legged warriors. It was said some never believed the tale, but other soldiers of old swore to the very end by what they saw, never denying the miracle of the flying warhorses. Some of the kids made fun of my name, poking at Sunbeam, "Whitewing? Where are his wings? Stupid name," they'd mock. But I was stuck with *Whitewing*. Sunbeam liked it. Yes, and so this tale was passed down and became a legend among the stablemen and warhorses, but was just a tale nonetheless.

"Best name on the island, Whitewing. The Tale of the Flying Warhorses," Sunbeam snickered. "Silly myths."

And she led me onto the secret path between the dark thickets of brambles.

"I don't see what's so bad in here," echoed Sunbeam's voice against the dripping caves. "Listen, Whitewing, my mother always told me, 'Never be afraid to see what you see.'" She steered us deeper into the forbidden darkness.

My hooves continued over the damp soil and crags. We walked in silence on a path where dead, brown vines hung in a row. Sunbeam liked the peace and quiet. The grey solitude enveloped and isolated her from all the voices and people of the island. She'd go there to think. There was not much to see: the trees were bare. Brown, jagged branches canopied over a wilderness of rock and muddy terrain. The wind whistled through the caves like it sung an ancient, haunting song. A little unnerved, I shifted my head slightly to see Sunbeam in the saddle. Surrounded in darkness, Sunbeam's golden hair shined brilliantly against the dead forest, and when she rode among the smoky dregs, it was as if she carried a mysterious light of life to it.

"If Gilda were here, she'd explore the depths with us. I miss her, Whitewing. I'm going to find her and bring her back," she said, tugging at the sore rib she just bruised. She hopped down from the saddle and sat on a stump.

If horses could talk to humans, I'd have told her to let Gilda go. Now, don't get me wrong, I'm not a cynical horse. I adored Gilda just as much as Sunbeam, and I grieved deeply over her. But five years ago, after she went missing, my sadness seeped over me like a grave sin, so much so that I didn't want to leave my stall. I didn't want to wake up. I was having a much better time asleep. And for a horse, that's really sad. It was then I knew I had to wake up. I had to snap out of my grief over Gilda. Why? Because as the saying goes: in this book of life, the answers are not always in the back. And I knew I may never know the answers behind Gilda's disappearance. Some of life's toughest questions go unanswered. Even animals know that. See, horses love their masters and mistresses more than life itself. I knew I couldn't *stay* sad. I had to be strong for Sunbeam. She was my best friend, and I was there to give her smiles.

It had been five, long years since Gilda went missing. Since Gilda disappeared, nothing had been the same. But I was determined to help Sunbeam move forward. I still hoped that Gilda was alive. However, Sunbeam had been tormented after Gilda was taken. And not a day went by that she didn't think of her twin.

"Whitewing, do you think she's still alive? It's my fault she's gone. Mother must never know."

She always talked to me. Even though she knew I could not talk back, she knew I heard her. I listened. My mistress and I spoke a close, unspoken language. The special, silent language between humans and their best animal.

"Whitewing, can you believe that annoying Gingerface?" She sighed and patted my head. "She'll never touch you again."

Sunbeam's efforts were sincere. But I looked at her, saddened. I didn't want to encourage her explosive behavior at school.

"Oh I know, Boy. I shouldn't have lost my temper. I couldn't help it. I got so mad I blacked out."

Yes, this was true. She was quicker lately—wild-like. And what I noticed during the last couple of months, was Sunbeam's unusual resilience during the Athletic Games at school. Her rapid speed during the running and long jump surpassed all the other students. Her accuracy with the bow and arrow was supreme. And she was becoming superior in fencing, even mastering the instructors, knocking their swords from their hands. She had even beat the boys at javelin and shot-put. The Athletic Games instructor said he'd never seen anything like it, especially from a girl. On the field, he'd shake his head and say, "This girl has superhuman strength!" He'd say it jokingly, but with a look of concern and uneasiness.

Perhaps it was because she was growing up. But whatever the reason behind her sudden exceptional, almost supernatural performance, I had noticed it, too. And apparently, so did Professor Plume, who always had his eye on her, studying her in the hallways, and watching her after school from his loft.

"I miss her. It's my fault, Whitewing. I should be the one gone, not Gilda." She looked out into the grey forest, and a tear streamed down her cheek. "It's all my fault, Whitewing. How can I live, knowing I . . ."

I lowered my neck to where she sat on the tree stump. She held on to my bridle, and as she wept, I thought she'd dissolve in her tears.

"If I don't get Gilda back, I don't know what I'll do." She put her face in her hands.

All of a sudden, as soon as she said "Gilda" something glinted in the distance, underneath one of the bare trees. It was faint. Subtle. But in its subtlety, it was intriguing and caught my mistress's eye.

"What . . . what is that? Do you see it, Whitewing?" Sunbeam slowly rose with her misery, her haunting memories about Gilda, and crept toward the obscured glow. With one foot in front of the other, she was drawn to the faint, warm glimmer ahead.

"What . . . what is this . . .?" she mumbled faintly, inching forward, her eyes drawn to it like a compelling magnet.

We rounded the tree trunk, and there, lodged between two dark crags and wedged in the earth's soil, lay a Golden Key. Trance-like, Sunbeam slowly lifted it out of the dirt, and wiping the smeared soil from it, we saw an inscription:

> *Called.*
> *This key will unlock any door in the world*
> *and beyond . . .*

"Whitewing, what is this . . .?"

Flipping it over, we saw something else embedded on the other side of the Key. To get a closer look, Sunbeam took her shirt tail and wiped the rest of the dirt off the brass. After she cleared away the smudge, we looked closer . . . only to find a FINGERPRINT. A fingerprint embedded and branded on the top part of the Key. Sunbeam looked over the Key like a skilled jeweler, studying it. Drawn to it, she ran her fingers over the Key, toying with the slim possibility of those prints being her own. *How impossible* she thought, yet she continued to brush her fingerprints over the engraving—when all of a sudden—the Key pulsed with a golden shimmer, magically aligning the curves of identity on her thumb with the one on the mysterious Key. With her eyes wide and her jaw dropped, she blurted, "Whitewing! This fingerprint is—is—mine? The fingerprint on the Key matches my own! Look!"

Skeptical, I lowered my neck to get a good look with my keen eye. Animals have clearer sight, and I knew Sunbeam, overly excited, was mistaken. She had to be mistaken about her fingerprint matching the one on the Key.

"See?" She stared and held it up to my nose. And as I studied it, lo and behold, there, in her hands, lay a Golden Key that unfurled her exact fingerprint.

"What kind of Key is this?" She muttered like she'd been captured under a spell. And then, she held it up, raised it to the sky like a prized trophy, and read the inscription on the Key—out loud:

"Called.
This key will unlock any door in the world
and beyond."

And while she read it, her voice carried on the air and echoed throughout the Depths of Cypress. Then suddenly, without warning, a mighty wind swept in from the East, a sound of bells rang like a ghostly choir, and grey mist rose from the earth.

Sunbeam's legs began to tremble. She looked for a place to hide. But the blinding mist crept up her legs and chained her feet to the ground. The mist rose higher and higher. The fuming fog blinded us. Our hearts would have stopped if it hadn't been for the fear pounding inside our chests. I thought we'd faint. Only sheer adrenaline kept us awake.

"Whitewing! Where are you?" screamed Sunbeam. Her hands reached blindly for me inside the fog. The wind howled. I stepped closer to her, and she grasped my mane tightly, and held on.

The wind picked up. The bells rang louder. The grey mist blinded us.

"Look, Whitewing! Look! There!" Sunbeam shouted and pointed to a narrow clearing in the mist. The cloudy fog parted into a thin path in front of us. And looking ahead, the tallest, loftiest Door appeared before our terrified hearts. And it was the most magical, ghastly thing my eyes had ever beheld.

CHAPTER 2

LORD WOLFORD AND THE GUILD OF GOLGUMS

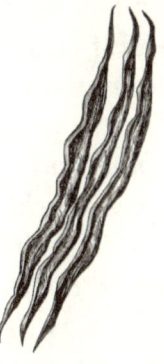

Long before my mistress was born, the forefathers of Ozmandia passed down a myth. The myth was later hidden and outlawed, so my mistress and I never spoke of it. I had listened in to the whispers of the old people sitting around their fires late at night when they thought no one heard.

According to the banned story, Lord Wolford rose to power in Ozmandia two hundred years ago, during a time of terrible drought and famine.

200 Years Earlier
(the myth)

He moved in swiftly. No one knew from where he came. Famine had eaten the land. The starving Ozmandians had gathered on the Holy Mountain to hear the Good Council of Oran discuss what could be done. For days, the council judges argued under the Sacred Lamps of the whitewashed portico, whether or not to place their trust in the God of Lights. Their stone table was long, filled with scrolls and parchments of ancient creed. Then suddenly, a tall, blond stranger appeared before them like an angel of light. He took his place in front of the portico, shadowing the Good Council of Oran, veiling the lamps with his large, handsome build.

"Men and Women of Ozmandia! I am Lord Wolford! Hear me! I will give you what you long for: rich succulent meats, fine buttered bread, cold, clear water, and more. Only accept my aid, and you will never be in want."

Yes, his statement was bold and generous, especially coming from a stranger. His blue eyes sparkled like refreshing waters to the thirsty congregation. And in their hunger, he enticed them.

"Who are you? From where do you come?" demanded Judge Aalock. "Why are you speaking as though you are a part of this Council?" He rose from his seat. Judge Aalok had served on the Good Council the longest. The entire assembly grew silent and watched the two men. The crowd of people stopped and stared. You could have heard a pin drop. Judge Aalok asked again, "I asked your purpose. From where do you come? Speak!"

Lord Wolford roamed his eyes over the large crowd on the hill. And they waited for his response. You could hear nothing, except the waves, lightly lapping on the shore.

"From where do you come?" demanded Judge Aalok. The light of the lamp burned like a halo above his head.

"Gehenna. The land of Gehenna," said Lord Wolford. "We have more resources than fish in the sea, to save all of you. Let me lead you out of this famine, and you will never suffer. Food, sweets from France, pleasures, the finest cloths and linens, jewelry from the West, and anything else you desire. Only let me lead you, and I will give you these things."

"Why should we trust you? Why do you care to help us?" said

Aalok. His dark eyes kindled under the burning lamps. "Cease—tell us what you desire here!"

"Enlightenment!" said the blond stranger. "My passion has driven me beyond my borders to enlighten the minds of men. I am a knowledgeable prince. Accept the knowledge I bring, and you will be as the people in Gehenna are—enlightened—without want."

The crowd thirsted deeper for his spellbinding blue eyes and the refreshing words he poured over them, for their hearts were as dry as a desert. And in that moment, he was filling them. Lord Wolford—he knew they hungered for what he offered.

"No!" shouted Judge Leona from the Council seat; her white robe flowed in the breeze as she stepped forward to Lord Wolford. The lamps caught a slight gust, and the flames blazed. Stepping in front of the entire crowd, she turned and looked Wolford straight in the eye. "Lying! Proud! Black-hearted son of a snake!" she said to Wolford. Then she turned and addressed the crowd: "How well this man speaks, as a skilled poet. But I tell you the truth, as your leader from the Good Council of Oran, this man is false. A merciless prince!"

"Wait, Leona," said Judge Bilhah. He rubbed his brow as if sunk in thought. Slowly he rose from his chair. "Our children and old people are sick. How do we know this man cannot supply aid to our island? Has it escaped you that we have exhausted our resources? The danger of this Prince is not altogether a threat, as it might appear."

"Bilhah, we both are devoted servants on this Council," said Leona, "and we both know these ruthless countries that call themselves superior are hateful to the God of Lights, and to all persons of insight." She turned briskly and pointed to the lamps of the portico. "Ozmandia has always burned these Sacred Lamps to the God of Lights, whom this barbarian prince hates. If you give this man authority here, or accept his gifts, it will end unprofitable."

"Quiet, Leona, I have had your beliefs and precepts flung at me all day!" shouted Bilhah, red-faced.

"*Compose yourself,*" *Judge Aalok interjected.* "*We shall win only by working together. We all know the lessons from the peace process here.*"

"*Sir, if I may?*" *said Lord Wolford, this time in a more respectful tone.* "*Why should this council think twice about keeping Ozmandia in hunger? I can provide all you lack. Let me show you. I propose and desire, that you grant me permission to stretch my arm to possess Ozmandia, and if you don't approve, I will draw it back undamaged if the plan proves harmful. This negotiation is reasonable?*"

"*Never!*" *said Judge Leona.* "*His tongue is crafty like a serpent's, but the poison of a viper flows from his lips.*" *She turned and addressed the crowd.* "*My beloved Ozmandians, this man is a liar. I've seen what barbarians do. He will take our good island only for his gain, waste it with fire and blood, and add it to his many provinces. Let us wait! The God of Lights will not fail us!*"

"*I OBJECT!*" *shouted Judge Bilhah, rushing to face the crowd.* "*This Prince, Lord Wolford, has spoken with knowledge and foresight. We can easily draw back his arm on our island if he is faulty—we will send him away if he proves false.*"

As the members of the Council of Oran raised their voices, an impatient movement swept over the crowd. Judge Aalok stood and tried to regain order. But in their hunger, like lost sheep who'd just found a shepherd, the crowd began shouting in unison: "*LORD WOLFORD! LORD WOLFORD! LORD WOLFORD!*" *until the Council had no other choice but to desist and allow the prince to give them what they wanted from his illimitable empire. They accepted his aid. And as the hungry crowd continued to lift up his name:* "*LORD WOLFORD! LORD WOLFORD! LORD WOLFORD!*" *delight filled his cool, blue eyes.*

"*The people have chosen,*" *said Leona. Her heart looked broken, yet the lamp's fire was still alight in her eyes.* "*You should not have given concessions to this man. Long will we regret opening our gates to him.*"

Lord Wolford received the crowd's desperate praises with noble grace. Then he mounted his horse, pulled silver and gold coins from his satchel, and flung them over the crowd like sparkling rain. And grasping their hands toward the silver shower, the people turned their backs on the Good Council of Oran. "There is money for your pains! To hear is to obey! The beginning of your enlightenment!" shouted Lord Wolford. Then he spurred his horse savagely and set off at tremendous speed, bound for his ships moored in a nearby harbor. Soon he returned with many shiploads of men.

And for a while, Ozmandia basked in his pleasures and flourished under his reign. Bit by bit, he seized control of the island, and sometime later, he closed the doors of the portico and put out all the lamps.

~ ~

Most people on the island consider this story an old-time myth. But a few still rumor it quietly as if it's true. The only truth we know for sure is that Wolford's power was passed down to his son, and his son's son—until his dynasty dominated every aspect of life on the island. And the story of how the *first* Lord Wolford invaded Ozmandia by deceit long ago was banned by the law. Anyone heard even talking of the myth is reported, punished, and exiled. And no one knows to where the myth-speakers are sent.

"My beloved people," Lord Wolford addresses the island after exiling a myth-speaker. "My Dynasty has only been to provide and protect. We must teach those offenders a lesson who wish to taint my name. Remember your foolish fathers! Long ago they led this island into famine! We today must be people of reason. We enlightened are rational. We believe only what is before us, the here and now, for only here and now matter. My beloved people, it was the Wolford Dynasty who saved this island. On that truth, remember!"

"To hear is to obey. To hear is to obey." The Guild of Golgums always chant as they stand obediently behind him in their long, black cloaks. To promise stronger protection, Wolford assembled the Guild of Golgums to patrol the streets. And since its humble history long go, the Guild had become strong.

Even more, to honor Lord Wolford, there is a Day of Ransom. On that day, the Golgums collect money to honor Lord Wolford for saving our ancestors from starvation.

My mistress and I are used to the sight of the Golgums. They stand watch at every corner and every high rooftop. Their eyes zoom in on every step we make, their ears lean into every breath we take. The shadows of their cloaks cover the city. On the Day of Ransom, the bells ring through Ozmandia. The Golgums march with their torches and their chants. Like a foreboding choir, their low hums echo off rooftops and through windows like a vexing song.

> He has enlightened you in his truth
> And when your fathers hungered,
> Lord Wolford fed the multitude.
> No one will cross over.
>
> We have come to take the census
> To ensure each head is counted.
> Each one must pay the ransom.
> The Day of Ransom is upon us.

The people silence their mouths because of the *other* types of Golgums. It is said these types are disguised. They masquerade and hide among the townspeople. These Golgums stay hidden by blending. They mingle and mask themselves at the local pubs and around nighttime fires: to spy, to report back to Lord Wolford any suspicion of rebellion, or any myth-speakers. But despite their disguises, once in a while we can spot one because all Golgums bear one thing in common:

The Mark of the Claw.

Every Golgum has this mark branded on the forearm: a three-clawed scar.

The only truth we all know now is that no one wants to be caught a myth-speaker. The Golgums are in place to protect us from the offenders. And boys and girls, together, are sent to the same schoolhouses to ensure all the young learn the exact same way, uniform instruction. This is the enlightenment Lord Wolford's dynasty brought.

Even though it's for our protection, Ozmandia can feel like a strange place. But stranger and darker still, throughout the Wolford dynasty, was the way Lord Wolford's power was passed down to his son, and his son's son, and all the sons who came after that. Their portraits memorialize the towns. I have often wondered: how can they all look alike? Through their two hundred-year line, every one of them carried the same name as their father, and each was tall and handsome with angelically blond hair and sparkling blue eyes. In fact, they were all identical.

CHAPTER 3

IN THE DEPTHS

Sunbeam and I still stood terrified, trapped under the heavy fog.

"Look, Whitewing! Look!" my Mistress shouted as the Key lit gold. We marveled in fear at the unearthly Door. The fog thickened. The bells rang louder. The Door beckoned. It stood high, with old petrified wood, the corners outlined with tarnished, bronzed rivets. We started to cross through. All at once, a ray of enchanting, horrifying light shot through the Door's keyhole. It seemed to beckon us forward.

"Whi-Whitewing," Sunbeam stuttered. She was still entranced. Her eyes glazed over. The light pulled her like a magnet to the door opening into cryptic Depths. I sensed danger. But there was no stopping her. I was determined to stick close to my mistress. Her heart raced. She lifted the Key and put it to the lock. The Door wore a face of old wisdom. And I'm sure it knew all things. I'm sure it had been there since the beginning of time. Slowly, she turned the Golden Key.

The ancient Door creaked. Reluctantly, it opened. In a second, it began quaking as if resurrected from a fossilized sleep. There was no going back. The vacuumous mysteries ahead engulfed us, mocking our attempt to turn away. We had no choice but to enter. A strange, powerful ray of light shone brighter through the open doorway as remnants of fog and dust floated in the half-light.

In fear, I shook my head. "Be quiet," whispered Mistress. Her hands trembled.

We crept forward until we were finally inside the hazy world we'd only moments before been outside of. We had crossed the threshold.

The air seemed heavier and the sky more grey and dim. Sunbeam fanned the fog to clear the way. When suddenly, the old, giant Door—slammed shut.

The door closed with thunderous force. Panicked, Sunbeam reached for the knob to get out. But the latch sealed shut. "Locked!" panted Sunbeam. Still grasping the Golden Key, she ran her hands over the door's grainy surface. She searched for the keyhole, but it had vanished. If the door could speak it would have said, "THIS IS THE END," in its old, wise voice. Startled, Sunbeam began panting and gasping for breath like she'd just crossed an entire desert. And I, I was trying to keep calm, but my jittery horse knees were about to give way. After a minute, we caught our breath. Sunbeam sat hunched over on the ground, trying to recover from the fright. Then she lifted her head and narrowed her eyes at me.

"We shouldn't have come here," muttered Sunbeam. Her eyebrows were raised, yet she looked aware of her surroundings, more aware than I'd ever seen her look before. In her hands, she still grasped the Key, tightly.

"It's alright," I replied.

For a moment, Sunbeam thought she was dreaming. I thought it, too, because the thoughts in my mind had just came out my mouth in the form of words! I wondered what had given me the supernatural power of speech! Sunbeam stared at me wide-eyed. I spoke again, "We will find a way."

Sunbeam stared at my muzzle, speechless. Her eyes were

about as wide as mine, and awe-struck, she blurted, "How did you learn to talk? Whitewing! You can talk!" She gawked at me.

"Dear Mistress, I'm surprised, too. But did you really think me so dumb and senseless?" I said.

"Where are we? Where animals speak?" she gasped.

"In the ordinary world, no animals can speak out loud. I assume it's for our protection. People would take us and make a display of us at carnivals and circuses. I'd be tied-up and caged forever."

"Why . . . ?" uttered Sunbeam, still gazing at me.

"Now listen, we can't tarry on any more questions. Not so loud, we don't know what is lurking here."

The fog lifted to reveal a dense row of trees beside us. My keen animal eye looked into the forest. When I felt it was safe, I gazed above to the ancient words engraved on the face of the old, wise Door. The Door that just locked us inside. There on the door were carved letters that read:

Valley of Bakah

"Bakah?" muttered Sunbeam under her breath. She examined the words.

"Bakah means pain," I blurted.

"How do you know that? You're only a horse." Sunbeam stared at me, her face astonished.

"Like I said, horses aren't dumb just because we can't talk in the real world."

It was true. I'd spent many days outside Sunbeam's schoolhouse window, waiting for her—and listening. There, I grew in knowledge watching over my mistress. On some days Sunbeam dozed off. But I hung on to every word the professors taught. However, I could see why Sunbeam was surprised I had any sense. What absurd and stupid horses some humans had! And even though I was sold as a foal because I didn't have warhorse strength like the rest of my breed, I had more wits than any horse on the island. But I also knew that at the end of the day, I was only a horse, and that was all.

"The Valley of Bakah," said Sunbeam, studying the door.

Suddenly, leaves rustled from the woods.

"Quiet. I feel a presence. Someone's listening," whispered Sunbeam.

"The rustling, it's coming from beside us, in those trees," I said. Horses' ears are very attuned to sound. Sunbeam's eyes widened and darted through the trees, bracing herself for danger. We heard the faint sound again moving in the bushes. Quickly, we crouched behind some nearby shrubbery—although it was a little hard for me to get low, as big as I am.

As soon as we hid, gentle footsteps pitter-pattered from the long, black shadow of cypress trees. At that moment, a tall, thin nimbly creature emerged from the trees and scurried to the great Door. His steps were swift, yet hushed and quiet. He stood before the great Door, tall and lean with suspenders holding up trousers that looked too big for him. His brown, shaggy hair resembled fur; some of it poked out from behind his pointy ears. He stood, both thumbs stretching his suspenders and leaning to the side like some nervous trickster. He wore a smirk on his long angular face.

We waited for the creature to speak. To move. To do something. Anything. But he stood before the Door, very still, but with tight tension on his alert expression. The nimbly creature squinted and stared harder than ever. Finally, Sunbeam mustered enough courage to rise and break the impending stillness. She slowly stepped from the shrub.

"Sir, can you help us?" asked Sunbeam. She watched him closely. He peered at us nervously, yet with a smug grin, like he knew some secret.

"The Valley," he said.

"Yes?" Sunbeam asked. "How do we get out of here?"

"There is no *out*, only *through*."

"Then how do we get through? Back to where we came?"

"Cresc-phos!" he blurted and broke into laughter.

"What does that mean?" she asked, annoyed he was laughing hysterically in the middle of her dilemma, with his nimbly face and nervous eyes. "How do we go back?"

"There is no going back. ONLY THROUGH!" His anxious eyes darted back and forth as if he were watching for some enemy.

"Can you show me the way?"

"Cresc-phos!" he shouted again, quick and sharp, like a dog's bark.

"What are you saying?" She started to breathe faster and tightened her fist.

"Once you've found the Golden Key,
You have made your choice, you see."

His menacing laugh grew louder, echoing through the air. He continued:

"To stay or go?
Only one more chance to know.
When you have found the riddle to,
The Golden Key will lead you through,
You'll then choose what you will do!"

"Lead where?" asked Sunbeam. "Tell me!"

While she demanded answers, the nimbly creature only laughed harder. Then suddenly he leapt from the door and broke into an agile sprint, pitter-pattering his quick and quiet feet until he vanished in his own laughter behind the dark row of cypress. And dissipating into his own echo, "Cresc-phos" carried in the wind behind him.

"Cresc-phos," said Sunbeam. "Whatever could that strange creature have . . ."

"Sunbeam, look. The Key!" I said.

Upon saying the word, *Cresc-phos,* the Golden Key lit up in her hand with great, golden hues. Hypnotized, we both stared, once again, at its enchanting warm glow.

"There's something on here," she said, squinting to read it. "Some kind of symbol. It looks like a circle with a spinning arrow. It's moving back and forth."

"A compass!" I said. "Its needle points the direction."

"Where do we turn? The needle won't stop spinning!"

"Turn it away from the door. The creature said you can't go back."

Sunbeam made an about-turn and shifted her body forward to face the unknown roads. The small compass embedded on the Key adjusted itself and pointed east.

"That's where we go," I said. "We'd better move before dusk."

"How do we know where it's leading?" said Sunbeam. Her green eyes were full of doubt. "Look at the mess it's led us into already!"

"There is only one way out. Forward. Hop on! You can't get near as far on your own two legs. I have four."

"You sure do have a lot to say. I'm not going to need a muzzle now, am I?" she snickered. She sighed, then climbed on my saddle—and my mistress and I set off toward the East.

こ ら

I'd been trotting east throughout the course of the shadowy afternoon. And because horses have eyes on the side of their head, I had a broad range of vision to keep watch for danger, which also allowed me to take in Sunbeam's in-the-saddle movements. With just a slight tilt of the head, horses can eliminate blind spots and see directly behind their tails. This allowed me to see Sunbeam very clearly on my saddle, and to watch for sneak-ups from behind.

By now, the tall row of cypress trees on the horizon was fading away. The hazy light that filtered around us seemed to grow more dim as if some ghostly sun were setting. We had crossed several murky streams, barren hills, then short slopes covered with old, dead vineyards. In the dead vineyards, black birds hovered and tore off the flesh of an animal carcass. Upon seeing the vultures devour the carcass, Sunbeam turned away, feeling ill inside.

But beyond the vineyards was something neither Sunbeam nor I had ever seen. There, beyond a great stretch, spread out far and long was something flat and grey. It was a river. Under the dwindling, late afternoon light, small ripples moved in its ghostly current, reflecting undertones of dark silver and grey. It was the eeriest river I'd ever seen: a deep mystery—calm, but as if something haunting and powerful lay underneath it.

"The compass," said Sunbeam. "It's pointing toward that strange river." Her hands started to tremble on the reins.

"What do you want to do, Mistress?"

"Keep going," she said. The further we went, the more hesitant she looked.

I continued forward. Instinctively, I could sense Sunbeam's heart pound with fear. I knew she secretly wished she'd never found that Key. Her pulse quickened, and so did mine.

"Where is it taking us?" she muttered, studying the Key. "Wait, Whitewing. The needle is turning south!" To her great relief, the compass shifted and pointed to an opening between another row of cypress trees. We veered away from the haunting river. The path became narrow as we walked deeper into a thick woodland of tall trees, which looked very dark and mysterious, for the sun was now falling behind them.

We moved along into the cypress. I was trotting south, and as the sun faded, it became quieter. We could hear that eerie river's current rolling in the near distance on the other side of the trees. Then suddenly, a gruff sigh came out of the bushes.

"Whitewing . . ." whispered Sunbeam. She pulled my reins to a halt. Before she could finish her sentence, a small figure whisked through the shrub. The only thing we saw was its backside: a hard, leathery mass with pointy shapes that stuck out like twisted forks.

Sunbeam sat up in my saddle as if she might order me to flee. "Be still," she whispered, for the thing had stopped just in front of us, behind a bush.

Was it an enemy? Another creature with a message? We froze, waiting. Then suddenly, its forked backside flitted off—and it was gone.

By then an ominous, full moon had risen over a sun that had totally set. As unnerved as Sunbeam felt, we pressed on into nightfall. Deeper into the cypress, the path melted away. In the twilight, a little stretch ahead, the moon's half-light fell on something that looked like large mounds of stone. I continued trotting until we found ourselves nearing a graveyard. And suddenly everything became quieter than ever. The gravestones, much larger than Sunbeam had ever seen, looked smoky under the moon. Altogether, they looked like giant, evil-hooded figures, like the Golgums, except much sterner. These were not the kinds of ghouls you wanted beside you in a dark cemetery all alone.

"I feel these things are watching us," said Sunbeam.

"I'll tread carefully, Mistress," I said.

Abruptly, a tall gate stopped us in our tracks. Through its bars we saw a trail leading straight between two rows of vaulted chambers laced with cobwebs. The air grew thick and ashen. A streak of moonlight laced the top of the old cemetery gate, which bore a small, cracked statue with parts of a face that had been torn off. Sunbeam became even more anxious and uneasy. In a few more paces she'd be alone—among those corroded stones, for the Key was pointing us straight into the resting place of the dead.

"Cresc-phos," whispered Sunbeam. "That nimbly riddler was trying to tell us something."

"Not back, only forward, we've done that," I said, recalling the creature's puzzling phrases. "When you have found the riddle to, the Golden Key will lead you through . . ."

"How do we know this creature isn't sending us straight to the gate of Hades?" said Sunbeam. Her pale skin glowed under the moonlight, bringing a mystical glimmer of life to the graveyard.

"We don't. But we also don't have anything else to go by, Mistress," I replied. I was just as skeptical. However, I was tried and true, a devoted companion to my mistress, and I never would have deserted her, afraid or not.

With beating heart she prodded me forward, so I lowered my head and pushed open the rusted cemetery gate. Its hinges creaked like a sigh of pain. We trotted deeper into the burial ground. The dry air smelled musty. There was something very unnerving about the moss billowing over those silent tombs. I kept walking with desperate hope leading me on.

It became very uncomfortable. My second sight was strong and sensed Mistress's distress. Sunbeam had been trying very hard not to think of the things lurking there. I slowly trotted around, circling around and through every turn, for the tombs were scattered in no particular order.

"Over there, Boy," Sunbeam whispered. There was something about the silence and dark stones that made you want to whisper. To talk in a regular voice would be intruding upon some mysterious silence that you did not want to awaken.

"There," muttered Sunbeam. The Golden Key lit up subtle gold, reflecting light over the corners of the stones.

"Wait, Whitewing. The needle has disappeared," said Sunbeam, alarmed. Sunbeam jumped off the saddle, and with the Key gripped in her hand, tiptoed lightly on the graveyard's damp soil. She ran her fingers over the tombs. I looked at the Key. The compass on it had vanished, but the Golden Key was still faintly lit.

"It has to be here. Whatever the Key is leading us to, it's close." She crept around the gravestones. "This one says, Judge Leona," whispered Sunbeam. She read off the names etched on the stones. "Look, over here, Judge Aalok of Ozmandia. These stones are the largest. I bet they were once important—like—kings or queens."

She gazed at the graves, wondering about the past lives of the dead. If the stones were sleeping, Sunbeam's hushed steps never would have woken them.

We walked a little farther. The Golden Key's light grew more intense, burning with deeper golden tones. And there, we saw something: a stone that had been rolled away from an empty tomb. On the great stone was a word written in some other language. The inscription read:

μεγαλύτερο φως

Sunbeam studied the ancient words. In the darkness, she lifted the Key. Its faint glow fell on the stone cryptogram. Suddenly, the stone tabulate began to unscramble, revealing what seemed like deep mysteries under the light of the Key, that now took new shape and read:

Cresc-phos

"Here's that word again. Cres-phos," Sunbeam whispered.

Then in a brilliant flash, the word transformed again, this time into our own language. Sunbeam and I read it aloud together.

"Greater Light"

"Greater Light?" sighed Sunbeam. "I don't understand. What's this supposed to . . ."

Suddenly, a breeze drifted through the graveyard, and Sunbeam felt something touch her neck. I stood still beside her. She shouted impulsively, then crouched very still with her eyes closed shut because she knew she'd be more panicked if she stood up and looked around to see what grabbed her. After realizing she'd shouted, she knew she dare not scream again. She didn't want to waken anything from the graves. She feared what might rise up or crawl out of them. So she sat there. Eyes closed. She was too afraid to run because then she'd have to go back through the entire graveyard and absolute blackness. She peeked with one eye. The large stones looked like huge ghosts. And she thought of any other place she'd rather be than among phantoms rising from graves, slithering around the ancient burial grounds.

"Sunbeam," I whispered. "Look behind you."

She was too frightened to turn around. But she finally mustered the courage to turn her head to find out what touched her: it was only a stray vine that breezed off one of the tombs, sweeping the back of her neck. Her heart surged with tremendous relief.

"Maybe this *is* just a nightmare," she panted.

"Where is the Key?" I asked, knowing it was our only hope of finding our way out of the ghoulish cemetery.

"Here. It stopped glowing," she said. She hadn't released her grip on it since she first picked it up.

"We must have found what it wanted us to find," I said.

"This cryptogram. It means something." She squinted at the words. "But I can't imagine what!"

Greater Light. I could not help but think of the irony. In the middle of the darkest graveyard was an ancient tomb that read *Greater Light.* How could we possibly find light? Even a speck of it for that matter?

Sunbeam was lost in thought when suddenly a shrieking, desperate cry wailed in the distance. She jumped up and gripped my mane. It was a deep troubling noise, one that seemed strange and foreign. "This has to be a nightmare. I'm sure of it," she gasped. "It never ends!"

Soon, the noise echoed again. It was a sharp agonizing cry, wailing on the other side of the trees—a horrific sound. Her heart felt as if it fell into her feet, and she tightened her lips to keep from screaming. She looked around at those chambers and blackness.

"We have to get out of here," she said. Her terrified eyes darted around for an escape in the moonlight. The mournful cry rang out again.

"Now!" She jumped on my saddle and led me through the other side of the graveyard. With one powerful bound, I leapt over the cemetery fence and out into another dense row of cypress. Now out of the graveyard, I hoped this "Greater Light" would suddenly emerge because it was so dark, I could not see a thing. The trees on this side of the graveyard were thicker and blocked the moonlight from shining a path. We kept on. The piercing cries echoed again and again.

All at once, we broke through the trees into a clearing.

"The noises. They're getting closer." Sunbeam trembled. "They're coming toward us."

She pulled the reins to halt my gait, then glanced around. She thought of turning me around, but that would mean going back through the loneliness of the tombs, and she changed her mind. Slowly, she led me forward into the clearing while the cries grew louder and louder. She was just going to make a dash for it until strangely, a procession of cloaked figures bounded into view.

"Get down," she whispered. She jumped off my saddle and led me behind a thicket of trees to hide.

The moon faintly outlined the cloaked procession. The figures looked very dark, and they wore long, black cloaks—the same cloaks worn by Lord Wolford's Golgums. We did not know what it was except that *this* was the place responsible for the harsh cries.

"Golgums," said Sunbeam. "What are they doing?"

"It's not what *they're* doing, but what's being done to *them*? Look, over there!"

⪻ ⪼

It was the most terrifying thing my keen animal eye had ever seen. A long procession marched gracefully under the silver moon, cloaked in black robes with hooded faces, up to a high place where pillars of fire rose into the night air. Then they split to form a ring around a young man who seemed to have just suffered a terrible ritual and beating on a high table. He cried wildly in pain.

After the man slid from the table and barely crawled away, it was another poor man's turn. The man stood petrified, yet determined, before the high table, where a crowned prince sat perched above on a throne. A mask covered the prince's face and he was surrounded by creatures that bared fangs and spoke and laughed like men. The masked prince on the throne looked to be a devil himself, but he was unlike the others, for only he had a claw. Only one claw, on his right hand. And in his hideousness, he looked to be half-man and half-beast. Through the eyeholes of his mask, his baleful, blue eyes glittered like ice.

And those somber Golgums, void of all expression, gazed hypnotically at the blue-eyed beast on the throne, chanting:

"O MASTER, O PLEASURE OF MY SOUL,

TO HEAR IS TO OBEY."

The Golgums chanted the words very drearily and not as if they had *true* pleasure in their soul. While they chanted, the man plunged himself headlong onto the high table. The man lay shivering in panic, waiting with submissive stillness.

The clawed prince stood from his lofty throne and raised himself over the young man: "This very night and hour of darkness, you are consenting to serve—for all the debt you owe your lord. By the law of magic, do you give consent for me to raise my arm, and cut with an incision of the deepest draft, to take your soul?"

The young man with sad eyes replied gravely, "Bid a sick man at heart. I love neither myself nor my life. I pay the ransom and make atonement with my life."

"I too despise life and all things in it except the praise and power of my throne," said the blue-eyed prince behind the mask, his voice alternating between excitable tones of high, low, and sharp. The prince raised his claw into the air, the tips glinting under the moon.

Then it became quiet—so quiet that Sunbeam hardly dared to breathe.

The clawed prince continued. "It is never possible that any living soul know of this secret guild and that we have met here this night!" shouted the prince to his solemn subjects.

"O MASTER, O PLEASURE OF MY SOUL,

TO HEAR IS TO OBEY."

The Golgums chanted in submissive agreement to the prince's mandates.

"O MASTER, O PLEASURE OF MY SOUL,

TO HEAR IS TO OBEY."

The prince, with his claw still raised high, shouted over the table to the young man. "It is so, my son, in return for the treasures I give you, that at the taking of your spirit, you will lose your soul. For in this alteration, I now bind you, not withholding my desire for your flesh!"

And with that, he plunged his claw down into the young man's chest. And before drawing it completely back, he seared his hot claw on the man's forearm, to mark him. The young man cried out wildly and writhed in pain. When he was finally able to stand, it was clear a terrible alteration had taken place. His face was indeed altered after the operation. It had become a copy to the Golgums' faces: blank and expressionless. And so he stood, gazing upon the prince's beastly mask and chanted, "The glory of my Prince is the pleasure of my soul. May you reign eternal, though you have completely overtaken me. To hear is to obey."

At this, the Golgums raised their torches and chanted in excitable praises around the prince and his lofty throne until the prince raised his voice to the young man, who now stood, without a soul, before his taker.

"Oh, my son," said the prince. "You shall quietly shed blood and drain as much from Ozmandia as you can." His cool, blue eyes sparkled from behind the mask.

"To hear is to obey."

"Go. Be swift, sly, and lead them back—shorn sheep!" ordered the prince.

"To hear is to obey," the man replied, his face drained of all color. Then he crawled backward on all fours from the high place and merged into the procession, along with the other Golgums, who marched away, down the high place chanting in unison:

"O MASTER, O PLEASURE OF MY SOUL,

TO HEAR IS TO OBEY."

"Ahhh!" shouted the prince. He licked a trickle of blood from his claw. "There have been some taken here tonight. I and my guild will fire through Ozmandia like an arrow from a bow. And I shall pierce *all* the hearts of Ozmandia. And I'll sit on this throne adding each soul little by little, until it is a great multitude. Guards! Call forth the musicians!"

Abruptly, a melancholy line of players with drums, strings and tambourines circled around the high place while the prince's voice became sad.

"Night after night I lie down but cannot sleep, and every morning the sun is a dark spot in my eyes because I know Ozmandia still walks free," he hissed.

"That man," whispered Sunbeam, panting. She could barely get out a word due to the trauma she had just witnessed. "The one who was on the table, I know him."

"Who is he?"

"He lives down the lane from our cottage," she whispered. "The one Mother sends me over to with food and drink—she said he always looks lonely, sad."

"Apparently, he's just joined the Guild."

"This explains why all the Golgums bear that mark," she said. "The mark of the claw."

"Keep it down. They mustn't hear you. We should not have seen this."

Suddenly, a terrible sound of hisses and mocking filled the thick air. We were still hiding among the cypress trees. We looked again at the dark ritual on the high place, and in the prince's hissing and shouts, he stood above on his throne. And lifting himself up, shouting muffled lines of "Mine! and Freedom! and Take! and Souls!" with that horrendous claw raised, he held what appeared to be a locket against the moonlit sky.

"What is he holding?" Sunbeam whispered, squinting to see it.

"It looks like a piece of jewelry—a locket," I said, zooming in with my keen eye.

In the next moment, the prince stepped down from his throne. His claw gleamed under the moon. Then, as if he caught a scent of some intruder, he lowered his chin and turned his icy, blue eyes in our direction. Sunbeam thought her heart had stopped.

"Don't budge," she whispered.

The prince dropped to all fours like a wild lion and crawled down the steps of his throne rapidly. Then as if stalking, he raised his nose like an animal smelling out its prey. Slowly, at the last step, he stood erect back on two feet. His procession gathered behind him. He began walking straight for us, his eyes like two rocks of ice blaring behind the holes in his mask.

Sunbeam and I crouched even lower into the thick bushes, which was very difficult, as big as I am. The prince and his guild marched by so close we could almost touch their cloaks. The beasts smelled like a mixture of ashes and rotten meat. Suddenly, the prince stopped. His blue eyes wild, he sniffed and growled. Now closer than ever, we saw clearly the locket dangle around his smooth neck. With that horrendous claw he reached up again and held the small locket; it glistened in the moonlight. Immediately, Sunbeam peered at the locket ever so intently; then became frozen until the prince swiftly set forward and marched out with his beasts fading behind him.

Sunbeam began to tremble, and her whole face turned pale.

"What is it, Mistress?" I asked, alarmed.

"That locket . . ."

"Yes?"

"That locket was the one I gave her."

"Who?"

"Gilda!"

Sunbeam became still, frightened and lost in thought. But in her hand, she still held the Key . . .

CHAPTER 4

THE CHASE

In the darkness, Sunbeam walked a good distance from the high place with me close beside her. She was on foot, leading me by the reins. She dared not go back through the tombs, so we trailed further into the woods until stopped again by that ominous, grey river. It channeled and wound through the Depths. Its calm waters rolled hauntingly along the edge of the woods. We couldn't tread further east, and we dared not step one foot in that river. So we moved along the riverbank.

Sunbeam hadn't spoken a word since new wounds were cut on that wretched high place, and old wounds were reopening inside of her after the beast held up Gilda's locket. Now a good stretch down the bank in the moonlight, those terrible hisses and chants had faded. But the noise was replaced with something else. Far beyond the trees, it sounded faintly like a . . . a . . . a flute? I listened harder. Yes, it was a certainly a flute!

"Where's that noise coming from?" she whispered.

"Sounds like some kind of song," I said, wary of what might happen next. "A flute player."

"How strange. This is not the time for music," she said. Thinking of music, her mind wandered to Harmon—his impressive musical talent and his bumbling awkwardness in class—then to Fawn with her peculiar ways and stray animals. School seemed so far behind her now, lost in another time and place.

The flute melody faded off into the night. And the sound of the river began to roll away the chaos. We walked on in silence. Sunbeam recalled the horrible sights she'd just seen: the Golgums, beastly fangs, and that masked prince with the claw. And as bad of a day as she had earlier at Thornridge, she'd rather endure Helga Hammerstone any day of the week than mess with these things. She thought of her mother, the moving boxes, and the trouble she'd stirred at Thornridge. She made up her mind she was doomed to be an outcast. And she accepted it.

In that moment all those things back home seemed trivial. For now, her heart beat for Gilda, and her spirit was broken down with images from the prince's high place. Sunbeam fidgeted with the Key, which she rolled between her fingers, lost in thought. After a moment, she took a length of thin rope from her pocket, which she often used to tie up her hair. She knotted it around the Golden Key, then tied it around her neck.

"We're bound to find the way out," I said, trying to distract Sunbeam from what I knew she was thinking.

"I can't go," she mumbled.

"Can't what, Mistress?"

"I've got to get that locket. It was the last thing I ever gave Gilda."

"But life in Ozmandia. It's not safe here . . ."

"I'm stuck, Whitewing."

We had come to a rough kind of terrain by now and making good distance. The river bank was broken by gullies and bluffs. But even though the road was rough, there was a stillness about the air. Everything else the past day had been chaotically moving and shifting, but the still woods started to counteract it. I continued along the riverbank. Suddenly, it became even more still in the air, like a thick, heavy, dark blanket being slowly draped over us, and it made you want to lie down and sleep, but not a peaceful sleep—a heavy and laden sleep. We were alone now under the drip drop of the wet trees.

"This road has to lead us somewhere," I said, breaking the stillness.

"Where is somewhere? Somewhere is just into taller trees and shadows," Sunbeam said, wearily.

She was visibly sinking under the heaviness of the air. I, too, began fighting the force of exhaustion suddenly being laid upon us. The Golden Key rested securely on her chest now, knotted on its stringed twine. The Key was the last thing I checked before veering from the riverbank. All I knew was that we had to escape the heavy air.

Suddenly, a slight movement jostled a shrub of leaves. Again, we heard gruff sighs that sounded like a bunch of hungry warthogs trying to be quiet.

"Who's there?" I said. I looked closer and caught another glimpse of a hard, leathery backside barely visible in the low bushes—the same pointy shapes that stuck out like twisted forks from before. But this time, there were more—about eight or nine of them. They stopped. Their thorny forks poked out of the dark green. It became very still. No sound but the river came between us and them—until they crawled off, the tops of the leaves flailing a wild trail behind them.

I began fighting my way slowly up the bank, zigzagging between cypress trees and broken trunks. The ground rose steeply through the thick underbrush. At once, a multitude of black birds swooped down from the sky. They looked to be the same wild vultures feeding off the dead carcass we saw earlier before sunset. They hovered in the air, then disappeared into the branches of the woods. I waited for the Key to light. To give us a sign . . . but . . . nothing.

"Let's stop and rest," said Sunbeam. Her eyelids began drooping.

"No, you must not go to sleep. You have to stay the course."

"Oh, what's . . . what's the hurry?" she replied, dozing off. Her walk became stumbled.

"We've got to get back before those Golgums find us!"

"We're miles ahead of them," she whispered, half-asleep. She plopped down on the ground.

"Get on Mistress. I'll carry you from here."

I bent my knee and kneeled so she could climb on easier. When she was safe in the saddle, I continued up the bank. The air grew heavier. And I, being a horse, am sensitive to certain forces in the air. Humans call it animal instinct. I became very nervous because I sensed darkness surrounding. Though I couldn't see it, I felt its presence.

"I . . . I just can't go on," said Sunbeam.

"Stay awake, Mistress!"

She was fading. And those haunting birds loomed above and peered down upon us from the branches of the woods. I fought the air of exhaustion. But in the haze, I struggled and strained up the slope of the bank. See, when horses have humans on their backs, they're made to keep going when their humans feel like they cannot.

Sunbeam was almost totally asleep now, slumped down against my mane. Her whole body felt limp, except for her hand, which was clutched tightly around the Golden Key.

The darkness grew stronger, but I still could not *see* the ghoulish presence I was *sensing*. The air felt a little like the tombs, but different. For the tombs didn't hide their hideousness. However, this darkness was subtle, yet looming.

Without warning, in the thicket of cypress, straightaway, something billowed from behind a tree. My eyes traveled down to the bottom of the tree trunk where the tail end of a long, black cloak trying to masquerade itself, caught in the wind and lifted from the ground, only a remnant of the hem barely revealing itself. I zoomed my keen eye to see. Just then, another cloak hem lining flapped from behind another tree, and another, and another, and another, until all at once, an assembly of cloak tails were billowing from behind all the trees a short stretch into the woods. But they never emerged. The cloaks stood silently behind the cypress, waiting, flapping subtly in the hazy draft. My animal instinct was right. We were being watched!

I froze. Sunbeam was slumped forward, asleep by now under the heavy air. I balanced my walk to keep her from falling. It was all I could do to prevent myself from freezing in fear.

Should I escape down the riverbank? Risk everything and speed forward in a wild gallop? Any good horse can get out of this. I hope . . . I . . .

The sound of the cloaks grew rapidly louder and beat in the wind. I paused to see which way to run. At that moment my ears were completely pulled back against my mane. The air grew heavier and the breeze blew a mist that never went away. Sunbeam must have felt the change, for she awoke halfway. She was breathing heavy, still weary but trying to sit up. As she regained consciousness, the Golden Key lit up around her neck.

"Mistress, you must stay awake!" I yelled.

"Halt, Whitewing. The Key is . . . is hot to touch," she groaned. "The arrow. It's coming back."

"Which way is it pointing?"

"I don't know," she said. "I . . . I can barely see a thing."

The sound of the host of whipping cloaks grew louder; however, they stayed disguised behind the trees. Only the mystic hem linings were barely visible. The dark birds watched and waited from the branches, which formed a haunting blackness throughout the tree tops.

"Check the compass again!" I said.

"I . . . I think it's pointing forward. But the trees are thicker *ahead* than I've ever seen them," she said, her voice still weary.

"Remember, you can't go back, only *through*!" I shouted against the gusts of wind. It was then I knew the direction to take.

And that relieved half of my distress. I braced myself, readying to set off at great speed through the fog and cryptic cloaks ahead. I knew what I had to do.

Then Sunbeam shouted, "The Key! It's bearing that word, Cresc-phos!"

"Greater Light?"

The very next moment, inside mist and wind, the colony of cloaks crept from behind the trees, aligning themselves like a strong, slow train. There were about twenty of them. They started raising their grey hands into the air as if they were performing some magical ritual. And when they raised their arms, their loose sleeves rolled down to reveal their forearms—all bearing that horrid scar: *the mark of the claw.*

"I can barely see!" shouted Sunbeam.

"Get out. Get out," they chanted in unity, creeping slowly toward us, expressionless.

Sunbeam's limbs were shaking, and I sensed a terrible ache was beginning in her stomach. She was too frightened to know what do to with my reins.

"Get out. Get out." They advanced steadily toward us, aligned in their black hooded cavalcade. The sound of their cloaks beat louder against the wind, and they seemed to grow taller with each step. As slow as they marched, we were surprised to find ourselves suddenly trapped, overshadowed by towering black cloaks, wind gusts, and somber chanting, "Get out. Get out."

The wind grew rapidly louder. Their ashen skin and hollow eyes were within only a few feet. They continued advancing, "GET OUT. GET OUT."

Panicked, my eyes shifted around the trees. I looked for a sign. I turned my head slightly to see Sunbeam in the saddle. The Key still lay on her neck where it gleamed more golden than ever against the blackness. In its halo of light, Sunbeam was pale and weak and trembling.

"Sunbeam! You have the Key! Is it leading us forward?"

I shouted against the wind. I wondered how I'd ever make it through the train of Golgums.

Her arms trembling, she clutched the Key in her hand and her eyes darted down on its Golden Arrow.

"Forward! Cresc-phos!" was all she could blurt. It was as though she did not know *what* she was saying or *why* she was saying it. She only read the compass on the Key.

Upon shouting *Cres-phos*, a little light, like a sun ray, broke through the trees. It broke through straight toward the advancing black cloaks. Against all odds, I knew to run toward the glow. Sunbeam must have known it too because she stared at the breaking light and yelled, "Whitewing, can you ride fast?" She pointed straight ahead.

"We'll run as hard as we can. Hold on!"

With great force I reared wildly back on my hind legs, bursting forth into an untamed gallop. And with the help of what must have been supernatural strength, I broke through the cloaked train. And we set off at tremendous speed toward the light.

"Run, Boy! Run!" shouted Sunbeam. To our horror, the hooded figures had shifted their sunken eyes and set themselves in our direction behind us. I continued toward the light. Its bright ray streaked down before us, illuminating our path. For what seemed like eternity, we sped through the trees. I ran as hard as I could on the glowing path.

Foamy sweat coated my flanks, and my nostrils wheezed for breath. Speeding through tree trunks, Sunbeam accidentally bashed her leg, injuring it against a jagged limb.

The race was very turbulent.

"Look! There!" shouted Sunbeam.

I rounded the bend. The streak of light shone over a hidden canopy of lush green hedges where everything became clear and colorful.

"There, Whitewing! Run!" Sunbeam pointed to the lit green sanctuary.

I sped forward into a secured garden, walled in by green hedges with colorful fruit that were at least twelve feet high. By now, I had lost the cloaked figures, but knew they couldn't be far behind.

"The Key! It's stopped glowing!" gasped Sunbeam. "This has to be the right place. I'm getting used to reading the signs," she said, slightly priding herself in her new skill. "Whitewing look!"

We stared forward and came upon something we didn't even have time to comprehend. In the center of the garden, next to a sparkling pool, stood a man with fine, lovely features. He was dressed in colors I had never seen before, but colors that looked like spring, all the way down to his sandals. Quietly tending the foliage and blooms, he had an auburn beard the color of wine and the kindest, golden-brown eyes I'd ever seen.

Sunbeam slowly dismounted, and with doubt and trembling, got down and walked toward the Quiet Gardener. She was limping on her left leg after it had slammed against one of the trees while running from the cloaked cavalcade. There were many cypress trees and branches to dodge, so to escape with only one injury was to come out well. I hadn't escaped without pain either because I had scraped up my horse knees and nicked my hoof. But that, too, was to run well, especially carrying a human on your back.

"Come in, my daughter, you are welcome here," the Quiet Gardener said. He was already helping her walk by carrying her weak side.

"Sunbeam, wait!" I said. I was unsure if we could trust the bearded man.

The Quiet Gardener looked over all the scrapes and the tear in her leg. I watched him closely, ready to scoop up my Mistress, lest there be any dangerous moves.

"Who are you? Where am I?" asked Sunbeam.

"There is no time for questions now," said the Gardener.

Then abruptly, without warning, my attuned ears heard the sound of the whipping cloaks. The wind grew louder. To our horror, the legion of Golgums, one by one, little by little, each slipped their heads inside the green enclosure, chanting, "Get out. Get out," and aligned themselves at the entrance of the garden archway.

The Quiet Gardener stood up. And at once, the cloaked figures came to an immediate halt. Sunbeam's heart seemed to race. She became very still, so still she could barely breathe.

"What do they want?" asked Sunbeam.

"Be still, Child," said the Gardener.

The Quiet Gardener's eyes stared at the hooded legion with an intensity that would cause even the strongest man to heed. Upon his stare, the cloaked figures moaned and groaned, then solemnly hunched over and crawled backwards down on all fours in the dirt, then slowly crept away.

"Come in, my daughter. You are protected in this garden by a high boundary."

The bearded man helped her sit at the edge of the sparkling blue pool. I quickly took in the sights of the blooming sanctuary, which was larger than I had realized. On the far side of the grounds there was a flock of sheep. They walked among the greenest grass I'd ever seen. The Quiet Gardener busied himself, filling a large, wooden cup with the sparkling water from the pool. He knelt down next to Sunbeam and began washing her wounds and tears. I watched him with a close eye, should there be even a hint of danger. Sunbeam was still shaken by the recent crisis and panting for breath.

"Who—who are you?" asked Sunbeam again.

"I am my Father's Son," replied the Quiet Gardener.

"Who is your father?" She stared at him.

"My Father owns the garden, and I keep and prune it," he said.

Sunbeam looked at the bleeding wound on herself and became faint.

"You are wounded. And your horse is tired. But do not be afraid," said the Quiet Gardener. Then he touched her bruised side and felt her wrists.

"I'm so sore. What did those things—those Golgums want?" asked Sunbeam. A peaceful feeling settled over her while he washed her wounds.

"My daughter, instead of catching you and sinking their claws into your skin, they fell behind, and you came out with only a few scratches. You've been protected."

He finished tending her wounds, then stood up. I hadn't taken my keen eye off him since entering the garden. Suddenly, he fetched a wood basin and brought it to me. He patted my mane and smiled, "Be at ease, dear horse. Here is something to eat. Have water and grass."

Now that he stood closer, I took in his countenance. He had an extraordinary expression, both serious and lively, so that those who looked at him would love him, but at the same time fear him. He was tall and well-proportioned. His face was without blemish and his cheeks had a light, ruddy color. His appearance was polite and joyful. His auburn beard was the same color as his hair, which hung down below his ears while his eyes were golden-brown and filled with extreme brilliance. He moved with wonder and grace, and his features were dignified. His arms were graceful as he patted my nose and fed me, and I sensed by my animal instinct, that he was the nicest of all men.

After a while, he fetched another cup of water and sat next to Sunbeam's weak side.

"Now, drink," said the Quiet Gardener.

She was extremely thirsty and drank the entire cup, and when she finished, she felt refreshed.

"I am looking for my sister, Gilda." Sunbeam stared at him. "Do you know . . . have you seen one that looks like me? My twin."

"My daughter, the days are numbered. Waste no more time on questions, just believe."

"I don't understand," said Sunbeam.

"Stand up on your feet. For your wounds are washed and bandaged."

He lifted her from the side of the sparkling pool. He steadied her weak side, and she felt strengthened. I, too, was no longer tired, but restored and good as new. The Quiet Gardener stood at the edge of the cool waters and looked to the sky.

"My daughter, you are still in the darkness of night," he said. "There will be thicker clouds and darker shadows. But your heart can be filled with sunlight."

"Will I see Ozmandia again?" she asked.

"Not by going back, only through," he said.

"I am not fit for this," she pleaded in a low voice.

"Be of good hope," the Quiet Gardener said. He raised his arm and pointed to the farthest side of the garden. "There is another door. Open the curtain ahead, further onward. Always onward. And keep running."

He then handed her a small, clear bottle filled with a potion as red as blood.

"I know by my name that you will find the right way. But there is only one. Will you drink this saving potion?"

Sunbeam stared at the red potion, as did I. For all I knew, it might be poison. My instinct told me the Gardener was a good man, but we hardly knew him. Everything in this unearthly world seemed designed to trick and mislead us.

By the look on Sunbeam's face, I knew these same questions were running through her mind, too, and in that moment, she froze. There was no knowing what the potion would do. She studied the blood-red bottle then looked into the Gardener's dazzling, golden eyes. He spoke with an authority one could not help but trust, for there seemed to be no fault in him. All at once, she knew she had to make a choice—to trust and receive his gift or leave it behind. For reasons she could not explain, her heart began to pound like never before with excitement and joy.

She stood in his presence, and against all sound logic, and without fully understanding, she raised it to her lips—and she *drank* the potion. My own heart fluttered in my chest as I watched her. I could barely breathe. I stood still as a stone, but ready to rear back and run with Mistress if the moment called for it. In a flash, to my immense relief, she lifted her face. She looked bathed in light and strength—absolutely radiant.

Then we looked, and incredibly, the bottle remained as full as before, as if replenished from an endless supernatural source.

"I—what—what is this?" She stared awestruck at the bottle that was mysteriously full again.

The Quiet Gardener sealed the bottle with a cork, then spoke. His voice was commanding as thunder, but pure and gentle as a peaceful stream. "Keep this with you, Child. You will need it. Listen to my words now. This was your first drink, but the next one will be your last."

"What do you mean?" Sunbeam asked.

"Do not spill it carelessly. Save the last of it for the final battle."

"Battle?" she asked, wide-eyed.

"Now run. Run forward," said the Quiet Gardener.

Sunbeam nodded her thanks. Without knowing exactly what lie ahead, she knew she had only one more time to use the saving potion and hid the bottle inside the satchel draped over my back.

"Thank you so much. For everything." She climbed onto the saddle.

We then set off forward at the Quiet Gardener's command.

CHAPTER 5

SUNBEAM HAS A DREAM

On the farthest side of the garden was an old hut under a skillfully thatched roof of palms. At the threshold of the doorpost hung a long curtain, vertically torn in half. Sunbeam dismounted and led me on foot by the reins. She crept carefully. The curtain swayed in the breeze and seemed to invite us in. The hut looked as if it were a deep and ancient boundary stone. Sunbeam looked at me with uncertainty.

"Should we?" said Sunbeam. She examined the Key, which still hung closely around her neck. But she received no signs.

"The Gardener said straight ahead. This is straight, Mistress. The Key led; you must choose."

Her breathing became rapid, and she started to pace. She turned around to find the Gardener. He now stood a long way off, barely a speck on the horizon, yet his penetrating, bright eyes felt near, and they urged us forward.

"Let's go," she said in a tone that let me know her decision was made. We walked toward the ancient threshold. For a second, I sensed Sunbeam's heart give way to intense doubt. She stopped abruptly. "I feel hot. All this I don't understand. I'm not cut out for this." She wound the Golden Key between her fingers.

She started to turn around, but then remembered the locket, and *Gilda*.

"Let's go," she said, and led me through the threshold.

Upon entering, all her fear melted away. I, too, felt a little relieved once inside. Sunbeam sat down on the ground to rest while I stood over her, keeping watch. She began to study the Key. With my warhorse second sight, I sensed what my mistress was thinking.

Once quiet and alone with her thoughts, she thought of Gilda. Then she thought of her mother's tired eyes, and the father she had never seen. She thought about the lost hope of Ozmandia, and the suffering people, and of the powerful Lord Wolford and the dark Golgums. Her heart felt like a hurricane, chaotic and heavy, for many heavy things had been laid upon it. Then she thought of the prince with that horrid claw. Who exactly was he? And she wondered what it all meant—and how on earth she ended up there. And now that she'd found the Golden Key, which led her deeper into dark and mysterious things, she wondered what she should do. And she wished she had never found the Golden Key. Because even though Ozmandia was a gloomy place, and her mother ran from things Sunbeam never understood, it seemed easier to just accept things as they were and live helplessly, rather than seek answers. It seemed easier to serve than to stand up and fight.

But at the same time, since finding the Golden Key, she seemed to be unlocking mysteries she now felt burdened to solve. Even though she didn't know what it all meant, she knew she'd seen a glimpse into something more. And she began drowning in more and more of her thoughts.

And in all the heaviness and swirling thoughts, she lay down tired, and drifted into a deep, deep sleep. And in her slumber, she had a *DREAM:*

In her dream, she was taken to an upper room of the ancient hutch. Inside, there was an air of all things new and light and refreshing. In the middle of the hut, sat an old table, carved from wood and the sweetest fragrance of incense burning on top of it, and next to it was a Golden Lamp. The air was the purest she'd ever smelled, even purer than the outside garden blooms, and when she breathed, it felt like power and life entered her bones.

She stood in a sanctum of flawless air and light. The next moment, a sound of voices, like a choir, sang from a far-off distance, beautiful melodies her ears had never heard. If she could see the music, the sounds would look like the Quiet Gardener's robe, full of wondrous color.

Suddenly, the music trailed off and the incense grew into a heavy cloud so thick she could not see, and then, the sweetest of all fragrances filled the air; it overpowered her. Sunbeam fell down afraid.

"I feel goodness and doom within me and . . . !" she screamed in the dream and trembled.

Before she could utter the rest of her sentence, the smoke dissipated. When it vanished, she saw the seat of an ancient throne, and the one who sat on it was so high she could only see the train of his robe, which filled the whole sanctum. The lamp on the table was now lit and flickering. Then a warm invisible hand seemed to caress her face.

"What is this hand I feel on me, but cannot see!" she cried, terrified.

"Child, do not be afraid." At the sound of the voice, the ground and doorposts shook. "See, my hand is upon you and has touched your lips. You are protected. Now stand."

"Who—who are you?" cried Sunbeam, looking up to the heights.

"I am the Ancient One." When he spoke, his voice thundered, not as if he were angry, but as though he was who he said he was.

"Stand up. I am the One from Ancient Days. Accept my mercy," he thundered. "My Child, why have you come here?"

Sunbeam slowly stood at his command. Even though the Ancient One sat so high that she could not see his face, Sunbeam felt he could see closely into the deepest parts of her heart. All at once, a change came over her and she screamed out: "Your royal highness, I am seeking my sister, Gilda. Can you help me find what—"

"Be still," he thundered.

Without warning, another cloud of smoke blew in and settled over the wooden table. When it wisped away, there lay a heap of bones. They looked like they had been long forgotten, like they were once lost and buried in a faraway desert. At the sight of these bones, Sunbeam's heart convulsed.

Were these Gilda's bones? Sunbeam drew closer, shuddering. Then she fell into a hypnotic state, staring at the bones, yet, fully aware of her surroundings. The bones evoked a sorrow so deep that Sunbeam felt like crying out in agony. She stared at the heap of deadness that lay on the wooden table. After a moment, the Ancient voice thundered:

"My Child, can these bones live?"

"Oh, Your Highness, I don't know!" she said, unsure how to answer.

"Speak to these bones and say to them, 'Dry bones, hear! This is what the Ancient of Days says: I will cause breath to enter you, and you will live!'"

Sunbeam watched and listened under the height of the Ancient One's voice. Then the whole sanctum began to shake. Suddenly, her heart began to race, as there came a loud rattling sound, and the bones joined together, bone to its bone. Tendons and flesh came up, and skin stretched over them, but there was no breath in them.

The next moment, the Ancient One spoke, "O breath, come from the four winds and breathe into these slayed bones!"

In that instant, breath went into them, and the bones came alive and stood up on their feet. From what had seemed only a small pile of bones, hundreds of ghostly men, women and children now filled the great hall.

Then the Ancient One said, "My Child, these bones are the whole island of Ozmandia. They say in their hearts, 'Our bones are dried up, and our hope is lost.' Therefore, speak to them, and tell them they are not forgotten. Tell them to believe, and light will again shine in the land."

In the dream, Sunbeam stood speechless and in complete awe before the wooden table, bones, incense, the magnificent robe and the thundering voice from the heights. She felt very confused in her mind, but somehow, her heart understood.

The Ancient One's voice boomed again. "I have seen the misery. The cry of the Ozmandians has reached me. Look now, go. I am sending you."

"Sending me? Who am I that I should do this?"

"I will be with you," said the Ancient One.

"But my sister! Gilda! Tell me where she is! I've come for her, not this!" Sunbeam fell down weeping.

"Child, do not despair. You came with your plans, but your steps have been re-ordered. At the end, all will be known."

"I'm just a girl," she repeated, crouching on the floor of the ancient hutch.

"I will send the helpers. You will know them. But listen very carefully, there is a Lost One. And the Lost One, must first be found."

"Lost One?"

"When the Lost One has been found, all will be complete. It is only when the Lost One is found, and all is complete, that you can defeat the darkness and receive joy for your pains."

"LOST ONE? I don't understand! Do you mean Gilda?"

"Have you the potion my Son gave?"

"Yes, I have it."

"Remember it and take it upon you. At the appointed time, you will know what to do."

"But how do I—?"

"Go, the answers lie in front of you."

With that, the train of his robe vanished behind a pillar of smoke, shaking the doorposts and the ground as it went. In the next moment, Sunbeam awoke from her sleep in a cold sweat, breathing rapidly. She sat up awake, trembling and lost in thought.

ॐ ॐ

"Mistress? Are you alright?"

"I . . . I don't know," she murmured.

"You were dreaming, Mistress."

"A dream, Whitewing. Or, was it a dream?" She looked down at the Golden Key, which glinted her fingerprint in the half-light.

"It's that Key," I said, concerned. "It's causing strange happenings."

"I must find—find . . ." she put her own finger over the lit fingerprint of the Key and pressed it down.

"Find what, Mistress?"

"Oh, never mind. There are answers. Tomorrow, we must go," she said, clutching the Key. Then she drifted back asleep.

She didn't know where we were heading next, and neither did I. All I knew was that ever since finding the Golden Key, things had gotten very, very strange . . .

CHAPTER 6

THE HELPERS

Early the next day, Sunbeam woke inside the hut at the edge of the green garden. When she trudged outside, she felt the warm sunlight on her face. She strained to make sense of the unnerving events from the previous night.

"What a nightmare, Whitewing," she groaned.

"Are you feeling better?" I asked, but she did not answer.

After a moment, she grabbed at her neck, and there, the Golden Key still lay on its cord. She clutched it in her hand; an air of relief washed over her face.

"I'm so tired. I can hardly move," she blurted.

"What about breakfast?" I nudged her.

"Never mind breakfast," she said. "Whitewing, I had a dream."

"I know, Mistress. You awoke briefly last night. I was concerned."

"I can't stop thinking about it. There was the most beautiful glowing lamp burning on a hill. And there was something about . . . a *Lost One*."

"Lost One?" I was skeptical and concerned for my Mistress's well-being.

"I . . . I don't know what it means yet," she murmured. She thought of Gilda.

I knew I had to nudge her along because she looked as if she might vanish in her own thoughts. "Mother must be worried sick about me not coming home," she said. "But imagine how joyful she'll be if I can find Gilda and bring her back. Surely that would make up for Mother's worry over where I've been."

"Yes, Mistress, I imagine it would."

"I've got to get the locket," she said, clenching her fist.

She recalled her mother again, and her mother's breakfast and realized she missed it terribly. She was hungry.

"Didn't you mention breakfast?"

"Yes. I'm sure you'll find something. Your mother put some food in the satchel."

"Good I'm starving! But we better move on a little first." She stepped in the stirrups and climbed on the saddle.

We set forward. As we neared the end of the green enclosure, Sunbeam looked back, trying to get a glimpse of the Quiet Gardener. But he was nowhere to be found. And with fear welling up inside her chest, she led me out of the Garden's boundary and deeper into the Depths of Cypress. And she knew, this time, she better continue her journey with extreme caution.

We trotted under the dark, twisted trees. Sunbeam, on the saddle, reached her hand in the satchel and found a slightly stale biscuit. She realized in that second just how starving she was, for it didn't bother her that the biscuit was a little stale, as long as it satisfied her hunger. She reached into the satchel for another biscuit, and her hand seized upon the bottle of red potion she'd been given. And looking up with a mouthful of biscuit, she blurted: "Whitewing, the potion! We must keep this safe!"

She pulled me to a halt, then dismounted to secure the small bottle of red potion inside her pocket. As she walked, her ribs still ached a little from Helga's "death grip." It had only been one day. But Helga already seemed like a distant memory and such a *small* matter now. For after finding the Key, she had much bigger problems to sort out.

With her rib aching, she sat on a large, broken branch and finished eating the biscuit. And I had a few more mouthfuls of grass. Usually, she ate breakfast at home with her mother. Sunbeam thought of how her mom must be sitting home alone at the kitchen table, worried sick. She recalled her mother's usual scolding every time she stayed out late. She could hear her mother's words inside her head:

"Sunbeam! It's not safe! I couldn't bear if anything happened to you, too!"

Guilt and sadness fell over her, and her heart became heavy, for her mother did not know the real reason why Gilda went missing and that Sunbeam was to blame. She harbored that dark secret every day and dragged it around like a ton of bricks. But she knew finding Gilda would set everything right. It was her fault she was gone. So, it was up to her to bring her back.

Trying to break the sadness I knew Sunbeam was under, I spoke up.

"We'd better get a move on, Mistress," I said, trying to lighten her mood.

"Whitewing, I must tell you of the dream. There was a lamp, a wonderful, glorious, burning light. And then a voice . . . a voice that told me to take the red potion upon me. And that at the end, all would be known. But reaching the end seems impossible," she sighed.

"Do you think this dream is some trick of the Golden Key?" I was cautious of the Key now and becoming suspicious of its powers.

"I—I have to find out," she said. Fear clashed with courage inside her stormy green eyes. "I just don't know how." She looked down at the ground.

As we finished our breakfast, I heard a twig snap a little distance behind us. Quickly, my keen eye investigated the surrounding trees.

"Get over behind the brush, Mistress," I said.

Sunbeam must have heard the noise, too, for she was already heading toward a heap of low hanging branches to hide. After only one night in the Depths, she knew danger lurked in the trees. And it was at the most inopportune time that it could emerge. In a moment, we heard soft music in the distance. Someone was playing an instrument! It was that flute we heard earlier on the riverbank. But this time, it was closer!

"Sunbeam, I think someone's shadowing us."

"What is it? A troubadour?" she whispered, somewhat sarcastically.

The music continued playing. It was a beautiful lovely tune. But whoever played it was either oblivious to our presence or trying to lure us in with enchanting music.

"Should we run for it?" Sunbeam whispered. She looked down at the Golden Key, but it did not light. It gave no sign. "Do you think they can hear us too?"

"They might be able to hear us as well as *see* us. Be still!" I warned.

It was daylight in the Depths now, so it didn't seem as threatening as the pitch-black night, but the haunting, grey sky over the large tree branches still gave dim light. The breeze carried the tune in the air. Sunbeam's heart leaped into her throat.

"Are you all right, Mistress?"

"No. I'm embarrassed of myself," she whispered. "Here I am shrinking like a coward. But I can't deal with anymore of those—those Golgums. I wish someone else had found this Key," she whispered.

The next moment, the music grew nearer—and nearer—and rounding the bend, to our great surprise, it was Harmon! And Fawn! They walked down the trail, Harmon playing his flute while Fawn walked a few steps behind him, petting some wild, furry, stray animal. The stray didn't look like an animal I'd ever seen before. It was about the size of a rabbit, with greyish-white fur that had specks of black peppered through it. The face looked like a mix between a rabbit and a husky. Its indigo eyes were large and round, with a blue-grey button nose and long whiskers. Every time it wagged its bushy tail, its pointy ears would pop up. Also, tiny birds flitted around her, and a squirrel followed at her heels. By the look of it, even the animals in the Depths seemed drawn to her. Back in Ozmandia, her parents owned a farm, and she'd bring the newborns to school: pigs, deer, baby chicks, and anything else furry and cute. And I, being a horse, noticed her love for me, too. When she saw me, she'd always run over to comb my mane or ask Sunbeam if she could take me for rides in the fields. Sometimes Sunbeam would let her, and we'd trot around the grass. She always fed me sugar cubes. I liked them very much.

Upon seeing those two, Sunbeam thought to herself:

Wasn't that just like them. Harmon with his music and Fawn petting some silly strays. But even more, what on earth were they doing in the Depths of Cypress?

Astonished, Sunbeam popped out from behind the wooded thicket, startling Harmon to death. He nearly jumped out of his skin—so much that he bumped into a branch, wavered on his knees, and dropped his flute. When he tried to pick it up, he fumbled and bumbled, "Oh! Sunbeam!" he shouted, squinting through his bifocals with a slight grin. "Fawn, look! We've found her!" In his excitement, he stumbled and nearly fell.

It was moments like these she could see why he was so unpopular at Thornridge. But she knew inside, he was true and sincere. Underneath his awkwardness, she'd seen a confidence that came out only when he played his music. When he took off his glasses, his eyes looked smooth and confident. He had a slim face with brown hair combed over to the side, and large, brown eyes that were deep set. His features were fine and pleasant, offset by a strong, chiseled jaw. He was handsome in a different sort of way. But behind the bumbling, Sunbeam thought there was a charming handsomeness, nonetheless. It's just no one could get past his awkwardness to see it.

Meanwhile, Fawn immediately set down her furry, blue-nosed stray and ran to Sunbeam. The stray ran behind her, pawing at her heels. "Sunbeam! You're alive! We were worried sick!" She hugged her. Then Fawn ran to me and patted my mane while Harmon stood there with his awkward half-grin, his eyes beaming with relief.

"What are you doing in the Depths?" Sunbeam said. "And what is this animal you have now, Fawn?"

"It started following me some miles back. Look at its blueish, purple eyes. It's so soft. I'm naming it Indigo!" said Fawn. The stray twitched its blue-grey nose and curled next to her feet.

"Indigo, huh?" said Sunbeam. "Well try to keep Indigo under control? We all know what happens when you take on more animals than you can handle."

As shocked as Sunbeam was to see her friends, she felt a little relief to see familiar faces. Seeing them brought a spark of happiness inside the Dark Depths, even for me. "How did you get here?" said Sunbeam.

"After the fight with Helga, we saw how upset you were, so we followed you," said Fawn. She picked up furry Indigo and was petting its pointy ears while at the same time, looked at Sunbeam with her warm, chestnut eyes.

"We ran after you!" said Harmon. "We followed Whitewing's tracks and knew you entered the Dark Depths of Cypress! We were afraid to go inside, but we could not let you go alone, so we trailed behind the tracks until we came upon a great Door. We kept following the tracks and knew you crossed through. And just as soon as we got there, the Door opened. Before we could think, we ran through it. We thought we'd find you inside, but when we looked, you were nowhere to be found. We tried to go back, but the Door slammed shut! And we couldn't get out!"

"You cannot go *back*, only *through*," said Sunbeam. "You two shouldn't have followed me here. It's dangerous."

As soon as Sunbeam said *dangerous*, a quick movement came from dark shrub near us. We looked, and the strange creatures were back again: the gruff crawlers with leathery backsides scampering in the bushes—with their same pointy shapes that stuck out like twisted forks. They were a little less than knee-high, small, but looked as hefty as hogs and strong as a tortoise shell. Each time they came back, they grew in numbers. And judging by the number of sharp pointers sticking out of the bushes, there looked to be about twenty of them. Everyone stopped talking. It became very still—until they romped off, rustling the leaves behind them as they went.

"What the—was that?" asked Harmon.

"I'm guessing some kind of strange species . . . maybe a reptile, but not quite," said Fawn, studying the bushes.

"Don't get so close!" said Sunbeam. "Stay away from the bushes, Fawn. Whatever they are, they keep coming back."

Sunbeam felt grateful her friends had come to her aid, but she didn't expect any help from them. She'd always got along fine without it. And she did not intend to start asking for help now. Besides, Sunbeam knew they would have no interest in her quest. It was dangerous. It proved too big of a burden for even herself, so it would certainly be too much to ask of her friends. Not knowing what to say, Sunbeam stared at the ground. Everyone looked at her. She swallowed. "Look, you two made a mistake coming here," she said. "You should head out. And I have to get moving. Let's go, Whitewing." She quickly turned and walked away into a row of trees to the edge of a nearby stream. Everyone followed her.

"What's wrong, Sunbeam?" asked Fawn.

"Gilda is in the Depths. I'm not leaving until I find her." She stared down at the stream.

As she spoke, she caught a glimpse of her reflection from the top of the stream. In the water's reflection, she thought she saw Gilda's face, but then realized it was her own. Being twins, they both had light hair and skin, with delicate features and piercing green eyes. The only difference was that Sunbeam's eyes were slightly darker, and her face was a little less round than Gilda's. But no one could ever tell them apart.

"You don't look so well," said Fawn.

"The water—I—I thought I saw Gilda."

"Well you two were identical, right?" asked Harmon. He walked to the stream and he, too, looked at his own reflection.

"Well Harmon, let's just be glad there aren't two of YOU," snickered Fawn.

Harmon dismissed her remark.

"Look," said Sunbeam. "If you two want to separate here, I'll understand. I'm sure you both want to get to Ozmandia." Yes, she knew they had good intentions, but she didn't expect them to follow her. It was risky.

Sunbeam's heart winced, and her eyes started to well with tears, but she would never let them see her cry. She turned her face away. They all fell silent, and a long pause hung in the air. Sunbeam, in the silence, waited. She knew for sure they would break it with why they'd have to go in different directions; that they'd have to head down another trail. After all, she couldn't blame them for wanting to escape the Depths. She wanted the same, just not without Gilda. She knew they had no time to bother searching for something they had not lost. However, she did. And that was her twin. Her other half.

"How do you know Gilda is in the Depths?" Harmon peered through his glasses.

"I saw her locket."

"Where?" Harmon moved closer, his eyes full of concern.

"At a very dark place. A place you two *aren't* going . . . where by the looks of it, a place you could die!" said Sunbeam.

"Die? Oh Sunbeam, you've already got us in a mess of trouble!" cried Fawn. She gripped furry Indigo tightly to her chest. "We have to get back to the island!"

"Watch what you say, Fawn. You talk rash when you're scared," whispered Harmon.

"You shouldn't have followed me here. You two can cut out as soon as possible. I don't want to keep you in this place," said Sunbeam.

"No. I think we should all go together," said Harmon.

"I don't know if there's much sense in going all together," said Sunbeam. "The more people, the more likely we'll be seen, right? Besides, you two shouldn't take the risk. This is my battle."

"But you're just a girl!" Harmon shrieked. He took off his glasses. His large brown eyes looked smooth, melting away the clumsiness from his face. He appeared strong, like he did when he played his music.

"What is it to you that I'm *just* a girl?" snapped Sunbeam.

"I'm sorry. I didn't mean it like that. I only meant that I would not leave a friend in this wild place alone. Why, it's only normal I'd try to help. Understand?" he said, his deep-set eyes looked serious, but sincere.

"I guess. But stop saying annoying things like that," said Sunbeam.

Suddenly, Fawn stood from the ground, petting Indigo and interrupted, "Listen, we're all friends. Let's try to talk *reasonably*?" She smiled.

"Oh come on Fawn!" said Sunbeam. "I can see you don't want to go."

"Look, I want to help you!" said Fawn, "but how do I know we're not going to die here?"

"You don't. And it's not worth it for either of you. It's a risk I'd never ask you to take," said Sunbeam. And she meant that.

It's already my fault Gilda is gone, she thought to herself. *I cannot be the cause for more lives lost. I could not bear it. It's up to me to find Gilda. It's my fault she's gone. It's up to me to bring her back.*

"I'll vouch for Fawn," continued Harmon. "You've been a good friend to both of us."

"Well . . . I . . . I guess it's settled then. We're all going together," said Fawn.

And as Sunbeam stood there, surrounded by cypress trees and the darkness of the Depths, and holding my reins, and seeing the faces of the only two friends she had from Thornridge, everything fell silent. It was like everyone's mouths were moving, but she could not hear what they said; everything moved in slow motion—like a dream. She grasped the Golden Key in her hand and looked down upon it. And all she could focus on was its sheer Goldenness. And she recalled the voice and vision in the dream from the previous night that boomed: *I will send the Helpers* . . .

And in that moment, she knew who they were.

And she felt great relief, but knew there were still many more answers that lay ahead . . .

&ev; &es;

As her two friends quibbled on about which way to go, I stood near my Mistress and listened. I thought how sometimes humans could bicker too much. We animals keep it simple. And that was fine for a simple horse like me because at the end of the day, I was only a horse and that was all.

Just then, I heard quiet steps from behind the trees. The creeping steps were hushed, but savage. I sensed danger, but the children were too busy jabbering away. I had to stop their quibbling, or we'd be heard. We had to get a move-on.

"Muzzle your mouths, children! Something is moving on the other side of the tree," I warned.

Upon hearing me speak, Harmon and Fawn looked stunned— then froze. They stared at me, wide-eyed.

"I—I must be delirious," mumbled Harmon. "I swear on my flute your horse just spoke!"

"I heard it too, I did! Whitewing, you're a talking horse?" blurted Fawn. The friends stood and stared in great shock.

"Shh! Not so loud," I replied. "There's no time to explain. We must hide!"

"This is no ordinary farm horse!" said Fawn, patting my mane. "This horse is top quality, this horse is!"

Harmon still gawked. "Whitewing, how did you—?"

"Now look, children, we must not waste time. We have to go. Hop on. I assume you both know how to ride?" I tried to nudge them forward, for I sensed danger. I felt we were being shadowed.

Sunbeam and Fawn had already stepped in the stirrups and were on my saddle. Fawn had Indigo buried in her lap and her feet pressed into my stirrups. I could tell she was a natural rider. But Harmon looked up, nervously.

"Do you know how to ride?" I asked him in a whisper.

"Oh . . . sure," he mumbled nervously. "I ride farm donkeys."

"You ride *what*? Never mind. You can learn as you go," I whispered. "Now, can you fall down?"

"Sure, what's so hard about falling?" Harmon struggled to get his feet in the stirrups.

"Listen, can you fall and get back up? And keep getting up over and over after you've fallen? It's the getting back up part that makes the rider," I said.

"I can do my best," said Harmon. By this time, he had finally made it on the saddle with the two girls. He was sitting behind them, near my tail. It wasn't easy carrying three humans, but I would certainly try. Suddenly, I felt Harmon lean forward.

"What are these for?" Harmon asked, grabbing the reins. He'd stretched his arms around the girls.

"Those are for steering," I said.

Suddenly, Sunbeam grabbed the reins from his hand. I suspected she wouldn't let anyone else do the driving on her own horse. "Don't touch them," Sunbeam said. "And you don't grab Whitewing's tail either. He won't like it."

"Well what do I hold on with?" said Harmon. He raised his voice, blushing over his lack of horse-riding skills. Although the girls didn't see it, I suspected he'd be a quick learner.

"Hold onto the back of my shirt," said Sunbeam.

"We'll make a real horseman of you in no time," I said urging him forward. "Now, straighten your feet and hold on. Don't slouch, raise your shoulders . . . sit tall, and keep your chin up." I knew we needed to move along.

"You come up much higher than I thought!" said Harmon.

"That's because you're used to riding donkeys, let's see if you can run with the horses!" snickered Fawn. Then she said, "Are you strong enough to carry us all, Whitewing?" She knew that though I came from a long line of warhorses, I was a bit smaller than the average horse and was sold cheap as a foal.

Frankly, with three humans on my back, I thought I'd be more labored. But just as Sunbeam moved quicker and sharper in the Depths, I, too, was given more strength to carry. My legs felt mysteriously stronger. Sunbeam's father had bought me because my breed was known for its loyalty and strength in battle, although I'd never once had to fight anything in Ozmandia. And I hoped I would never have to fight. After all, the man who sold me said even though I could run fast, I'd never be a true warhorse. But it was as though the Depths brought out survival skills in me that had gone unused. I suppose it's only when you're forced to go forward against the odds, you see what you're really made of.

And with that, we moved forward into the Depths. But I sensed strongly, there were still footsteps shadowing close behind.

CHAPTER 7
THE UNINVITED PROPHECY

We'd been trotting for some time, I with my mistress and her two friends on my back. The day melted into a dusky sunset. My mistress led us deeper into the forest. We had endured the day's journey with extreme caution. As for Harmon, he wasn't doing so bad learning to ride. He'd only fallen twice between trots and a small jump. But when he fell, he quickly got back up.

The moonlight, especially bright, had risen over the trees and lit paths in streaks of silver. I wondered where we were headed and what might meet us there. By my animal instinct, I suspected we were heading south. The Key hadn't lit our direction the whole day. Sunbeam stayed quiet most of the journey, like she did when she was deep in thought, twiddling the Key through her fingers. And Harmon played his flute lightly. It was Fawn who did most of the talking, asking questions about the Depths—questions no one knew the answers to.

"We might as well give ourselves up for lost!" said Fawn. "Can't we stop and rest?"

"Well, it is late and we're all tired," said Sunbeam. "We'll stop here." She pointed to a low canopy of branches good enough for hiding. "We must all keep together. No wandering off." She was afraid to lose one of them. She vowed after losing Gilda, she'd never let that happen again. Ever. These were her friends and she'd do her best to help them out of the Depths. After all, this was her journey, and they were there to help her.

They all dismounted and settled inside the canopy of branches. Sunbeam reached into the saddle bag and fetched the leftover biscuits her mother packed for her lunch before getting lost.

"Here," she said with a mouthful and handed some to Harmon and Fawn. "We're all starving but we have to make it last."

"Wait, I have this, too." Fawn pulled out a small handkerchief from her pocket with dried beef wrapped inside. "I never eat all my lunch. My mother always sends too much."

"Put the leftover food in the carrying bag. We'll need it for the rest of the way," said Harmon, busying himself to make a fire.

Watching him gather wood, the way he moved when building the fire, Sunbeam saw Harmon's clumsiness fade away. He was skilled in the outdoors. That was evident by the way he rolled the spindle sticks together to spark an ember under the nest of tree bark to light the wood. It was during these moments he surprised her. Then Harmon sat down and began playing his flute. His large, brown eyes seemed to dance in the firelight. Sunbeam took in the sights, and watching her friends under the moonlit sky, decided she was glad they were there. And she thought to herself:

There are some friends you have for a short time. Moving from town to town, she knew that well. But she suspected these friends, she would have forever. For her other friends showed their love when times were a little happier. But these showed their love in her greatest trouble.

Suddenly, her thoughts were broken by the sound of quick and desperate footsteps, the same footsteps I'd suspected were trailing us since morning. I raised my ears.

"Put the fire out," whispered Sunbeam. "Whitewing?"

I ran to my mistress, ready to scoop her up and run. Harmon moved quickly and doused the fire while Fawn latched onto her button-nosed indigo she'd been carrying the entire time. The furry indigo also became alert to the oncoming presence we could hear but could not see.

"Quick, hide under the canopy," Sunbeam whispered. I stood close, camouflaged among the branches, but ready to run at any second. "The Key feels hot," said Sunbeam. It lit up in its golden tones. The steps grew closer. The branches parted and rattled, whoever was trailing us was good—like a tracker looking for its prey, and not giving up until he found it.

"Get down," whispered Sunbeam. We peered from behind the branches. Sunbeam barely breathed while Harmon gripped his flute and Fawn squeezed her stray indigo to her chest. Then lo and behold, the tracker stepped from behind some trees off a dirt trail and came into view under the moonlight. It was Professor Plume, their teacher from Thornridge.

"Professor Plume!" Harmon gasped and stepped out from the canopy. Once seeing the Professor, Sunbeam and Fawn followed. Harmon turned quickly to Sunbeam. "He was not with us! We had no clue he was behind!"

Professor Plume stood tall with his hair as black as a crow and dark, beady eyes. He held a tote bag of books, among other things a professor might carry in his teaching bag.

"Do not be afraid," he commanded. "Sunbeam, I've been studying you for quite some time. I believe you are in grave danger."

"You don't say?" she smirked.

"Sunbeam, this is no time for amusement. I have strong indication that you are The One."

"The One?" she asked.

"The One Called," he replied, his long, black coattail whipping in the wind. "You must be protected."

"I'm not leaving. I'm not leaving until I find my sister!" Sunbeam snapped. This was not school, and there was no way he could tell her what to do, especially in the Depths.

"How do you know your sister is here?" The professor lifted his chin.

"I saw her locket," said Sunbeam.

"Where did you see the locket?" he asked. He stood on a large stone, hanging on the fringe of the group, distant, yet close enough to hear them. He seemed preoccupied for a second as he stared, lost in a moment of thought.

"Back at a dark place. A place you'd never want to go," she said. She recalled the images she'd witnessed on the high table with the beasts and dreadful Golgums, and a heaviness fell over her shoulders.

"Was there a Prince?" asked Plume. He stepped off the stone and stood upright.

"Yes, and he had some horrible claw," said Sunbeam. At the thought of it, her pulse quickened. She couldn't bear to think of the things those demons may have done to Gilda.

"Did the Prince see you?" asked Plume. His black, beady eyes stared at Sunbeam. Before she could speak, he turned and jerked a book from his carrying bag. He had many books in there, like a professor would. "You must stay far away from him!" he warned.

"How do you know of the prince?" asked Sunbeam, still trying to understand Professor Plume being there. *He's just another professor trying to meddle. What does he want?* She thought to herself. The last thing she needed was another scolding teacher in the Depths. This wasn't the time to keep up pretentious nonsense in front of another teacher.

"I have my reasons," he said. "You must not question. Trust me. I am here to protect you!"

I was wary of Professor Plume. Why had he been watching her at Thornridge from his loft? I had noticed him shadowing her for the past month. My animal instinct sensed something I couldn't pin. I was skeptical. I knew to keep a close watch over Sunbeam. It seemed within the last day, my mistress needed me now more than ever. No one could be trusted. Ever since finding that Key! But I was prepared to carry her, as any loyal horse would.

Suddenly, holding the old book in his hand, Plume advanced toward Sunbeam. As he got closer, the Golden Key began lighting up again.

"The Key! It's burning me!" blurted Sunbeam.

I trotted briskly to my mistress's aid. My hooves skidded to an abrupt stop in front of her, blocking Professor Plume's advance. I stood tall and raised my head high. My ears were pulled back, and I looked hard at Plume. He stopped and stared cautiously. For I gathered he knew I was a horse ready to rear back on my hind legs. Plume stopped frozen in his tracks, like a lion that had been thwarted, just before pouncing on its prey.

"The Key. It's still hot," Sunbeam said. Her eyes darted around the trees. The last time the Key felt hot to touch was just before being chased by those dark hooded Golgums the previous night.

"You are all prisoners in enemy territory!" warned Plume with caution.

"Prisoners?" said Fawn, dropping her furry indigo. She clutched onto Harmon's arm.

"I'm dreaming. This is a dream," said Harmon, and began playing his flute, which only added to the chaos because this was *not* the time to start playing a flute.

"You are simple, common little children!" shouted Plume. He stood tall, still holding the old book in one hand, while with the other hand, pulled his long, black cloak into his chest. "You do not know the danger that lurks here!"

As he spoke, Harmon nervously continued playing in the background, which only seemed to make Plume more furious. He shouted to Harmon, "Stop! Loud, common little boy! Listen, you are in grave danger! And if caught, you will all be captives to a terrible master! I am here to protect you!"

He whipped the old book open. The Golden Key was still warm to the touch. I knew it because it was still faintly lit in her hand.

Engrossed in his book, Plume slowly walked backward and plopped down on the stone. The further away Plume got from Sunbeam, the less the Key burned. She backed away from him a few more steps, and the Key cooled down.

"What is in your hand?" asked Plume, his dark eyes narrowed and focused directly on the Key.

"The Golden Key," said Sunbeam, securing it tighter under her fingers.

"Let me see it!" He rose from the stone.

My instinct was sensing a tremendous threat as he stood and stared at the Key.

"I think I'd better keep hold of it," she said, although she was unsure why she felt afraid to release it to him.

"As you wish," replied Plume. Then, without taking his eyes off the Golden Key, he slowly crouched down and sat on the stone. Then swiftly, he turned his head back toward his book.

"What is that book, Professor?" asked Harmon. In the next moment, they all slowly gathered behind him to get a glimpse of what he was reading. On the pages lay many secret symbols that looked like deep and ancient mysteries. Sunbeam thought of the tombs. The words looked like the ancient writings she saw on the old gravestones the previous night.

"Those symbols. What do they mean?" asked Sunbeam.

"There is no doubt you are the One Called. We have pieces in this book to help us, but the pieces must be put together," he said, gravely. "I've devoted my life to the study of these books."

Plume ran his fingers over the pages, and his dark eyes scanned the book. Beads of sweat dripped from his face, and his black hair shined slick as a crow's wing. Sunbeam felt a little scared but drawn to him at the same time. In all his peculiarity and strangeness, there was something familiar about him. She decided it was because he was a teacher. Plume continued:

"My grandfather gave me these books when I was only a boy. He told me a great secret: he was a protector. And before he was laid to rest, he passed the books on to me. He confided that I was the next male in line—the next protector. He instructed me to study the pages. To learn them. To be aware. To be on guard. And above all, to follow my instinct. He said the books were only guides, that I would know some things only through my instinct. My senses led me to Thornridge. Then later, I understood. When I saw you, Sunbeam, I questioned at first, but after more observation, I believed you were Called," he said. Although he showed emotion in his voice, his eyes looked void and empty. Sunbeam could not look at his eyes too long without feeling a little afraid.

"Your mother must be worried," said Plume. "I hope she is alright."

"How do you know my mother?"

"I—I don't. But I do know mothers in general. And I know they all worry about their children." Then he turned away and looked up at the trees. "The journey will be long. Rest here until I return. For now, I need to be alone," he said. "You must trust me." And he stood up and faded into the woods, his coattail trailing behind him like a ghost.

"You've got us into a lot of trouble this time, Sunbeam!" said Fawn. "What are we going to do?"

"Fawn, it's OK," Harmon said. "It's not her fault. Remember we're all in this together."

"You two should clear out!" Sunbeam said. "I told you this was dangerous. I don't want anyone hurt on my account. I'm the one who found this cursed Key."

She stared at the ground, trying to hide the tears welling up from her terrified chest. She was beginning to feel a little ill and turned away.

"No. We're staying with you," Harmon said.

"OK. He's right. We made a pact. We're going through—together," said Fawn with a shaky voice. As she sat on the ground, a pack of foxlike animals scuttled out from the trees and settled around her, as if they came out of the night to comfort her. They had short, tan fur and began pawing her as if letting her know they were her friends. Fawn always had a way with animals back home, but in the Depths, it became more-so. It seemed the creatures here knew she felt scared and offered help. They shared an unspoken language. We watched as they nuzzled close to her.

Suddenly, without warning, the Golden Key burned hot against Sunbeam's chest. It glowed brilliantly on the thin rope around her neck. Alarmed, she peered throughout the trees. In a moment, Professor Plume shot out from the woods, running madly, his coattail whipping furiously behind him in the wind.

"Traitorous hounds! Run! All of you—run! They have found us!" he shouted, sweat pouring from his slick, black hair.

We turned back, and to our horror, about twenty hooded Golgums emerged from the woods. Then suddenly there came a deep, somber chanting out of the cypress. "Get out. Get out," they chanted. The figures crept slowly, but steadily toward us. The heaviness in the air grew. And that thick blanket of sleep, once again, lay upon us in a fog. The whole forest became grey. I was sure now their chanting songs were spells that cast weariness. They continued their somber hexes.

It was urgent. I knew we had to move fast! Although these Golgums crept slowly, they'd be on our tail in an instant. They chanted in unison, "Get out. Get out," as they did before. But this time, one of them was sitting on a large, hideous creature. It looked to be half-beast and half-wolf, with red, bloodthirsty eyes.

The rider appeared taller than the other figures, and he carried a bone battle horn. The beast he rode had the streamlined body of a lean wolf and the head of a growling tiger. Its sandy-grey hide was matted with blood. It had distinct black stripes only on its hind quarters and swung a long tail. Each time the rider whipped its flanks and jerked the reins, the large tiger-wolf snapped viciously at its iron bit.

"Hurry, Whitewing!" shouted Sunbeam.

The Key flashed its golden tones. Instantly, Sunbeam, in one leap, whirled on the saddle, gripping the reins, ready to dash forward. Like at school recess when she was outperforming everyone else, her movements had quickened, and she was even swifter since being in the Depths.

"Where is the Key pointing?" I shouted.

"Straight ahead," she screamed. Her eyelids started growing heavier; the fog thickened.

Plume was almost to us now and waving his hands wildly, motioning us to run. Sunbeam grabbed my reins and fighting exhaustion, screamed, "Ride! Whitewing!"

The Golgums' cloaks beat loudly against the wind, so loud we could barely hear ourselves think. Among the dark, moving cloak-train, she almost forgot about poor Harmon and Fawn, who looked up from the ground, frozen in fright. Then suddenly, Harmon braced his flute and held it like a weapon while Fawn sprang up, her stray indigo and pack of foxes rearing and hissing at the dark figures creeping out of the Depths. Sunbeam knew she couldn't ride without them. For a second, she wondered if their company would be more trouble than it was worth. They were already slowing her down. But she couldn't leave her friends behind.

"Can you carry more, Whitewing?"

"I can try, Mistress!" I shouted. The wind picked up speed and blew in from the direction of the hooded legion. The fog was rolling over our backs.

"Go! Go!" shouted Plume, who without warning, leapt up from behind me and landed on my back!

"Get on the horse, children!" he demanded.

Harmon and Fawn, fighting exhaustion in the hexing fog, leapt on my saddle and doubled up on laps. There was no other option than Sunbeam sitting on Harmon's lap, and Fawn sitting with Plume.

"I've got you," said Harmon, wrapping his arm around Sunbeam. With the other arm, he braced his flute like a sword.

She pushed his arm away.

The cloaked figures were gaining on us. Then, more turned out from all directions of the trees. Their cloaks fanned around us in the moonlight. My back was very heavy carrying a load of humans, but I braced myself, ready to run. I would try my best. Any good horse would. I had to find a way out of this. In a moment, I felt unusual strength surge through my legs. Was this what warhorse strength felt like? The strength the line of thoroughbreds I came from were said to have?

"You must start at once!" shouted Plume.

"What's our direction, Mistress?"

"They're everywhere. What do they want?" cried Fawn.

Suddenly, the flock of black vultures swooped down from the sky and landed in the trees. As I started to run, there came a horrible shock—my hoofs were stuck! As if someone chained them, I could not move! Then, the grey fog turned to black.

"I can barely see," muttered Sunbeam. Her voice sounded wearier by the second.

"Stay awake, children!" shouted Plume, who seemed completely immune to the foggy grey spell.

"I can't move! My hoofs are stuck!" I panted.

Suddenly, inside the blinding fog, a spellbinding haze appeared in the far distance of the cypress, surreal and wavering grey, like a cloudy mirage. Nearly sunk in sleep, Sunbeam wondered if she were dreaming. She could see blurry, beast-like forms busy at work, moving around a larger figure at the center. My keen eye zoomed in closer. It was the prince!

He sat on his throne surrounded by his beasts, and his blue eyes peered at us through his mask. He examined our presence like he was being interrupted from some important mission, and we were intruding upon it. Then, he zeroed in on Sunbeam, and his eyes narrowed on her. He tore off his horned mask and began glaring at her with a severe expression, twisted in fury. He raised his claw and cried out in a deep, booming voice that seemed to come from the bottom of the earth, "You fools! You've taken the wrong one!"

He glared at Sunbeam with a hungry expression in his icy, blue eyes. One of the beasts next to him winded a horn, but it was very faint, due to their distance.

"Bring me the girl!" roared the prince and slammed his great claw down on the arm of his throne.

"Run! The enemy is upon you!" demanded Plume.

"I can't move!" I shouted. The heavy fog was still gripping my legs.

The rider whirled his tiger-wolf around and trembled at the sound of the prince. Without thinking, Sunbeam raised the Golden Key into the air. It was ancient gold against grey. The compass needle swayed to and fro, and she read the Key aloud: "Cresc-phos! Greater Light!"

In a moment, a boom like thunder struck down; light broke through and parted a path for us—a path leading straight ahead. At once, my legs unstuck, and I plunged out of the fog.

"The Key! It's pointing east!" shouted Sunbeam. She jerked my reins.

"Due east it is! Listen children! Don't lean to the side and keep your face straight into the wind! Don't look down. If you start to fall off, just press your weight into your heels, shorten the reins and hold on. And? Forward!" I brayed wildly and carrying more humans on my back than I ever had before, shot off at great speed toward the East.

And as we plunged forward, there came another sound of a battle horn, and the prince's voice bellowed and hissed furiously from the Depths: "IT HAS BEGUN!"

My warhorse second sight was very strong. And shifting my head slightly to see behind me, the surreal haze began to vanish, but not before the prince with the torn-off mask revealed a face that furiously hissed at his hooded legion, and it was a face I *thought* I had seen before.

Plume muttered something in a very low whisper under his breath. His face sunk down into hollow grayness. He gazed at the prince as though his very life had been sucked out, and his face, now pale, looked hesitant to run away. But then swiftly, against much resistance, Plume forced his head forward, and turned his back on the prince.

"Sir?" I shouted against the wind, catching him whisper something with my attuned ear.

"Nothing," Plume muttered. "Nothing."

❧ ❧

I had been galloping for a long distance. The cypress trees zoomed past us. Thick bushes and branches were scattered everywhere. I tried my best to dodge ruts and rough terrain. Everyone held tight, and no one uttered a word. All their focus was spent steadying themselves on my back, for we were running at great speed. We ran and ran until the dark hooded Golgums became smaller behind us, turned aside, and melted into the trees. All but one: the one who rode the growling tiger-wolf. Breaking from the hooded train, the tiger-wolf shot forward and trailed close behind us.

"Hurry! He'll get his teeth into you!" shouted Plume.

"Come back. Come back." The dark rider chanted. The tiger-wolf ran with deadly accuracy. Its hooves beat the ground, rapid and sharp, contrasting against the dark rider's slow and creeping mantra: "Come back. Come back."

I was fast. But I had to admit, the tiger-wolf was quick, too. He was a challenge. I was panting for breath. Carrying four humans on your back is no easy feat. But even a horse knows that sometimes you have to give total effort, even when the odds are against you. And especially, when something as hideous as a fanged tiger-wolf is gnashing its teeth at your legs. This was my race. And in this moment, I was my mistress's only chance for escape. Indeed, her life depended on how skillfully I ran. But I knew if I stayed the course, and didn't hit any slopes or water, I could outrun him.

I swiftly shifted my head back. He was very close, gnashing his yellow teeth and snapping his fangs while the rider whipped its flanks to shreds. It was then my eye caught something that made my heart leap. I knew in a moment the tiger-wolf was preparing to launch. But the beast wanted more than a fight. See, animals read other animals. We know whether a creature means to fight for dominance, or instead, means to kill. And by his eye—the beast meant to kill.

"Run! Whitewing!" shouted Sunbeam.

"Listen, I have to let you off! All of you!" I shouted against the wind.

"No!" cried Sunbeam.

"I must! It's your only chance to survive!" I knew once the tiger-wolf pounced, which it was about to do at any moment, one swipe from his claw or fang would render them useless, or worse, kill them. This was no ordinary creature; it was beastly, savage, and quicker than any one I'd ever seen back home.

But I had a plan. Up ahead, a small channel of water ran between the trees. Seeing the channel of water, I knew what to do.

"Listen children. Hold on. We're going to run down the bank. The water will slow him down and give you all a chance to dismount," I panted. "When I hit the water—Swim! And scatter in different directions. This will deter his direction. Careful! The beast is treacherous!"

The race was very severe. And though they knew more or less what to do, no one knew what would happen. From the top of the bank, I looked back and saw the dark mass lurching toward us. I sped down the bank.

"Quick! Quick!" Sunbeam shouted to everyone. We all hit the water and scattered. It was then, by the look in the tiger-wolf's eye, I knew who the beast wanted to kill: Sunbeam.

I had to protect my mistress. Torn from my family of thoroughbreds, I never had to fight any animal in my life, but that did not matter. If the beast wanted Sunbeam, it would have to get through me first. I was back up on the bank before the tiger-wolf was in the water.

Narrowing its eyes, the tiger-wolf bared its teeth and growled. Its face contorted into a wild state of attack. The beast dove at the water toward Sunbeam with thunderous force until I rammed him from the side and knocked him down. The rider roared and lashed at me with his whip while the tiger-wolf scrambled back to its feet. After getting back up, the tiger-wolf lunged at me, and we ended up splashing hard into the channel. He clawed at me under water. We swam and wrestled to the other side of the channel, until facing each other on the bank.

The run had been tiring. I didn't think I could possibly continue, but I had no choice but to try for more strength. See, in order to get a second wind, you have to push through the first. And with a fanged beast growling for my blood, I was bound to find out if I'd get one. The tiger-wolf circled, and so did I. We eyed each other, each looking for an opening to attack.

Sunbeam swam to the bank and lay on the edge of the water, gasping for breath. She looked up to find me challenging the beast, and she cried out, "Whitewing! Run! You're not a warhorse! Run!"

I had to protect Mistress. But to my horror, the dark rider was sliding toward Sunbeam through the water like a predator moves when it's stalking its prey—slow and easy but determined to catch it. The tiger-wolf blocked my path, so I couldn't defend her. Sunbeam's thoughts ran wild. Then she remembered the voice in her dream: *Take the potion upon you. At the time, you will know what to do.*

With trembling fingers, she drew the red potion from her pocket. Upon seeing it, the rider froze, reversed in the water, then hit the ground on all fours and crawled backwards into the woods. She stared into the forest, fearing the rider would soon reappear. But I could not reach her. I had to fight the beast.

We stood face to face, animal to animal, ready to engage. The tiger-wolf crouched back and bared his fangs with a great growl, ready to pounce. Simultaneously, I reared back on my hind legs and flailed my front hooves wildly. I let out a mighty scream, which shot adrenaline through my legs. I didn't know if I could take the beast. I had to only protect my mistress from smaller things before, through the usual horse skills of running and jumps, but never—never like this. I remembered my breed and knew I was rejected from a long line of warhorses—who deemed I'd never be one. But now, faced with a combat, I could feel unknown strength rising up in my legs. And for a second, I wondered if that's what warhorse strength felt like.

In the next moment, everything felt consumed by sounds of hoofs and growling. For the beast had lurched. He tore into my side and sank his teeth into my flesh. His eyes beamed red and his lips curled above his fangs and snapped together in a loud clap while his fur stood straight up on his back. He moved fast. He crouched and zipped around with sculpted and quick muscles. He ripped into my side, and I felt searing pain. I knew I had to throw him off. With great might, I kicked up my back legs, and the creature's agile body hit the ground. In a few seconds, he streaked across the turf, a streamlined, moving striped mass, and struck again. He growled and hissed, then leapt forward with all fangs, clipping sharp snaps at my hind legs. The beast knew my strength lay in my back legs and sought to tear me down where I was strongest.

"Run, Whitewing! Run!" shouted my mistress while the savage beast tore into my hind legs. She cried and shook on the bank, fearing for my life.

I was growing weak and for a moment, thought there was no hope inside the snarling growls and flailing hoofs. The beast was foaming and tearing and snapping at my body. My torn flesh burned, and I was winded. And for a second, I was crouched as low as a horse can get, trying with all my might to steady my legs, until I looked up, and was staring straight into the beast's wide-open, roaring mouth. The beast had me cornered. My legs were giving out.

"Stop! Stop!" screamed Sunbeam from the bank. Harmon was on the edge of the water with his arm around Sunbeam, while Fawn cried and cried and cried. And Plume watched from a far distance at the edge of the trees, pale-faced. For they saw I was doing all a horse could do, which was not quite enough. I was losing blood, and fainting.

"Help! Fight, Whitewing! You must fight now! You must!" Sunbeam screamed, tears pouring down her red face. The Key was in her hand and flashing gold. "You're a warhorse, Whitewing! You *are* a warhorse! My warhorse!"

In a flash, before I knew how hurt I was, I rose up on my hind legs and let out one of the most awful noises in the wild—a battle horse's cry. I flailed my legs. Then I charged toward the beast, being driven by some inner strength, like I was leading a rushing brigade. Like a powerful war stallion, I trampled and bit, kicked and turned at the right seconds, so that my hoofs struck down on my enemy in the swift blow of a mighty battle-axe. I was now over the beast and he was stooping low. His sharp claws swatted at me but missed. With my hoofs in mid-air, I knew if I hesitated for one fraction of a second, I'd lose. With my keen eye, I aimed it at the beast, and slammed my hoofs down with such force on top of his head, that he rolled over and hit the ground. He was now staggering. I then rose up over the brutish beast and struck again.

"Away from here, beast. Away!" I bellowed.

The beast stammered, hurt and astonished, until it turned tail and rushed away into the trees. I watched him vanish. And by my horse's instinct, I sensed it was long gone.

I was now standing on my weakened legs, trying not to faint.

"Whitewing!" Sunbeam rushed to me. "Look what you did! You are a warhorse! You are!" Her face was streaked with tears. Seeing me still standing, waves of relief washed over her. Harmon and Fawn weren't far behind. They embraced me and patted my mane exclaiming a bunch of, "You're the best of all warhorses!" and "We're safe!" and "You saved us!" all intermixed with jumbles of hugs, kisses, and sighs of relief.

Meanwhile, Plume inched over and looked from a little distance. His forehead was scrunched, concerned. I assumed he, too, was shaken from the fight.

"Drink, horse," he said, gesturing to the water. "We must get to safety. They are gone, but I am certain, that they'll be back."

❧ ❦

Sunbeam examined my bleeding wounds and took out the red potion, thinking it might heal me.

"No," I said. "It's for you, not me. The Gardener gave it to you."

"I wish I knew why," she said, stuffing the bottle of potion back in her pocket.

Fawn knelt and washed my wounds with water from the stream, then tore strips of cloth from the lining of her sleeve to bind my deepest cuts. All the while, Sunbeam patted my mane, and Harmon played his flute for me. After resting on the bank a while, I felt ready to go on. The moonlight still shone through the trees. The Key lit up and then began to point us through the direction of the night.

"You are hurt, Whitewing. We have to get you better," said my mistress. She took my reins and led us ahead on foot.

We walked silently through the trees. We all felt exhausted, and looking ahead, we saw only more and more cypress. Harmon had been playing the flute lightly as we walked, which by the look on Plume's face, agitated him.

"Keep it down, Boy. That music!" said Plume.

"That's what they want to do—to kill my songs with that somber chanting," he said. Harmon got serious when he spoke about music. He actually did know his stuff, and his clumsiness would disappear even talking about quarter and half notes, measures and beats. But in this moment, he put his flute away.

We walked on.

"Whitewing, your legs. You're losing too much blood," said Sunbeam.

"Look, there," Fawn interrupted.

We looked straight ahead: a beautiful, green circle of fruit hedges formed a boundary, very much like the Quiet Gardener's sanctuary. Had we traveled in a circle, I wondered? But then I looked closer, these hedged walls were a little different: a deeper green with larger fruit that seemed riper, with a sweeter scent. In the middle of the high green wall was a gate. And between its silver bars, we caught a glimpse of what was inside: lush, colorful blooms and refreshing waters which reflected the silver moon. Sunbeam thought of the Quiet Gardener. She held the Key and still had the red potion tucked safely in her pocket. She recalled the Gardener's words:

Take the potion upon you. You will know what to do.

She recalled his gentleness, his dancing, brown eyes and joyful presence, and his graciousness to her, which when thinking about it, gave her hope and strengthened her walk.

"Let's hurry," Sunbeam walked toward the green threshold. When she found the gate locked tight, she said, "We'll have to climb over!"

"You all go on," said Plume, sinking his shoulders. He halted at the wall of green fruit hedges. "I am not entering."

"Are you sure, Professor?" Sunbeam asked.

"Yes, now go," he said. "I'll wait out here and stand watch for the night." He quickly took out one of his books and flipped his fingers through the pages, squinting to try and read by moonlight.

"Be careful, Professor," said Sunbeam. She turned to face him.

Plume looked up from his book and stared at the Key that dangled from the rope around her neck. The Key glinted in the silver moonlight, and he studied it as long as he could, until Sunbeam turned away, grabbed hold of some vines and disappeared over the garden wall.

CHAPTER 8

IN THE GREEN

As soon as Sunbeam dropped into the garden, she realized the climb over the wall was well worth it. The fruit trees bore fresh oranges, dates, juicy red apples, and the greenest grass glistened in the half-light. This garden was different from the sanctuary where she had rested before. This one had more pools and more fruit trees. The garden was filled with cool, fresh air. And though only the moon shone down from the night sky, she felt like she'd taken in a breath of fresh sunlight. Beside the nearest pool, a large ancient tree spread its mighty branches, casting shadows over the water. Fireflies floated through the branches, stirring the air with a restful ease.

At once, Sunbeam ran to the high gate to let me inside, but to her surprise, she found the gate had already been opened. Standing at the open door was the man dressed down to his sandals, in his tunic of splendid colors that looked like spring. It was him: The Quiet Gardener. His auburn beard formed a soft silhouette against the glistening pools, and his dazzling eyes sparkled. He looked very joyful to see us and smiled at each one of the children like he'd known them all personally. After everyone else, he looked at me. Seeing my scrapes and tooth-marks, his eyes became serious. In an instant, he took my reins and led me to the edge of the sparkling pool so that I could drink the pure water. Then he turned to Sunbeam.

"Come drink, Daughter," he said to her, and "Come here, my children," to Harmon and Fawn as they ran up to him. Then he turned and fixed his gaze at Sunbeam.

"Now, how are you getting along, my daughter?" he asked.

"We were chased! Attacked! My horse is hurt!"

"Be still. You are protected. They will not pass through," the Quiet Gardener said. His face was joyful, which brought a peace to everyone's frantic hearts. They began to calm down a little. Standing at the edge of the pool, the Gardener unfastened my harness. He took my bridle and saddle off, and having pity on me, he cleaned my wounds and scratches so well that it looked as if I'd been groomed for a great King's chariot.

"Who—who—who are you?" gasped Harmon. He plopped down next to the pool to quench his thirst with handfuls of water.

"I am my Father's Son," the Gardener said. He busied himself to put my saddle back on.

"Who is your father?" Harmon said and wiped his dripping chin. The Gardener faced us serenely.

"Are you a King?" asked Fawn. We noticed more stray indigos had come out of the bushes and lay at her heels. She also had about four or five deer, rabbits, and birds surrounding her.

"Yes, but my kingdom is not here. I take care of all that has been given to me," he said. "I tend and prune everything that is in my care." Although he wasn't dressed like a king, he moved like one: graceful and dignified, yet humbly.

"How did you get ahead of us?" Sunbeam asked. "I last saw you a whole day's travel behind. And how many gardens do you have?"

"Daughter, if you look for me, you will find me," he said.

"What kind of king is this?" muttered Harmon, staring at the Gardener's magnetic eyes.

"My Son, waste no more time. For you are hungry and pale. As for the horse, his wounds are dressed. He'll be ready to run. Now you must all eat and rest."

As he said this, next to the sparkling pool, he lit a lamp. Its flame burned and flickered with vibrant embers.

That lamp, Sunbeam thought to herself. I've seen that flame before.

In the next moment, the Gardener fetched wooden cups of more water and gave them to the children. Then, turning to me, he fastened my harness, and patting the side of my nose said, "You are a very fine horse. A breed of champions. Now, have water and grass."

"Will Whitewing be the same again?" asked Sunbeam.

"Though the cuts are many, your horse warded the beast off. There are wounds, but not deep enough to be dangerous. Your horse fought bravely, and with skill."

The Gardener continued patting my nose. I drank his water and immediately felt strength fill my legs. In fact, I felt better than ever. That unknown strength returned. I ate more grass while the others sat on a grassy slope near the pool, watching the fireflies flutter over the ripples.

From the ripest tree, the Gardener picked fruit and served my mistress and the others. By the look in his golden-brown eyes, it gave him great pleasure to refresh them with delicious pomegranates, oranges, and figs. Although taking a servant role, his form and features looked noble and dignified. To look at him you'd immediately love him but fear him at the same time. His face radiant, he sat down beside the children on the grass. He was smiling. The children ate and rested; then lay on the grass and stared silently at the sky, exhausted from the day's events.

In that quiet moment, their fears melted away. Safe in the green hedges, the night was soft, blue pools and cool air under the stars. The pleasing aroma of fruit blooms wafted through the gentle breeze. Then the Quiet Gardener turned his attention to Sunbeam.

Strangely, the Gardener's eyes drew out deep emotions from Sunbeam's chest. She thought of the dark secrets she'd locked inside her heart, and of Gilda. No one knew of them. No one would ever know. At least not until she got Gilda back. No one would ever see the huge bricks of guilt and sadness weighing her down more and more every day. She could never forgive herself. In fact, there were some days the sun seemed so dark that Sunbeam barely had the strength to go on. But she hid it well. No other human knew her—truly knew her. But the Quiet Gardener seemed to see directly into her secrets, and he did not despise her for them. And with his eyes piercing into the deepest drafts of her soul, a feeling of light and air filled her heart. And it made her want to cry, but not a bad cry, a good kind of cry. But then remembering her friends sitting next to her, she turned her face to the side and hardened her expression.

"How are you getting along, Daughter?" he asked her.

"My side is a little sore, that's all," Sunbeam snapped.

The Gardener knelt to her weak side and felt her wrist and forehead.

"There is no sign of sickness. You will go forward in good health. Drink from this well," and he gave her a bit more of his refreshing water. She held it to her lips and drank all of it. She felt better. After drinking, her weak side became stronger. The more she drank, the better she felt, going from strength to strength.

"This water," said Sunbeam. Her eyes gleamed in delight.

"You must all be strong and do the work," the Gardener said, "for the way gets much harder from here."

"We're all running as hard as we can," said Fawn.

"Yes. But you must be sure to run in the right direction. Forward. Always forward," he said. "Now, have you the potion I gave?" he asked Sunbeam.

"Yes, but there are things about it I don't understand," Sunbeam said.

"You have little wisdom of things to come but be of good hope. I know by my name that you will find the answers."

"Do we have far to go?" asked Fawn. Her eyelids looked heavy; she curled up with her fluffy grey-white indigos and a deer.

"The farther you go, the more war is waged, but the more you will learn along the way. You already have what you need to do the work. What you've been given, you must unlock," he said.

"I—I don't know—what do we unlock and how do we find it?" asked Harmon. He stared at the Gardener, confused. Then he turned dismissively and began playing his flute lightly under the stars.

"You will know," was the Gardener's reply. He listened to Harmon play a lovely tune, one only a fine musician with the greatest skill could play. The Gardener faced Harmon serenely, then nodded at the flute. "You carry the gift of music. That is a great gift."

Next, the Quiet Gardener looked at Fawn with her collection of furry stray indigos, foxes, and deer nuzzled around her. The Gardener patted Fawn's shoulder. "Child, your heart beats with the wild creatures." More animals from the garden were gathering around her.

The Gardener turned to Sunbeam. "I see you have good companions. They will serve you well." He watched her twirl the Golden Key between her fingers. He studied her agile movements and swift feet.

"Daughter, you must unlock what you've been given." He said it with authority, as though her life depended on it.

In the next second, he paused. He turned his face toward the boundary wall and took a long, piercing stare. He seemed to look directly through it. "There is one more, traveling?" he asked.

"Yes," said Sunbeam. "Our professor. He didn't want to come in."

"I see," said the Gardener. He stared harder at the boundary wall.

"Will we ever see Ozmandia again?" asked Sunbeam, gazing at the sky. "Will I find what I came for?"

"If you don't, I will go back!" said Fawn. "I never chose this! I'm homesick, and you two are just . . . I want to go back!"

Harmon stopped playing his flute. "What? Back to slavery? To that terrible island? And Lord Wolford?"

"There is no going back, only through," said Sunbeam, squeezing Fawn's hand. "Will we get on the other side?" she asked the Gardener.

"Children, the darkest of night is yet ahead. Therefore, I cannot tell you if Ozmandia will be alive before the setting of the last sun. For you are now among the wolves. But take courage; the shepherd is here. You must strive forward. Unlock the power you hold," he said. "Now, be still and rest. Let tomorrow worry about itself."

At this, they were all too exhausted to speak, but yet, they looked peaceful. The Quiet Gardener's presence seemed to give them confidence. It was clear no one understood everything at once, but they did know one thing to do: not turn back, but only go *through*. Then Harmon murmured, "I feel somehow, there's a reward for all of this."

Under the full moon, Harmon and Fawn fell asleep on the soft grass, but Sunbeam lay at the place between reality and dreams, that place where you're just before sleep but still hanging onto the last remnant of the day. With my warhorse second sight, I sensed what she thought. Just before her eyelids closed, she saw the Quiet Gardener in all his magnificence. She thought he looked beautiful against the majestic, orange flames burning from the lamp. His fine features beamed humbleness and peace, but with a king's power. And suddenly, she recalled the images from her vision. As she crossed over into the place of dreams, she mumbled lightly: "Those lamps. I've . . . I've seen them . . . in my dream." Then she drifted into a deep, sweet slumber. And in her slumber, she had another DREAM:

~ ~

In her dream, a cloud of incense rose into the air. When it vanished, she saw again the seat of the ancient throne, and the Ancient of Days who sat so high she could only see the train of his robe. A lamp on the table burned brightly. Then she lifted her eyes. When the Ancient One saw her searching, he called to her:

"Sunbeam," his voice boomed, shaking the ground and doorposts.

"Here I am!" she cried and fell down on the floor. She hid her face and was afraid, for she feared him seeing down into her dark secret about how Gilda went missing, which she sensed he saw at that moment.

"Stand up, my child. Receive my mercy."

When Sunbeam stood up, the lamp burned frantically in majestic embers. Sunbeam stared at its beautiful glow, and in it, everything was clear and radiant. But suddenly, in the middle of its warm light, the fire was snuffed out, and everything became completely dark and still. In pitch blackness, Sunbeam grew terrified and screamed out:

"Your Highness! I cannot see!" She trembled and shook.

"My Daughter, do not be afraid. In the darkness, hear my voice!"

"Here I am!" she cried.

"My Child, do not be negligent now, for you are Called. You stand in the darkest of night because your fathers fell by their own sword. And for it, Ozmandia is now slave to the dark one. For long ago they turned their faces away from the light. They closed the doors of the portico and put out all the lamps. And this was their downfall and the downfall of all Ozmandia," he thundered.

"Your Highness! We have looked for light, but all we see is darkness. We look for brightness, but we walk in grim shadows." Sunbeam cried, thinking of her mother and the moving boxes and sadness of the island.

"Sunbeam, the people do not know the way of peace. Their paths are lies. Like the blind, Ozmandia gropes along the wall

feeling their way in the dark, like men without eyes. They have followed the dark one and are prey to his powers.

"But now, be warned: there are some among you who are very strong but like the dead. You have seen them. In their hopelessness, they moan mournfully because they've lost their souls. Be on guard, for they now run to take yours. These strong dead ones fell to the Dark Prince who put on a breastplate and a mask, who shoots from dark shadows and wraps himself in a cloak of deceit. He prowls now like a lion, seeking to destroy you. For he knows you've been called. You have come far, but the way from here grows more treacherous."

"Who am I to stand against this powerful force?" she cried, and she fell down weeping for the island and for Gilda.

"My Child, what are you doing down on your face? Stand up!" he thundered. "Surely my arm is not too short to reach down and save. Go, I will guide you."

"Where—where can this light be found?" cried Sunbeam, blind inside the pitch-black room.

"In the darkness, hear my words! I will cause light to enter you, and you will again see."

Suddenly, a sound of thunder struck loudly and the room shook with great power. Sunbeam was still crouched on the floor afraid, but when she opened her eyes, the lamp had been lit. The lamp burst into dazzling flames, and its light burned wildly. And once again, Sunbeam could see, but this time, she saw more clearly than before.

"My Child: It is only in the light, you see light," said the Ancient One. "Now, you must find it, for that is the hope of the whole island of Ozmandia. You must return this light to them. Do not be negligent."

"But how?" she cried.

"Find the Lost One. Then you can defeat the darkness, and this light will again be in the land."

"But how can I find her? I am the weakest of the two!"

"Have you the potion my Son gave? It is very sacred. Do not pour it without reason. It is a sacred potion. Whatever touches it will be saved. You are to consider it pure—a potion of the gods. It will defeat the battle that will take your life. It will reconcile you to the Light. You cannot conquer this battle without it. Do not put it on anything except what I've commanded. Whoever spills this potion carelessly will be cut off. Use it at the appointed time. Be watchful, for you are but a step between life and death," he thundered.

"Will you give me a sign?" Sunbeam asked, wiping her tears. *"A sign that I can do this?"*

"I will guide you, but you will always bear the means of making the final decisions. Go in the little strength that you have and save Ozmandia from the hand of the Dark Prince. It is only in going that you will find the answers," he boomed. *And with that, the train of his robe vanished in a haze of smoke, shaking the doorposts and threshold as it went. In the next moment, Sunbeam awoke from her dream with a loud cry.*

❧ ☙

Already, the dawn was warming her face. It was early. The sun barely broke through the tops of the trees that swept the horizon. In the Depths, the dawn looked more like grey dusk, but there in the garden, it kissed the air with rosy light.

Despite the dream, her sleep had been sweet. As she slowly came to, she realized her weak side felt stronger than ever. It seemed as if a century had passed since her fight with Helga. Under the dawn's rays, she rolled her shoulders and stretched out her arms. In the midst of great trouble, indeed, her body was healing.

"Good morning Mistress," I said. Though I too had rested, I had slept with one eye open and kept watch over her all night. I had done that every night since she was very small, a responsibility I would carry out until the end of my days. I knew I had to gently nudge her up. Just like back home, before school, she dreaded getting out of bed to face the smirking kids and Helga at Thornridge. However, I was her best horse; I was there to give her smiles. Any good horse would never resort to a stable and let their mistress stay down. Because if any good horse carries a human, they know it's a lifelong friend.

Horses must stand on their feet. But as for my mistress, sometimes I wondered if the only thing standing her up on foot was her drive to find Gilda. And this haunting desire kept driving her forward, opening new doors, and finding new things. It kept leading us down new paths. By my animal instinct I sensed these paths had the power to swallow her life. But to my best ability, I'd uphold my mistress all the way through.

"Whitewing! Look at you, you're all better," she said, rubbing her eyes. The Quiet Gardener had groomed me; I beamed as shiny as a great king's horse.

Harmon emerged over a small hill with streaks of morning rays behind him, the edges of his glasses beamed fractions of sunlight. Seeing her awake, he hurried over.

"How are you feeling? You gave us a scare last night." He reached down to help her up.

"I'm fine," she said, a bit annoyed he was there so early, helping her before she could barely open her eyes. But that was Harmon. In a moment, Fawn came into view. She was skipping a little distance in the grass, followed by a troupe of animals.

"Sunbeam! Aren't they adorable?" laughed Fawn, petting a family of badgers that had gathered next to her. She now had about ten or twelve wild creatures following her around.

"How long have you been awake?" asked Sunbeam.

"A good while. We let you sleep because you woke up screaming in terror last night. We tried to talk to you, but you just stared off into the night, like you were sunk in some serious thought, and then, you just fell back asleep. Here, you'd better have breakfast," Harmon said and handed her some figs and fruit.

"No, I'm all right." She refused his offer.

"OK, there will be more in the satchel bag if you get hungry. I took some food from the garden. It should last us a while," Harmon said. "We better get going while it's early. You know how the Depths get at night." Sunbeam thought he stood tall and handsome against the sun, his dark hair to the side, and his flute tucked inside his belt loop like a sword.

"Yeah, we'd better! We all know how you need to practice your horse riding!" laughed Fawn.

"Quiet, Fawn!" he stammered. "I've—I've ridden before!"

"Yeah . . . *donkeys!*" she giggled.

Harmon raised his chest, then turned red-faced and walked away. He never stood up for himself against Fawn. Against anyone. It was times like these Sunbeam saw why it was so easy for others to jab at him. She watched him walk away, his shoulders up, with the dawn against his back. And she wondered how one person could have two totally different sides at different times: One minute he was shying away, and the next, running toward her with his charming, brown eyes.

Suddenly she snapped to. She shook her head and wondered why on earth she was thinking about Harmon. She had much bigger things to think about. With the sun now breaking all the way through the trees, the Golden Key reflected its rays on the thin rope around her neck. Gripping it tightly, she stood and faced the Dark Depths of Cypress. Time was slipping away.

∂❧

By now, rested and awake, everyone had gathered food and made their way to the end of the garden sanctuary. As we approached the silver gate to leave, Sunbeam searched for a last glimpse of the Gardener, but he was not in sight. Her heart pounded, and a wave of fear traveled all the way down to her toes. She grasped the Key. She secured the bottle of red potion in her pocket. Her dream from the previous night sent fear crashing like a hurricane inside her chest. But then, she thought of the Gardener's eyes urging her forward. In that moment, everything fell silent, and the voice of the Ancient One echoed through her mind.

In the darkness, hear my words . . . Go . . . you bear the makings of the final decisions. Keep watch, you are but a step between life and death.

Then clutching the Golden Key, she opened the gate and entered into the misty fog of the Depths. As soon as the gate closed shut behind us, we heard the rattle of the iron gate intermix with rustling bushes. Indeed, the bushes continued rattling; then they parted. And rapidly, out jumped the nimbly creature from days before.

He stood very still. He smirked at us with one side of his mouth grinning and other side drawn tight, like he knew a secret but would not tell us. His eyes roamed quickly around the Depths, nervously, until they glared at a clump of bushes. We turned to see what he looked at, and there, a horde of leather-backs bristling like hungry warthogs with twisted forks were camouflaged in the leaves. They were back, but this time there were many more. Then he tilted his pointy chin and side-eyed Sunbeam.

"Bogwallows!" said the creature quick and sharp, then giggled.

"Bogwallows?" asked Sunbeam, already annoyed with the creature again.

"Those!" he whispered and flitted his nervous eyes toward the twisted-forked crawlers blending quietly in the bushes.

"What are Bogwallows?" asked Fawn.

"Shh!" snapped the nimbly creature. He continued:

"What you want *not* the enemy to know
Don't speak it amongst a Bogwallow!
Their backs are hard and stingers sharp
They creep, crawl, and make report!"

"Report? Report to whom?" said Sunbeam. She stepped toward the nimbly creature.

He smirked, then tightened his face and zipped his eyes side to side. He bent forward and whispered:

"The one who's come to take your soul,
He'll make you like the ones you know,
Alive, but dead, all sorrow,
He is to whom the Bogwallows go!"

Suddenly, in an explosion of rustling leaves, the leather-backs' forks stuck up behind them as they scurried off into crevices of the forest.

The nimbly creature's ears stood up, and his long fingers curled around his suspenders, laughing nervously:

"To him they go, to him they go,
The prince, the dark one, the one they know,
Oh, be leery of the Bogwallow!
You must not stay here, leave—GO!
Don't say I never told you so!"

With that, the nimbly creature raised his pointy jaw until it opened in a wide cackling laugh—and he scampered away, his laughter echoing behind him until he vanished in the trees.

"Ah! He aggravates me," said Sunbeam.

"I think he was trying to warn us, Mistress," I said.

"I know what he meant. But I wish he would tell us straight," she said.

"It's those Bogwallows!" said Fawn, "I felt a strange energy from them, so did my animals."

"OK everyone, keep your eyes out for the Bogwallows!" said Sunbeam. "We have to focus. Let's go."

CHAPTER 9

THE SECRET
AT THE
END OF THE ROAD

Deeper into the thick cypress, it was a horrible shock. The heavy fog seemed to watch them with hollow eyes through the branches. Slow winds whispered in steady haunting riffs. The trees looked taller, more alive, like their branches reached down to swallow them, for they seemed to go on forever. The air felt even more stale and decayed.

It was a big weather change from the cool breezes of the Garden. She thought of the Quiet Gardener, his gracious eyes and how they'd seen into her secrets—into her guilt over Gilda's disappearance. She felt like he was there, as an unseen companion, walking beside her.

We continued forward at a slow walking pace. But just as Sunbeam rounded a corner, she felt a chill go down her weak side. A deep, heavy sigh came out of the darkness, breathing beside her. It was Professor Plume. He had met them down the path, well outside of the Garden gate. He stepped from the trees.

"Professor! You scared me," said Sunbeam, clutching the Key; it was slightly warm. She looked around through the trees.

"I have been out in the dark all night. What have you seen inside the wall?" he asked. His beady eyes looked intense, but his shoulders sunk in fear, as if ashamed. He stared at Sunbeam, but Fawn interrupted:

"It was the most beautiful garden I've ever seen!" said Fawn, who'd now had even more stray indigos, foxes, and squirrels following her. "And the kindest man I've ever met. He was very nice!"

"We're all better," Sunbeam said. "And Whitewing is groomed and ready to run."

"There is food in the satchel bag, Professor," said Harmon, and began playing his flute.

"That music! Stop it, rude boy!" Plume said. He seemed to wince in pain. "Give me the name of the man inside the high wall!"

"The Quiet Gardener," said Sunbeam. "His Father's Son, is what he told us."

Upon hearing the name, a sort of trembling came over Plume. His eyes, hollow and empty, shuddered and his skin went ghostly pale. But yet, he looked sort of glad, too. He slightly smiled but his cheeks looked sunken in, and his beady eyes began blinking rapidly. Sunbeam felt afraid when she looked at his face.

"Do you know of him, Professor?" asked Harmon and kept playing his flute.

"Yes, in my books. And I have never seen anything more terrifying or beautiful," he whispered. And looking pale and ill, he swiftly hid his face. He leaned against the tree, ill and hunched over. All we could see was the back of his cloak as he fought for breath behind the tree-trunk.

Harmon, looking uneasy, started playing his flute even louder. He always did this when he was nervous or didn't know what to say or do. Abruptly, Plume reemerged from behind the tree and snapped, "Boy! That music! You are all in the darkest of hours! And you're marching around like you're free!"

I began sensing a threat. What were Plume's intentions? I couldn't quite pin him. I watched the way he stared at the Key, the way he flipped furiously through his books. Most of all, his peculiar reaction to the Quiet Gardener troubled me. I knew for certain, with him around, that there was one more reason to stay close to my mistress. And with my keen eye, I watched him without flinching, like a good horse does when danger broods near.

"You are all in peril! Your lives are in jeopardy!" he said gravely, his coattail flowing behind him as he held up the ancient book to show us. On the page, in the middle of ancient writings, there lay an image of an archaic lamp in the finest gold. Sunbeam's eyes traveled all over the page, and she immediately recognized the artifact. It looked like the lamp that burned zealously in her dream the night before.

"That lamp. That fire!" said Sunbeam, recalling her dream.

Plume quickly spoke: "I've been translating this all night. If my studies are accurate, we must unearth it. The lamp is old, but its light is sacred. If I am right, according to the prophecy, it is a crucial piece to our freedom. The problem is, it lies hidden in a Valley. You must cross the Valley of Dry Bones," he said, breathless.

"Valley of what?" shrieked Fawn. Dropping her stray, she sat on the ground and clutched her knees.

"Dry Bones!" Plume said. With that, silence overtook the air.

Harmon lowered his flute, looking concerned.

Sunbeam raised her hands in annoyance. "This is *not* the sort of place to be talking about valleys and dead bones."

"It is only the One Called who can enter the Valley with some hope to stay alive," Plume said, sweat beads on his forehead.

"What does this mean?" said Fawn, while Harmon stared from a distance and put down his flute to listen. Suddenly, Sunbeam felt a little sick. Then looking at Plume, she sensed that familiar feeling as he stood over her, with his books and his urgency to protect her.

Plume flipped the pages rapidly until he stopped on an old map that looked tattered and almost torn on the page. "This map. This is our ground plan," he ordered.

Everyone gathered around him while he taught them how to read the writings from old. Sunbeam thought he looked just like he did in the classroom at Thornridge. And she had to admit, despite his strangeness, no one could deny he was a brilliant teacher. Plume continued: "The journey is in stages. By looking, it appears to be River, Valley and then—the Mountain!"

"No! I'm not looking for some lamp. I've come for Gilda! That's priority!" Sunbeam said, feeling sick. She imagined the horrible evils that might be lurking in the Valley of Dry Bones.

"We've suffered too much. Now this? To remain this long here—?" said Fawn.

Sunbeam sat down and put an arm around Fawn. "You're right. This isn't your problem. I wish you hadn't followed me."

"I'm still with you," Harmon said.

Fawn wiped a tear and then rolled her eyes. "What choice do we have? We don't know the way out."

Plume flipped to another page. His finger slid across the old writings as he taught. "Know, children, that the year our fathers lost freedom in Ozmandia, there was a famine. They were overtaken by a powerful enchanter. And this evil in the land was brought to pass by his wicked charms. And those same wicked persons now call themselves Rulers and Lords of our island. I have a strong inclination—these are not men, but some kind of walking dead, who live only for the Dark Prince."

"Dark Prince," Sunbeam shivered. "I've seen him. The man in the mask with the horrible claw. He had Gilda's locket. I believe he's the one who took her."

"Sunbeam, even if you do find Gilda, you will not escape the Depths without unearthing the Sacred Lamp," Plume said. "You'll *both* die here!"

"WE'LL ALL DIE?" Fawn shrieked and got to her feet. Harmon pulled his flute from his belt and grasped it tightly.

In the next moment, Plume turned to Sunbeam. "You are Called. Only when you reach the Holy Mountain, with the lamp in hand, will there be hope for any of us—or for Gilda. Trust me. Under the Prince's spells, you have no chance without finding the oath. You are the prophecy," boomed Plume. "It's in the book." His black hair waved against the haunting winds.

Sunbeam was now sicker than ever and turned away. I trotted to her. I knew my mistress. She was visibly sinking and looking as though she'd collapse. Her knees faltered, and she leaned against my neck, gripping the reins and trying to catch her breath.

"I—I—you've got the wrong girl," she murmured, thinking of her guilty secret about Gilda. "You don't know me. I can't be Called. What if I don't accept the call? Your translations are wrong. Get away from me. All of you—Away!"

"Compose yourself, Sunbeam!" Plume said. He stood and stared at her while Harmon moved close to her shoulder. He took his glasses off, and with confidence in his brown eyes, he took her hand.

"I'm not going anywhere," Harmon whispered. This gesture only made Sunbeam feel worse. She would never let him see her cry, or any of them. And with that, like a strong force of lightning she leapt on my saddle and sped me off into the trees. She moved strong, fast—powerfully, like a thunder bolt.

"Come back Sunbeam! They wait to strike you from the shadows! Come back! Come back!" echoed Plume's voice as he called out after her. "Sunbeam! Come back!" he ordered until his voice faded away, and she dashed alone deeper into the trees, feeling heavier than she'd ever felt before.

☙ ❧

Sunbeam was alone. Anger and shame pounded her heart. She managed to find a long-abandoned road and came to the end of it. She drew me to a halt. When she dismounted, she found herself in darkness, for the trees blocked off all the sun. "I'm going home," she said in a low voice.

The corners of her mouth turned down, and her eyes welled up until tears streamed down her cheeks. She looked around in the darkness at the high trees and large stones at the end of the road. The stones made her think of the graveyard, and that set her thinking of the Valley of Dry Bones. Now, as strong as a girl she was, her heart quailed.

"I wish we hadn't come here."

"Mistress, rest on the tree a while," I encouraged her.

"I'm just going to sit down against it," she cried. Tears flooded her face. With her back resting against the trunk, she gripped the Golden Key. She missed her mother terribly. She knew she must be worried sick by now. With thoughts of Gilda and her mother, the decision to move forward or backward collided in her chest. She had to make a decision.

What do I do? Where do I go from here? She thought to herself, over and over again like a steady mantra.

Until getting the answer, she froze. She couldn't move. She looked down at the Golden Key. And with her face toward the ground, a tear drop escaped her cheek and splashed on the round of the Key. Suddenly, as if it swallowed her tear, the Golden Key lit up. And with the help of some force, a vision was cast before Sunbeam against the darkness. Sunbeam's eyes fixed on its golden brilliance like a magnet that pulled her in. As though under a spell, her eyes glazed over and stared straight at the vision. She couldn't turn away:

"It's Mother! I see Mother!" cried Sunbeam, looking into the hazy vision of the Key.

In faint, obscure form was her mother, sitting alone at the kitchen table back home. Her head was bowed, and her shoulders sagged forward. In the next moment, her mother's eyes bounded into full view, terrified and more defeated than before.

"Mother. I'm here. Don't worry anymore. I'm coming home," Sunbeam cried, barely above a whisper, for she was pulled deep into the vision.

Then, Mother's tired eyes morphed and faded away, for the Golden Key cast another sequence of the vision. Next, it showed her mother's feet running across soil. And her voice shook and cried out in loud wails against the trees, "Sunbeam! Sunbeam! Where are you? Come home. Sunbeam! Sunbeam . . . !" Until her mother's voice vanished, still searching as though the search would be a never-ending maze of misery, until she found the only daughter she had left in the world.

"Mother! I'm here! Don't worry! I'm coming home. Mother—Mother!" Sunbeam cried.

"Mother . . . I didn't mean to—!" But she couldn't make her mother hear.

Then just as suddenly, the vision vanished, leaving behind only darkness in the whispering trees. For a moment, Sunbeam remained transfixed in the place between vision and reality. On the Key's golden surface, her fingerprint brightened to dazzling light on the round of the Key. Her eyes gazed at it.

"My fingerprint, Whitewing," she rubbed her eyes, still somewhat in a haze. "Mother . . . Gilda . . . this tragedy began with me, and it ends with me. I caused all of this," her lips barely mumbled, coming out of the vision cast by the strange powers of the Key. And with the collision of forward or backward still raging in her chest, she knew what direction to take:

"I cannot go home until I bring Gilda back. Only this will give Mother joy for her pain—pain I've caused," she cried.

"So which way, Mistress?" I asked.

"The professor says we need the lamp to save Gilda."

"Not only Gilda, but all of Ozmandia," I reminded her.

"If I must go through the Valley, then so be it, even if it means my death."

And mine, I thought, but didn't say it. Whatever my mistress chose, I would carry her through. Coming out of the vision, she felt tired. She hadn't eaten in some time, and the combination of exhaustion and hunger made her feel so bad for herself that tears poured down her cheeks. "I've got to be cursed. The most cursed girl ever born," she said, lying against the cypress.

"There's some food in my saddlebag," I said. "You should eat."

"Gilda should have got away. Not me. Why was I the one who was sent on?" she continued as the tears rolled down her red face.

What stopped all of this was an abrupt footstep, or at least it sounded like one. I sensed someone was hiding near us. It was black as the dead of night. We could not see a thing at the end of the road. And the prowler crept so softly that I could barely hear its footsteps, but I heard the quiet steps, nonetheless. Then I heard the thing sighing. And I began to realize the sighing was so subtle and insidious that for all I knew it could have been watching us the whole time. Then it got closer, and Sunbeam heard it. And she started thinking of the disfigured Golgums and that horrid Claw. And too terrified to keep crying, she stopped—and froze in horror. The footsteps crept so faintly that Sunbeam wondered if she truly heard something or just spooked herself, like people can do all alone in the dark. But then, only a step from her, she felt the breath of a heavy exhale. And a chill went down the back of her neck.

The Golden Key was now hot to the touch. I stepped very close to my mistress, but being so dark, we did not run, for we risked running into the very thing that we could not see. We stayed very still. Sunbeam barely breathed. But after a few moments, she couldn't bear the strain.

"Who's there?" she said.

"It is me," said the voice. Sunbeam thought she recognized the voice, but it had a gentler tone.

Then suddenly, stepping from the trees like a ghost, emerged Professor Plume.

"It is me," he said, speaking in a gentle tone that Sunbeam never heard him speak. She was used to his commanding, abrupt teaching voice. "Tell me your troubles," he said.

Sunbeam felt that familiar feeling again while he sat next to her. She felt a little scared, but drawn to him, too. But she felt like that with most teachers because she never could tell what they would do next: be kind or scold her.

"Sunbeam, I've seen your sadness." He had the book of old in his hand and opened it. "You are in the darkest of hours, but the hope of freedom rests on you. If not for you, then do this for Gilda, and your beautiful mother," he said, his eyes looked intensely hollow in the murky night.

The Golden Key was very warm to the touch. And she had felt another exasperated sigh the Professor exhaled. He seemed desperate to get freedom. Sunbeam sat in silence. It was still pitch dark. Very dark. But then, breaking her thoughts, there came more footfalls from the brush.

"Sunbeam! Is that you?" It was Harmon, tripping on roots as he groped his way through the dark forest toward her. He was playing his flute.

"Stop it, Boy! We're sitting at the end of a dark road, and you're marching around with that flute like you're in the light of day! Loud, simple boy!" Then he turned to Sunbeam. "Compose yourself, Sunbeam," rising over her with his long, black cloak. "It's time to stand," he ordered, holding his book under his arm.

Fawn was behind him leading her menagerie of wild animals, which continued to grow in number. Sunbeam couldn't so much see the little creatures as she could hear their paws and hooves scuttling around in the dark.

"You all didn't have to follow me. I mean . . . I shouldn't have run off like that. Look, you don't understand," Sunbeam said, wiping her cheeks to remove all evidence of crying.

"I told you, we're doing this *together*," Harmon interrupted. She could barely see him or Fawn, but enough to see their movements in the dark.

"Yeah—together—unfortunately!" Fawn complained. "You can't run away from us or I'm going back!"

"Fawn's just scared," Harmon reassured. "Right, Fawn?" he said, nudging her.

"I want to go back home. We all do. And we can't do that without you, Sunbeam," she complained. "You're the one with the Key!"

"And what if I didn't have the Key, Fawn? You'd be gone, right? I can see you don't want to go." Sunbeam sank down on a tree root and shook her head. "I wish there was another way."

Fawn stammered, "No . . . I don't know . . . it's just . . . I miss the farm. I'm . . ."

"She's afraid," Harmon said.

"Let me finish talking," Fawn interrupted. "You know I want to help you find Gilda, but I don't know if I can. I don't want to die!"

Sunbeam could see her trying. This was hard for Fawn. She liked to keep things light. When the mood got too heavy, Fawn would disappear. She knew Fawn was out of her element. And if it were up to Sunbeam, she would want her friend back home, safe. "It's OK, Fawn. We will be OK," Sunbeam said with more confidence than she felt.

Fawn, looking down, continued, "I've only known your smiles, Sunbeam. It's going to take some getting used to . . . to understand your tears."

"Tears? What tears?" Sunbeam said, turning her face away hardened. With her face turned, the tears rolled down her cheeks again. She swallowed and raised her eyebrows upward to block the cries trying to escape, but she couldn't hold them back. The tears rolled and rolled. She could sense Harmon's concern, and the professor's desperation, and Fawn's strays, and all their eyes on her.

"I—I'm not good enough for either of you," Sunbeam's heart quailed.

"What? Of course, you are," Harmon said. "You've always been there for me."

"Compose yourself, Sunbeam!" Plume said again, "It's time to stand!"

Sunbeam, in the dark, swallowed her tears and attempted to stand. But her knees faltered because the secret of how Gilda went missing was pushing her down; it rendered her useless. She could not move.

"Let me be alone. All of you!" she snapped, knowing in a little moment she might be alright if they just went away. She'd catch up to them later.

"Why? So you can run away? Not again!" said Fawn. "You've got that Key and we're not getting lost out here forever!"

Harmon advanced toward her. He stuck his flute inside his belt and rested his hand on her shoulder. "Sunbeam, we're standing in the shadows with you. I'm not afraid of your dark."

Weak and trembling from holding in her secret, she felt overpowered by his kindness. She did not like the fact she felt like this. "Let me help you up," he said, and reached down to help her stand. His kind, soft voice was all too much for her. When Harmon took her arm, she pushed him away.

"It's my fault Gilda's gone. I'm to blame for all this!" she blurted. She had said it before she knew what she said. The secret broke out of her prison and escaped in the dark, right there at the end of the road.

"I've waited so long for you to talk," said Harmon and drew her into his arms. "You must have carried this so long, Sunbeam." He touched her cheek then tipped her chin up, and she felt the soft brush of his lips move briefly over her eyelids. "You've built your walls so high, no one could get inside. But I'm gonna try," he said. She was trembling, but yet, after telling the secret, relief washed over her. His words surprised her. He must have observed her with a lot of attention to understand her so well. She'd never seen this side of him.

Suddenly, what stopped this was Fawn's shout: "What happened Sunbeam? What have you done?" she demanded. With that, Sunbeam came to her senses and stepped to the side, releasing herself from Harmon's embrace.

"It's true," she began, "I'm the reason Gilda's gone. I forced her to play The Game," her eyes darted to the ground.

"Sunbeam, you do not have to reveal this," said Plume. He walked closer and stood near her, his black coattail waving. "This is not your fault. This prophecy is much bigger than you."

"No. Let her talk," said Harmon. "Can't you see she needs to get it out?"

"What game?" asked Fawn, confused and holding onto her creatures.

"The Game," Sunbeam continued, breathing rapidly. "I—I forced her to play it." As she began to reveal the secret, layer by layer, she felt heavy but lighter all at the same time. And while her friends and the professor looked on and listened without flinching, she plopped down against a tree, and confessed everything:

~ ∻

"See, Gilda and I used to play the Game. We were twins. We were young, and it was funny. We liked to swap identities. We were good at it. I could fool anyone into thinking I was her, and she was me. So, when we felt like it, we'd put the other person on for a day. All our friends and professors would call us by the other's name, and Gilda and I would smirk and exchange winks, loving the fact that we could fool them. But at the end of the day, we knew it was only fun.

"So one night, Mother had a new nanny watch us while she went away. This thrilled me, and I decided to play our infamous Game. And I said to Gilda, 'Let's see how good this new nanny is. Let's switch beds! I'll sleep in yours, and you sleep in mine!

So when this nanny wakes us for breakfast, she won't know who is who.'

"I said this to see if the nanny could tell us apart. After all, she was going to help Mother. And she'd have to know us as individuals.

"But, that night, Gilda was not up for playing. She thought switching beds and names would be mean and confusing to our new nanny who looked overwhelmed with her responsibilities. But I . . . I demanded that she play.

'O c'mon Gilda! Don't be boring! A boring halfwit!' I yelled at her. But she kept refusing. She told me she had a bad feeling. This was the first time Gilda never wanted to play the Game. And I didn't understand. It made me angry. I kept persuading and yelling at her, and she'd beg me to stop and plead, 'No, Sunbeam. I just have a bad feeling about the Game tonight,' with her green eyes that looked like mine, only much kinder and gentle. Mother always said mine were more piercing and mischievous than hers. And that's how she could tell us apart during the early years.

"But I wasn't stopping. I thought I was doing good by breaking the nanny in. And finally, Gilda relented. 'OK, Sunbeam. I'll play. But I don't have a good feeling about it.'

'Gilda! What's wrong with you tonight?' I poked at her. So that night, we swapped beds. I slept in hers, and she slept in mine. I was never so excited. I couldn't wait to see if this nanny was sharp enough. But the next morning . . . when we woke up . . . the nanny entered the room. She . . . she pulled the covers back, and I peeked from under the blanket to see her reaction. But after pulling the covers back further . . . and further . . . the bed was found empty. Gilda was gone.

"At first, I thought Gilda might be hiding or would walk in from another room, but that never happened. My heart began to pound rapidly underneath the blanket. The nanny turned to me and asked, 'Gilda, have you seen Sunbeam?' not knowing I was *really* Sunbeam. My heart was now in my mouth, and I did not know how to respond, and I hoped this was all some trick. But this wasn't something Gilda would do.

"I jumped up, and my pulse was so rapid, I couldn't even speak. And the nanny called to me, 'Gilda, Gilda, have you seen Sunbeam?' she kept calling and asking as I ran and searched every crook and corner of the house. My stomach felt very ill and I ran back to the room and jumped in my bed . . . *my* bed. The nanny followed after me and asked again, 'Gilda, where is your sister?' with desperate eyes. 'Tell me Gilda, where is Sunbeam?'

"I screamed and cried. And looking very confused, the nanny peered down at me. I never intended the Game to go that far. I never knew this would happen. It was a horrible nightmare. She was taken from my bed, forced by me to play. Gilda was stolen from the bed that was mine, and I, disguised as Gilda, was left behind . . .

"And in that horrible moment, I wish I really had been Gilda. For I was the one who should be gone, not her! Not her! And I will never be me again, without her!"

❧ ❧

My mistress wept and wept at the end of that dark road. The road where she'd run to hide, but instead, where a piece of her past was found by her friends and a strange professor with a book. No one spoke a word, for words could never be sufficient at a time like that. The best thing we could do was listen. And in the next moment, Harmon moved toward her. For the first time, he didn't reach nervously for his flute. Instead, he placed his hand on her shoulder, and sat there, silently.

Meanwhile, Fawn seemed unsure of what to do. She was good with animals and farm handling, but not so much with human tears. She looked on, not knowing whether to go toward Sunbeam or walk away. Then all at once, she walked toward her friend, and embraced her.

"Well Sunbeam, it might take me a while to understand you. But it was just a mistake. Don't blame yourself."

"It should have been me," Sunbeam whimpered.

What put a stop to it all was Plume who, looking upon with his beady eyes, ordered, "Sunbeam, you are Called. Act like it."

Sunbeam sat up straight, feeling a little embarrassed. She looked around and quickly pulled herself together and stood on her feet. Then she looked to the sky: "How can I make this right?" she said.

"You are the One Called," Plume said solemnly. His skin was pale against his black hair. "The book has more to tell us. Come and see."

They all gathered around to see more ancient mysteries on the page of the book. In the middle of the inscription was a horned mask. Sunbeam thought it looked like the one the prince wore that night on the high place.

"According to this, there is some kind of hidden message," said Plume.

Plume ran his fingers over the pages and held it up like a teacher: "I will translate:

There is one, whom you will find
That demon from old
Who's walked the earth since
The beginning of time."

"The Dark Prince," Sunbeam said. "This is the mask he wore on that high place, with his claw in the air, stabbing people. He— what he did to them . . ." That horrid claw made her shudder with fear and anger.

"If my interpretations are correct, whatever we're dealing with here is no mortal man. We've landed in a war between the gods, and we're casualties of it, and so is all of Ozmandia," said Plume, gravely. "Our freedom depends on your decisions, Sunbeam. You must go through the Valley to find the Sacred

Lamp. At the Holy Mountain, there you will relight it. This . . . this is how you're going to make it right. The ancient oath—is today's freedom," said the professor, running his fingers over the dusty pages.

Sunbeam nodded. "Whoever this imposter prince is, man or not, I believe he has Gilda in his clutches. I'll go."

"And I'll go with you, too," Harmon said.

"Right, we all will," Fawn added with a hesitant shiver.

"Yes, we'll go with you as far as we can," Plume said.

And with that, we all broke through the end of the dark road and moved deeper into Cypress. And Sunbeam, grasping the Golden Key, recalled her dream and hoped in the deepest parts of her soul that she would find the *Lost One*. Because only then, would all things be complete. And bearing heavy burdens, she stepped forward, knowing whoever this masked imposter was, he wanted her life.

CHAPTER 10
UNLOCKED

My mistress and the others walked on, except for Harmon who rode on my back. He focused hard on mastering his riding skills. He'd made some progress, but still had more to learn, still falling a few times a day during gallops. But the boy was determined. He'd stick his flute inside his belt like a dagger and get back up.

After many miles of walking, everyone stopped talking altogether. I sensed something was strangely different. Mistress's shoulders began to droop, and she wouldn't look up. The others sunk in the same low posture.

"Harmon, how about playing a song?" I said.

"I . . . I don't feel like playing."

"Fawn, how are the indigos?" I asked. My question seemed to go right through her, unnoticed.

"I don't know, Whitewing. I'm thinking about this suffering and our possible death—will we conquer these horrors?" said Fawn. She didn't look up.

Then Sunbeam said, "And loneliness—loneliness—the one who truly knew me is lost."

They all seemed to find themselves feeling lonely—very

lonely. They'd been walking together as a close group, but suddenly, they looked heavy and detached among the deadness of the trees. The air gradually grew thicker. It grew so heavy, they looked like they could barely breathe.

The next moment, I heard rhythmic footsteps that seemed not to step, but to slide along the leaves like a snake. Along with the slithering steps, a flock of black-winged vultures opened their wings and circled the children. And the lonelier and sadder the children looked, the more eager the birds' eyes gawked. Slowly, they swooped down and settled in the branches. Different from the day before, larger scavengers added to their flock. My senses heightened, and I stepped lightly, like a horse: a horse on edge, just before an ambush. Then, in the next moment there came a wicked shock. To my horror, peering through holes in the branches, perched more vultures. There must have been a hundred eyes studying our every move from the trees. They loomed like a feathered blanket, ready to cover us up for an eternal sleep.

The feet slid just beyond us. They moved in constant rhythm: steady, watching, following. I braced myself, ready to scoop up my mistress and the others to dash away.

"Mistress, climb up," I whispered and stooped low. But before she could climb on, a great shock hit the back of my legs. I began to experience a strong feeling of fear for my mistress. I had a strong sense that something horrid was just beyond the field of vision. And the horrid thing, though unseen, did not mean to send us running. It meant to murder.

Just then, my mistress barely spoke above a whisper: "Whitewing, the Key. It's scalding hot. Hotter than ever before," she trembled in a low voice.

Harmon and Fawn barely budged. They did not say a word. The slithering sound grew closer. Sunbeam, still on foot, grabbed my reins and stopped, and though her heart pounded in her chest, she masked it behind a calm face. The thing was close.

"Don't panic. Keep your heads about you," whispered Sunbeam, trying to stay focused in the dark, heavy air.

In a moment, Plume, just above a whisper, ordered, "There is an enchanter among us. Do what I tell you. You stand on the edge of death." He opened his book quietly and did not make a sound. The Golden Key was flashing. Then abruptly, before my mistress could take another step, everyone heard an impatient movement of feathers inside the trees. Then, a deep low hellish groan—and following it, came two dark Golgums armed with glaring knives.

It immediately became evident it was fatal for anyone who got in their way. Their sunken eyes roamed the area, then passing by everyone else, they fixed the front of their writhing bodies toward Sunbeam. Inside their hollow deep hoods lay one thing: death.

Immediately, fighting the heaviness in the air, Sunbeam stood up in a way I'd never seen before, and spoke in a strong voice: "What do you want here?"

"The master wants to meet. Come with us to the High Place of Reason," they moaned together.

I knew it was a set-up; had she gone willingly, she would have *never* made it to this High Place of Reason alive. Before Sunbeam could answer, they advanced. The hooded figures crept, sliding in circles around her. I stepped in front of my mistress to shield her. In a second, one of the Golgums slung his knife, which barely nipped my throat-latch, and sent a little blood trickling down my neck.

"Whitewing! No! They'll kill you!" Sunbeam turned, and grabbing hold of my mane, said, "This is my fight. You stay put." And as much as I did not want to obey my mistress's order, I did.

Without a second's delay, my mistress's eyes narrowed. They became sharp, ready for combat. Her shoulders raised and her knees bent so that she looked ready to strike like a thunder bolt. Like when she fought Helga, only with much more stealth and sharpness. Her hidden athleticism rose and was thrust to the forefront; she moved like a warrior: accurate, with purpose. Meanwhile, the children stood awestruck, frozen in horror. And strangely, Plume turned the pages of his book quietly, somberly.

"The master wants you at the High Place of Reason," the Golgums moaned in unison. Then without warning, they raised their knives into the air.

Sunbeam knew there was not a moment to lose. The hooded Golgums stood on each side of her. She was staring straight ahead and felt that foreign, supernatural force electrify down both arms. In a blaze, she jutted her arms forward, and held her palms out facing them. They stood very still. All one could hear was their deep hisses and groaning—until the blades came down.

Swiftly, the two dark figures began jabbing their knives with quick, downward slicing strokes toward her. And with the aid of some wicked sorcery, their knives sent out a blinding glare that made Sunbeam's eyes burn, but she knew as bad as it stung, she must *not* shut them! The blades came from opposite directions and closed in on her. In a flash, Sunbeam ducked and rolled forward so that the swinging blades that were meant for her, clashed into each other instead.

Before the hoods could turn back around to slice her, Sunbeam's eyes targeted their slithery cloaks. With one swirling strike from her fist, she sent them toppling over on their backs. They hit the dirt. Hard! A cloud of dust rose from their fall. But through the fog of dirt, you could still see the glare of their knives, which rose again with great clashing from the ground. The hoods stood upright, writhing faster and steadier like dancing snakes. They struck again. But this time, they began gliding toward her like a dark dance, left to right—left to right, in perfect rhythm, jabbing downward, slicing strokes at rapid speed. And to my horror, they had added two larger knives. We were swallowed inside the sounds of slicing blades against wind, hisses, and blinding silver glares—all moving steadily toward Sunbeam.

"The master wants you at the High Place of Reason," they moaned in unity, steadily gliding, left—right, left—right, toward her. Meanwhile, the hundred pairs of vulture eyes peered out from small holes in the trees. It was then Harmon lifted his foot to run and help her; then reluctantly, Fawn did too. But Plume snatched them back by their collars.

"Do you two want to die? You're no match for them. Only the One Called has a chance!" he shouted. Harmon and Fawn flailed in the professor's strong hands, desperately trying to help. But Plume had a strong grip on them.

With that, Sunbeam backed against a tree until the Golgums glided closer and closer, slicing faster and faster. They had her cornered. A left or right step was not an option for Sunbeam because the mud was deep and slippery, and she knew one slip on it would be her death. In horror, her eyes darted in all directions for an escape. Her back was wedged against the tree-trunk. And she was almost in despair before she remembered the red potion in her pocket, and amidst the clanging knives, recalled the words:

Do not spill it carelessly. Use it for the battle that will take your life.

The sounds of the knives built into a deafening crescendo. And at any second, those knives cutting through the air would soon cut into her flesh. Panicked, she was stumbling and panting and lagging against the tree. She didn't know whether to release the potion or not. Though in despair, she sensed the strength to get out of it herself. But she hesitated too long. That was always her downfall.

At this point, I dared disobey her order and galloped toward my mistress's rescue, only to be stopped by muddiness and a trickle of water in the soft, deep mud. I'd found myself slipping, as well as the others, who stood frozen in shock—shocked by the silver, swinging blades and Sunbeam's new superhuman force that kept the hellish things at bay. Sunbeam grasped the potion. She had less than a second to decide.

"Mistress! Don't hesitate! Make your decision! Now!" I screamed. For I knew that was her only chance. But this, this would be a miracle. For her only escape was to jump with great force clear over the top of the Golgums' heads.

With that, she stuck the potion back inside her pocket. It was then I knew she planned to jump. Then, she stooped as low as she could bend, and letting out a scream, burst forth from the ground like a cannon-shot. In a second, she was soaring through the air at a great height, until she hit the ground and landed behind them. And knowing her life was only a second from ending, with great force, reared back both arms and struck each of them on the crest of their heads. The dark hoods staggered and moaned to get back up, but indeed, *were* getting back up. In a flash, she ripped the knives from their black sleeves, and jammed it through the center of their chests simultaneously. The Golgums shuddered and fell down in whining moans, until melting slowly beneath the train of their cloaks. Then, regaining her bearings, my mistress panted for breath until she blurted, "Don't ever!—EVER!—throw knives at my horse!"

After a moment, Sunbeam plopped onto the ground, breathing rapidly. Her pulse still beat hard from the fight. Harmon and Fawn stood silently until the air had finally settled. They barely found words to speak.

"What the—Sunbeam I have never—ever seen you move like that!" Fawn said wide-eyed.

"Sunbeam, are you alright?" asked Harmon.

"Your powers are becoming evident," said Plume, standing tall, but with a gaunt expression on his pale cheeks.

"These devils just keep getting faster," Sunbeam said, wiping her brow.

"What was that? Who are you?" muttered Fawn. Her animals were nuzzled against her, more numbers than before. Sunbeam dismissed her questions. It wasn't the time for over-thinking things. She'd just slayed two walking deads simultaneously. And she didn't know how on earth she did it.

Meanwhile, Harmon's wide eyes peered at her through his glasses. He grasped his flute tightly. He had no clue what to say or do after his friend, Sunbeam from music class, just destroyed two knifed Golgums. The friend who was a *girl*. The girl who, only a moment before, was crying in the dark. He raised his flute to his lips uneasily.

"Don't even think about it, Boy!" thundered Plume. Harmon dropped his flute next to his side.

"We should probably get going before more come," said Sunbeam. As she said it, she looked down and her eyes fell upon something of intrigue. It was a shock. Lying on the dirt next to the melted black cloaks, there lay, a *LETTER*.

"Look, a letter!" Sunbeam said. On the ground next to the knife blade was a folded message, sealed with a round, silver inscription that bore the Mark of the Claw in red. The same mark the Golgums had branded on their forearms. She stared at the letter, debating whether or not to reach for it.

Sunbeam reached down to pick up the letter.

"Careful," said Plume moving toward her quickly. "It is sealed. Open carefully."

Slowly, she tore the round silver seal, tearing through the red Mark of the Claw inscription that overlay it. She smoothed out the crinkled paper and un-creased the edges. The hand-written words looked as though they'd been slashed across the page with the point of a sharp claw. Then, to her horror, in the middle of the letter, lay *Gilda's locket*. It beamed in the middle of the clawed ink, reflecting a broken branch, hanging from a tree above her. She thought of the prince with the horned mask. She picked up the locket. Sunbeam's heart began to pound violently inside her chest. Trembling, she read the *Letter:*

Subjects,

There is one who has come to the Depths to promote the welfare of the Ozmandians. What are those feeble children doing? Will they restore their island? Will they finish in three days? Can they bring the lamplight back to life—put out as it is? What they are trying to set ablaze—if even a slight breeze came, it would blow down their torches of light!

They will not know it or see us, until we are right there on them and will kill them and put an end to their work.

I am determined to stretch my hand out even farther. Intimidate her. It is well known that girls are weak and changeable as the tide. Now, tell her we will send back the other one.

I have made clear how you will deliver to me The One Called. It will help me to overthrow Ozmandia. The people are enslaved, powerless. For the dark gods have withheld the light from them.

On the third day, I will spill every last son and daughter's blood, so not one will stay alive, but serve as the walking dead. And I will have it forever.

Your Prince,

Sunbeam stared at Gilda's locket. She clutched it in her hand and felt like the broken locket: Incomplete. Half–Alive.

"We are in way over our heads!" shrieked Fawn.

"Yes. And you will become taller because of it," said the professor. "Sunbeam, you are at the forefront. It is time," he stood gravely with his book under his arm.

"Lord Wolford! Our island's leader? Who is this man?" said Harmon.

"I think we've found out. And he is no man, I suspect. And his supposed sons, well, are not his sons. No son looks exactly like his father, and his father's father for centuries. It's the same Wolford from centuries ago. He never dies," said Plume. He opened his book. "It says here, 'That demon from old, whose walked since the beginning of time.' This war is between the gods, and we've landed right in the middle." Plume began to move slowly; his eyes glazed over and looked hollow.

Just then, there came a large sound and a great gust of wind. And yes, even though Sunbeam had just slayed two Golgums, I sensed this fight was not over. It had just begun.

For in the very next moment, the birds' eyes, still watching in the trees, widened and glared fiercely; then came flapping of feathers and high-pitched squawks that sounded like battle-horns. With that, all of Fawn's indigos, foxes, and the rest of her strays lifted up on their hind legs. They hissed and pawed like enemy soldiers against the vultures diving low. Instantly, her creatures formed a circle of protection around Fawn like a ringed shield. But the evil scavengers' sharp wings flapped more wildly. Their talons opened up like weapons. And then, to our horror, came that dreadful chanting, "Come home. Come home."

At this point, I wanted to carry my mistress off and go back on the entire arrangement. For, standing before us was a land of perpetual darkness and cypress colonized by demons and sorcerers. Emerging from all directions of the trees stood at least a hundred of them, creeping slowly, moaning straight at us—a bewitching choir: "The master wants to meet you at the high place. The master wants to meet you at the high place. The Day of Ransom is upon you. The Day of Ransom is upon you," the Golgums crooned.

The air grew heavy and the children's eyelids began to droop.

"Get up," moaned Plume slowly; his eyes went blank and grey as he searched his books. "Stand Sunbeam. You must!" he wriggled against the wind. But oddly, his screaming began to sound like chanting, exactly in tune with the hexing choir moving upon us.

I galloped to Sunbeam and lowered my mane ready to run. But I was too late. She was falling asleep, succumbing to their dark spells.

"Hold on, Sunbeam! I'm . . . I'm . . ." Harmon shouted. He ran to her, fighting sleep.

"I'm holding on . . . and . . . and . . . people are always leaving," she mumbled, out of it, her eyelids closing. "I'm falling . . . " she muttered.

"I'm not leaving you here alone," Harmon screamed. He fought his way toward her. He reached out to catch her. "Fall into me," he screamed before he caught her, and Sunbeam crashed into him. Meanwhile, Fawn was slipping away too.

"The Key . . . Sunbeam . . . the Key . . ." Fawn mumbled. For it was lit on Sunbeam's chest. In its Goldenness, a keyhole formed, as if the Key wanted her to unlock something.

"Now. Now. Now," chanted Plume, the only one immune to the hexes. "Unlock it. You have authority. It's in the book." He writhed around and moaned like a snake.

"I don't understand," muttered Sunbeam.

"You don't have to understand. Just believe!" I brayed to my Mistress.

Without a second's delay, taking her last breath awake, Sunbeam raised the Golden Key into the air. And reading the inscription on the Key, muttered: "Lift up O Ancient doors. Come in to lift our heads."

In a second, a clap of thunder shook the grounds as it went by. And as the thunder trailed off, my mistress, along with Harmon and Fawn, slowly rose to their feet. But they stood differently. Transformed. New—with Authority.

At once, Harmon raised his flute to his lips. His chest lifted to maximum height. He drew in a great breath, and then blew out a very lively tune that hit the back of my legs and made the hair stand straight up on my back. It was music my ears had never heard: lovely, beautiful, sharp, powerful. High notes, low notes, all resonating into one glorious song. His music awakened fire in the heart. And his song was the match that struck it. And you wanted to move, but move in a good way: lively, rhythmically. The tune was palpable. It quickened everyone's pulse—and indeed, was counteracting the heavy chanting spells.

Suddenly, the dark figures turned to Harmon. They glared fiercely at his flute. And although they did not stop chanting, they came to a complete stop. Standing before us were about a hundred of them: humming and trying to infect us. But they were held back by the collision of Harmon's musical notes and tunes colliding into the air. For his one-man symphony burst into theirs with great force. It was casting away the heaviness. Their sunken eyes turned and locked on him, as if perceiving a great threat. A face-off.

At once, I looked around. Professor Plume had slunk down and crawled into the walking deads' foggy choir; he peered at us with caved-in, beady eyes, then suddenly—vanished like a ghost into the trees.

Alarmed, the hooded Golgums turned their bodies. Then they stood around us in a circle and raised their hexes louder— louder—and LOUDER!—trying to drown out Harmon's song. Then they lifted their black sleeves and grey, wrinkled hands into the air and called out. Immediately, the black vultures landed, one on each of their shoulders.

There was not a moment to lose. For their musical chants were swallowing Harmon's melodies, and the hexes began winning and sleepiness was settling in again.

"Louder Harmon! Play! Play!" shouted Sunbeam, fighting weariness.

With that, Harmon drew in another great breath. At once, his music slammed into the airway. It burst rhythms and force as he played harder, his fingers moved quickly and swiftly over the flute like the most skilled musician.

"Play, Harmon! Play!" Sunbeam screamed, for his tunes were swallowing their spells. His melody clashed in the air, note against note, beat against beat.

And then, all together, the Golgums crawled down on all fours like the lowest of creatures and chanted:

"Carry her off. Carry her off.

To hear is to obey. To hear is to obey."

And then, to our utter horror, the vultures rose. They lifted off each one of their shoulders. In a second, they spread their wings and squawked wide-open beaks—gaping and oozing red. Their talons flung open like hooks: hooks all pointing at Sunbeam.

"Mistress! Get Down!" I yelled, rearing back on my hind legs. I hoofed wildly at the birds swooping to hook her. I fought with all my might, but I was outnumbered by a sea of black wings and pecking bird heads.

Fawn's strays hissed and pawed. And suddenly, without thinking, Fawn raised her palms to the sky. And she raised her voice and shouted, so it echoed on the wind:

"O four walls,

Be broken!

I command you—burst from each corner,

Like creatures from a stall!"

With that, a loud wind rushed through the trees and a great multitude of four-legged creatures shot across the turf and others dashed down the trees and stood with Fawn from left to right. They whipped around swiftly, baring pointy teeth and claws at the Golgums, hissing at their dark enemies. Her strays bristled their tails out like a wide fan and arched their backs. Their fur stood straight up on end. And the pack of indigos' eyes opened like round cups of purple fire. And their ears turned flat then straight up into a point.

Perceiving this threat, the Golgums' vultures cawed like battle-horns; they then hovered to face Fawn's creatures and formed an enemy line.

Sunbeam came up from the dirt for she'd been dodging the vultures. And lifting her head, she stared at the horrors of the night. Then suddenly, she stood tall. Her eyes livened again, her shoulders raised and her movement quickened. It was then that the Golgums in the front of the brigade drew knives. She thought of the previous moment against the tree where she was almost sliced to pieces by the end of one of their blades. Now, there were even more glinting at her. In a second, my mistress looked around and wondered what was the least fatal thing to do—fight or run. But surrounded at every corner, she knew she had to fight. The next moment, those devious sorcerers raised their daggers. Those horrid knives—and chanted:

"The curse of the master is upon you.
The curse of the master is upon you.
Your doom is nigh.
Your doom is nigh."

It was then, with a great stroke downward, their blades cut in unity across the battle line. And the clamor of light and dark clashed against each other in music, beasts, and bladed battle.

Although there were many weapons and vultures going on, they all moved steadily in one direction: at Sunbeam. But she was transformed. She stepped and dodged like a warrior. I was already galloping to my mistress's aid when suddenly the dark deads linked the hem of their cloaks like a train and spewed out of their mouths:

"Thunder in the strike of twisted daggers,
fall down upon you,
four-legged beast!"

And with that, a multitude of short, wrinkled-up creatures with ugly, scrunched faces, hard as leather, rushed out of the cypress while others ran down trees and landed one by one all over me. Although rough and stumpy and grunting like warthogs, they moved quick, and bore sharp stingers that stuck out of their backside like twisted forks. It was the Bogwallows! They invaded around my breast collar and my saddle. They stung me continuously, gnawing on my legs with dirty, sharp teeth while others turned over, their backsides ramming venom inside my flesh with their curled, forked stingers.

"Whitewing! Run! Run! It's poison!" my mistress shouted. I flailed and hoofed wildly to throw off the Bogwallows. For they were running down one by one in a steady pace, keeping me from reaching her. I felt the venom hit my blood. I was growing weak.

Suddenly, Fawn, seeing my dilemma, stood high with brightened eyes—and shouted into the air:

"Every winged bird,
That moves and sees good,
Enemies of the dark gods,
Take flight!
Remove this poison from our sight!"

What came next was astonishing. A flock of bright-winged eagles swept in from the Eastern sky. And following it, a war drum was heard, but no one saw from where it came. *BA-BOOM! BA-BOOM! BA-BOOM!* It roared across the skies like distant thunder, as if it were being signaled by gods from a far-off land.

Upon Fawn's order, the bright eagles dove in sweeping motions from the air. Like hunters after prey they swooped down, swallowing the smaller bogwallows whole, and hurling the bigger ones through the air with mighty talons. I continued rearing and kicking the ugly things off my body. This battle of the wild ensued. And I hoped to come out alive, after the deathly venom.

By this time, the Golgums were about to overrun Sunbeam. The enemy line—the front of the force advanced. And the Golgums' dark vultures flew in loops, squawking and flapping violently. They flew into Sunbeam's face, trying to peck her eyes out with their beaks and wings. And together, the entire wicked army moved in rhythm, like the timing of a dark, sad song—slow, but powerful—the vexing song Harmon was trying to kill with his flute. Just one slip of his lips off that instrument, and the whole rhythm would break. And Sunbeam would be left broken. He played and played and played. He was breaking their spells.

Quick as lightning, my mistress raised her arms in a fighting stance. Her eyes opened wide, darting quick and sharp. And although her heart pounded with fear, she hoped she would be brave. For she had never seen anything that made her blood run so cold as the line of Golgums whose grey faces peered at her with eyes like bottomless pits. They circled and moved around her in a ring. Then suddenly, with the help of some strong sorcery, their blades glinted in her eyes. A blinding glare shone out, and there was a strange little noise coming from their mouths. Her eyes hurt terribly, but she knew closing them would be her death. Suddenly, one let out a whimper, and flung a blade from its sleeve. And following that dagger, the whole line raised their blades. Their rushing was like the breaking of a tsunami: Sunbeam nearly fell over.

Then a strong force shot through Sunbeam's body. Her strength increased. For she was now staring death square in the face. She leaped and dodged out of reach of their blades and settled into the rhythm of the fight. A few of them dropped to the dirt and began writhing on the ground and swept at her from crouching positions.

"The master wants you at the high place. The master wants you at the high place," they hissed and moaned.

"Away, you demons!" Sunbeam shot back, kicking at their jabbing daggers. While this was happening, suddenly, a deep strange noise started rising out of their mouths and an entire line of them levitated from the ground. They idled in midair!

Their grey eyes turned black like holes: holes that swallowed you into deep pits of nothingness. Slowly, they moved in with little faint whimpering noises. They invaded her. They came from high and low, from air and ground. If they couldn't kill her with skill, they'd kill her with numbers. For she was outnumbered indeed.

By now, I'd managed to throw off the majority of Bogwallows, and with the little strength I had left, galloped to rescue my mistress. The levitating Golgums all turned and glared fiercely at me. By my instinct, I knew I must decoy the ones levitating in mid-air. Instantly, I remembered hearing my father say that no other thing, except the mighty sea or a gleaming spear, can match a true warhorse. And not having any battles behind me, I rushed into the levitating demons and called out: "Here! You Devils! Over here!" I reared and ran upon them. This turned them away from Sunbeam, for now they had hoofs and bucking and teeth to deal with all in one swift charge.

While all this was happening, Sunbeam was dealing with two strong Golgums that wouldn't let up on her. She ducked down and swiped her leg out in one brisk sweep and sent the two of them toppling over their heads. They tumbled over, which gave her a slight opening. At this point, she knew it was either escape or die.

"Sunbeam! Catch!" yelled Fawn who'd managed to reach down and pick up a random blade on the ground from the fight. She quickly tossed it to Sunbeam and went back to directing her animals.

Instantly, Sunbeam rolled over and grabbed the blade so fast, you might have thought she was a gold streak of lightning. The two strong Golgums were already back up. They crawled on all fours toward her.

From their sleeves flashed something cold and blinding—like dark wizardry. But before they could unleash it, with one foot, she held down one of them by the hem of its cloak. It couldn't budge. In a second, she thrust her arm over the side of her body and drove the blade down into the middle of its cloak. The thing wailed out in sharp bellows and squeals, until it melted away inside its moaning. However, the other one was still moving. When she turned back to the left, it came and passed and was so close that its shoulder was pressing down against hers. It invaded, and like heavy smoke, it overspread its cloak. Its knees were digging into her chest. It had her pinned to the ground. And Sunbeam felt something crack in her weak side. She was panting and exhausted. By now she looked up and could see right into its face. But it didn't look like a face she'd ever seen. And she knew she may not live to see the next breath of life.

She was in despair. "Flee you Devil!" cried Sunbeam.

But the face was cold and blank—hollow—like pleading for your life against a stone boulder that's crushing you.

"To hear is to obey. To hear is to obey," it chanted and grabbed Sunbeam by the throat. Its cold, lifeless hands squeezed and squeezed until Sunbeam was slamming her fists into the thing with great force. She gasped and panted for air, but it had her good and tight. It squeezed harder and tighter until she saw nothing but shiny blue light. "Your life will be brief, but your death slow and tortuous," groaned the cold, placid voice that sent a chill down to her toes. Half-conscious, she remembered the red potion. In a flash, she reached for it. But before she could spill it, she heard a great clash and shattering like thunder.

"Take your filthy hands off her!"

It was Harmon. He had struck the thing so hard with his flute that it toppled over, giving Sunbeam the second she needed to save her life. She had one second left to slay this demon. In a flash, she leapt up feet first, her body in an arch, until she landed upright. With the last bit of fight she had in her, she grasped the blade. With all her might she drew back her arm, and brought it down in a thunderous stroke, and drove it so hard through the dark thing's cloak that it split in two, right between the torso. It howled and writhed and mumbled in a low voice, "Why? Why? To hear is to obey," and with its confused hollow eyes, as softly as a child, it rested its grey face down in the dirt and never moved again. Then it melted into nothingness, leaving only the hem of its gown billowing in the haze.

Now, two lay dead, pierced by their own blades. Others lay gashed by hoofs and some were pecked blind by the bright eagles' beaks. But there were more. And we needed to retreat. Fast.

"Whitewing!" my mistress screamed, exhausted. She could barely stand. Her strength was giving out. The choking had taken a toll on her.

"The master wants to meet you at the high place. The Day of Ransom is upon you," the ones left alive chanted. Just then, to ensure it was still there, Sunbeam took the red potion from her pocket. And once out, the dark figures saw it. They froze; then dropped down on the ground, cried out and wailed: "No! Hide us! Hide us from him! Go away!"

And they hid their faces in their cloaks, so it looked like they had no heads. And seeing them retreat into the Depths, we stood awe-struck, but knew this journey ran much deeper than originally thought. For there was no doubt Plume had been right: we'd been thrust between a war of the gods. And those wicked, Golgum sorcerers had scoffed and hid from the god they did not follow, but yet, were afraid of.

With that, we turned slowly forward, for there was no going back. And for a long time after the battle, no one could muster an emotion or utter a single word.

And after a good stretch down the road, Harmon broke the stillness, and trudging ahead in a low voice muttered:

"Where is the Professor?"

CHAPTER 11

THE SACRIFICE: SERVE OR DIE

After the fight, everything had changed. The Golden Key rested quietly on Sunbeam's chest. The Key was a quiet storm: silent but stirring things—unlocking mysteries day by day. There was no need for talk or questions. We all saw the plans laid were much bigger than we'd thought possible.

Unlock the powers you already hold.

Sunbeam remembered the Quiet Gardener's words. And she finally understood what he meant. She knew for sure now he was a king, but not of the earth—a god. And the children, they knew it too. He had tried to tell them what they were, but their fears of the unknown limited their vision. However, just a few steps down the road after his warning, they had unlocked their powers. And it was valuable. See, hard times have the effect of waking up your gifts, which in easy circumstances, would otherwise lay dormant. Even a horse knows this.

We all walked on, resuming the adventure the gods had sent us.

Sunbeam rode on my back. Her side was sore. And I noticed a quiet strangeness in her face since she had recovered Gilda's

locket. My mistress kept gazing at its reflective beam—
pretending her face was Gilda's.

"I should be you, and you should be me," I'd catch her
muttering to her own reflection that mirrored her twin in the
gleam of the locket.

Harmon rode too and sat behind her. He practiced his riding
skills, so Sunbeam let him hold the reins. She let him, not in an
effort to be nice, but to take a break while she recovered from a sore
neck after that walking dead nearly strangled her to death with
his stone-cold hands. If Sunbeam had felt better, he wouldn't be
doing the steering. I had to admit though, all Harmon's practice
paid off. Sure, he needed more training, but he was becoming
quite a horseman.

"You'll get through this," Harmon said.

"I'm fine," she said.

Suddenly, we came to the edge of the haunting, grey river
again. The same deep, grey river that looked like a current of
hideous myths and legends. Sunbeam and I had seen it before,
but only skirted its bank once, the night we'd seen the prince
ramming his terrible claw into people's flesh at the ritual on the
high place. The thought of stepping even one foot in its murky
water seemed to cause the hair to raise on the back of everyone's
necks—much less the thought of ever crossing it. Its current
moved steadily like a ghostly hum, like the rhythmic spells of the
Golgums' chants.

"Where do we go now? Is there a way around this dreadful
river?" asked Fawn. "Anything—anything would be better than
crossing *through* it. I can't even . . ."

"We'll stop here. I think everyone could use a break. We're all
exhausted," said Sunbeam.

"We have to find a way around this river soon, Mistress," I said.
"I assume the Golgums will be back."

"I'm starving!" said Fawn. She'd plopped down next to a tree.
A few indigos curled into her lap.

"You know where the food is," said Harmon. He unsaddled and tossed Fawn a fig from the satchel. Then before Sunbeam could dismount, he had lifted her off the saddle so that her feet were completely off the ground. Her head was pressed against his bicep as he whisked her. Before she realized, he'd already set her on the ground in one swooping motion. His eyes sparkled brown, and he seemed lost in thought—more serious than his usual manner. Then he walked to get the satchel.

"I could've got down myself," she said. She watched him walk away. Sunbeam thought he looked taller somehow, and that in this moment he was *not* Harmon back at Thornridge. His other person was taking over more and more each day.

"Here," Harmon said, and dished out leftover biscuits and figs he'd saved from the Garden. He sat on the ground. Sunbeam sat down next to him.

"Sunbeam, your side," said Fawn. "How are you feeling?"

"It will heal." Sunbeam dismissed it.

"And might I add—what was all *that*?" said Fawn. "Back there? Those powers. And Harmon, I mean, that music! It was beautiful . . . thrilling. And Sunbeam, what you did . . . I don't even have words. And I . . . I've never felt so alive and terrified at the same time!" She pulled in one of her indigos. "I was speaking their language. I had dominion over them. And they listened. What happened to us?"

"We must find out and not be afraid," said Sunbeam.

"Do we have to? I mean, it's exciting, but it's scary, too," she said. "I'm not sure how to use it so well."

"Of course, we must find out," said Harmon. "This art . . . power . . . whatever it is . . . is something useful. The Gardener said so. We have to keep going, then we can get a clearer look at it. We need the professor. He could tell us."

"Where is he?" asked Sunbeam.

"Probably off reading one of his books. You know he's always been—private," said Fawn. The children squabbled on about Plume's whereabouts, but I sensed danger: the way he'd melted into that grave choir so perfectly, the way he writhed on the ground, stared with his beady eyes, then scurried off like a phantom into the woods. After that, I feared seeing him at all.

"I just want to get back home." Fawn scrunched her eyebrows. "Sunbeam you're too young . . . we're *all* too young . . . to go out in such a bloody end! Who knows what else we'll face tonight!"

"I know. And I'm sorry, Fawn. I wish you'd gone back," said Sunbeam. Her eyes looked tired.

"No, no!" said Harmon. "I don't care if the devil himself shows up. I'm sticking by your side, no matter what you say! Aren't we, Fawn?"

"Yes, but there's no reason to get so riled up about it." Fawn rolled her eyes.

"What good is it to keep talking about going back?" said Harmon. "We can't now. And we've got powers from the gods for doing it."

Everyone ate. No one spoke anymore.

Dusk settled in, and we were engulfed by eerie sounds of the rolling river on the riverbank. It was that time of day when the moon and sun cross each other, and the sky is blue twilight. Each wrapped up in their own silence, Sunbeam turned on her side. She pulled out Gilda's locket and stared at it.

Breaking the silence, Fawn spoke out, "I hate to bring this up. But I would like to get out of here before I die an old lady! How are we going to get around this river?"

"Fawn, just . . . just give it a minute, will you?" said Harmon.

"Can we just let this day end? Let's think about that tomorrow," said Sunbeam. She stared at her moonlit reflection again, gleaming from Gilda's locket. She began drifting off to sleep.

"OK, Sunbeam. But you've got that Key, remember. And we're all in this with you. I guess I'm forced to take this chance." Fawn rolled over and sighed.

There she went again. Fawn meant well, and she was great with animals, but sometimes she could be so nitpicky with humans. Sunbeam always said she acted this way when she got hungry or tired—and paid no mind to it. With that, they lay down on a heap of leaves, and winding down from the adventures of the day, fell asleep.

They looked very peaceful in their sleep. But I knew better than to doze off. I decided to stand watch. As the others slept, I found myself very thirsty. It was then I realized I hadn't eaten or drank anything since we'd fought for our lives against the army of knifed Golgums.

It was pitch-black by now, and I wouldn't have been able to find food, but to my relief, the moon had bounded into view over the trees and lit a path. I walked a short distance to a little stream that trickled into the river and had water and grass. As I ate, I thought of how glad my mistress was to have Gilda's locket. But her eyes, the way she stared at the locket—the way she hung her head in her hands when the others weren't looking—that locket was pulling her further into a dark past she never broke free from. I suspected for her sake, she had to let go of it. For in order to rush forward with the strength she needed to win, she couldn't look back. I'd have to nudge her along.

Just then, I felt a creeping sensation hit the back of my legs. I swiftly turned my head to see. It felt like the biting Bogwallows from earlier, but without the sting. I kicked and turned to look, but there was nothing. It was only a sensation: a strong one. My animal instinct alerted to a presence.

Immediately, I galloped to my mistress. And amid the horrors of the night, to my utter shock, Sunbeam was gone . . .

෧ ໑

In less than a second, I let out the most horrible horse's cry. This woke the others and they sprung to their feet.

"Mistress is gone!" I brayed. I raised my head and zoomed my eyes all over the trees, high and low.

"Wh—what?" Harmon stuttered, waking up. He tried to open his eyelids while flinging his boots on. "Sunbeam? Sunbeam!" he called out. "No! This is a nightmare!"

He'd already gripped his flute in his hands like a weapon, ready to play it in case the Golgums' hexing songs drifted through the trees. While all this was happening, Fawn was coming to, and half-awake ran off at the mouth, "Is she up to this again?"

"No Fawn. This isn't the time," said Harmon. "Get up. Look!"

Everyone looked. And there, before our terrified eyes, lay Gilda's locket on the ground where Sunbeam had slept. Everyone's heart seemed to stop beating.

"She never would have run off without Gilda's locket. She's been taken," Harmon said. His eyes were wide, but determined, trying to decide which would be the best direction to search.

Fawn reached down and picked up Gilda's locket from the dirt. "I'll hold onto this." She grasped the locket in her fist. In the mix of all this, Fawn's indigos began hissing in the direction pointing west. "West! Let's go," said Fawn. "They know!"

In a flash, with my heart beating as hard as ever, I let out a wild cry and shot west into the trees. I hoped with all my heart we would find her. And if we did, that we'd find her alive. And if we didn't, I should be disgraced to a stable forever if I let my mistress go down in this battle at my side.

Just then, a dark figure shot across the trees. It hid behind a cypress, but the whites of its eyes glimmered in a silver streak of moonbeam. It cast a tall shadow on the ground. It was large and breathing exasperatedly. We all froze. But when it stepped into the moonlight, before us, stood Professor Plume.

"Where do you think you're going?" he demanded. His eyes were now black pits in the half-light.

We didn't move. Slowly, Plume crept closer. "I asked, where do you think you're going?" We stood still as statues. Then he roamed his eyes around us and gravely asked, "Where is Sunbeam?"

"We thought you would know. She's gone!" said Harmon. He gripped his flute.

"What? No. No! No!" he sighed, his face turned from grey to white and his eyes, although hollow, stared alarmed. "You all were to protect her. And for heaven's sake, put down that flute, Boy!"

"You should have been with us, Professor! Why did you leave?" said Harmon. "This may not have happened if you'd been—!" Suddenly, judging by Plume's crunched, pale forehead, Harmon thought it best not to finish the rest of his sentence.

"There is no time for questions. You must trust me," thundered Plume. "How long has she been missing?" He plopped his book over a rock and flung it open.

"About a quarter of an hour," I said.

"We need to find her before . . . before they take her to . . ."

"Take her where?" asked Harmon.

"To the high place," Plume said gravely. "That's where they disarm and strip and tear you to pieces. He'll cut into the deepest drafts of her soul and take it. It's the only way to stop the One Called before the Valley of Dry Bones."

"What are you saying? Tell us straight, Professor!" said Fawn.

Plume continued, his cloak whipping wildly, "Once the One Called crosses the Valley of Dry Bones, she's an even greater threat because it's near the Sacred Lamp. He'd *never* take her through it. I suppose he'll take her back. That viperous snake always takes you *back!*"

"Back where? Where do we look? We're lost in a maze of dark trees out here!" said Fawn.

Plume rubbed the bottom of his chin and squinted hard: "His high places lie everywhere: in low provinces . . . with tables for operations and dark wizardry. He secures these strongholds in corners, wedged between rows of cypress, behind rocks and inside caves, like little dark fortresses at every turn that come upon you when you least expect it. Like quiet traps a hunter sets for an innocent bird, to snap its wings when it's flying on course, to catch and bind it, beat it and break it. In the fringes of light, he slithers in the shadows. Treacherous snake!" Plume said.

"How do you know all this?" asked Harmon.

Plume flipped to a page and read, "It's in the book: 'Watch. Be on guard. See to it that the demon from old doesn't cut in on you, to disqualify you from reaching the end,'" he instructed. "Once in a high place, one of two things will happen: he'll either break her, or kill her." Plume looked like he was reliving every hideous detail.

"Break her?" asked Fawn, wide-eyed.

"Break her! Break her to serve! One who's Called is a powerful force against him. But if turned the other way, the One Called becomes the strongest force of obedience to him—for his evil. If he succeeds, it'll be too late. The alteration cannot be undone. And no sane person who wants to stay alive will go against one: a broken Called One. They're stronger than the others. Powerful. Lethal. A force to be reckoned with."

"He won't break Mistress!" I said.

"Then he'll kill her. If he cannot break the One Called to serve, he'll trick her into her own death. He will tempt her to serve him, or to sacrifice her own life for all of Ozmandia. It's in the book. We must hurry!" ordered Plume.

"Sacrifice?" said Fawn. She raised her eyebrows.

"Yes. The Called One's life is of high value. If he cannot break her to serve, he'll kill her to glean revenge against the God of Lights, whom this Prince hates. He'll try and trick Sunbeam into believing *she* is the ransom—the *sacrifice*—the highest debt owed to Wolford for saving them from hunger—her life in place of *all* of Ozmandia."

"Well isn't *she* the One Called? Wouldn't that be true?" said Harmon.

"No. The Prince is a liar and a twisted tongue from old," Plume said. "He will lie and seduce her under his wizardry. Yes, she is the One Called, but her power comes from a sacrifice that has *already* been paid."

"Then who paid the ransom? The sacrifice?" asked Fawn.

"He's in the book," said Plume, shuddering.

With the humans squabbling, I listened. All I thought about was Mistress. What Plume said made sense. However, I didn't trust him. I couldn't put my finger on why. But we'd have to take our chances. We had nothing else to go by, for Sunbeam was the one with the Golden Key.

"Look!" said Fawn. We looked, and her strays were hissing and standing over a piece of ground. "Tracks! They're still pointing west!"

"As I suspected," said Plume. "We must hurry."

"Wait!" yelled Fawn. "It's dark out here! The tracks only give us a starting direction toward a desert of wide-open darkness!"

"Yes, and sometimes it's not until we are lost in the dark do we begin to start seeing things," Plume thundered.

"Do you think we'll find her in time?" said Harmon.

"We have to, or it'll be too late," said Plume sternly.

"It's settled!" said Harmon. He seemed to try all he could to be brave, and he raised his flute in the air.

"Don't start getting ideas in that head of yours, Boy! Because we know common sense isn't your strong suit," shot Plume, irritated.

"I'm just thinking of all the good I can do with this!" said Harmon, clutching his flute, which only made Plume look squeamishly angry.

And with nothing but pitch-blackness spread before us, we set off quickly toward the West.

∼ ✺ ∽

We'd been searching for hours under tall trees and faint streaks of moonlight. The climate had changed, and we ran hard against cold winds. We ran so hard we could barely catch our breath.

"Water! I need water. My tongue is sticking!" said Fawn.

"You must not stop!" ordered Plume. "There is no time. We

are the only thing to shield Sunbeam from the Prince. After the alteration, it will be too late!"

Beads of sweat dripped down Plume's pale face. His eyes, like two empty black holes, searched for Sunbeam. Meanwhile, Harmon ran fast, his flute tight inside his balled-up fist. And Fawn, she ran too, with her furry strays; she seemed to try hard to conceal the doubt that was trying to spew out of her matter-of-fact mouth. But she couldn't hold it any longer:

"I give up! We're never going to find her! It's pitch-black out here! The tracks stopped miles back!" Fawn panted.

Yes, Fawn did have a point. The trees had cut off all moonlight, and darkness enshrouded every step. The only thing visible were our clouds of breath from running in the cold. It didn't help we had no real direction. It was like shooting a target in the dark, hoping you'd get lucky enough to hit the bull's eye. And I sensed whatever *thing* took my mistress was traveling fast—real fast—because I was running at top speed, and we still saw nothing in what felt like an isolated black oblivion.

"My animals are stumped! It's a sign! We're going the wrong way!" cried Fawn.

"Maybe we're not going the wrong way. Maybe we're just going about it wrong!" Harmon wiped sweat from his forehead.

"No, no!" I said. My senses were strong. I felt we needed to keep searching west. But maybe we needed to do it in a different way, for we weren't getting anywhere on our own. We needed help. I remembered my father said a good warhorse always trusts his instincts. And though I'd never lost my mistress before, I would have to try and trust myself now like never before. They never considered me a warhorse, but I hoped the breed and blood I came from would prove me one. My mistress needed me. And whether I believed I was a real warhorse or not, I at least had to act like one.

"Maybe the darkness is a sign that we're going the *right* way," I said. "Maybe this dark haze is precisely where we need to be.

Perhaps it's a decoy to throw us off."

"Right, Horse!" said Plume. He perked up and patted my head. Inside his hollow eyes sparked a gleam, like he'd just found a missing piece to a puzzle he'd been trying to solve. He quickly pulled out his book and flung it open. He flipped through the pages. He searched the old ancient writings. "The dark . . . the lost . . . the dark," he muttered under his breath, searching.

"Sunbeam has the Key, does she not?" Plume asked quickly, his head still in the book.

"Yes. She has it. Only Gilda's locket was left behind," Fawn said. "I have it in my hand."

"If she guards the Key right, they can't take it from her. Let's hope she's still holding on to it!" Plume said. "It's our only chance!"

He stopped on the old tattered page and read aloud like a stern teacher instructing. "It says here:
When you seek on your own, the natural way,
You will lie down in torment and pain.
Hold on to the Key! Abide in darkness,
Knowing HE is present,
And will guide your way.

"Horse, perhaps you *were* onto something," said Plume.

Suddenly, Plume took the back of his hand and smeared away a film of dust on the old page. And there, in the middle of it bore faded edges and lines, which faintly outlined the face of a man. A man I recognized, with the face of a king, but the nicest of all men.

"That face!" Harmon blurted. He squinted to see the faded face barely outlined. He recalled the Quiet Gardener but didn't know for sure why he did.

Suddenly, getting a closer look after wiping away more dust, which bore more angles of the face and features of a god, Plume began to shudder and tremble. And across the forehead of the face was written:

He did not come to be served, but to serve,
and to give his life as a ransom for many.

"Is this the face you saw in the Garden?" moaned Plume. He looked sick and hunched over.

"I think so! And he talked to Sunbeam about something . . . a red potion," said Harmon.

"It's him!" Plume hissed. "It's him!" he writhed and moaned. "I can't—I can't—this is our one chance of getting her back!" And though he yearned to look at the face on the page, he couldn't. He was growing terribly ill. His eyes began to roll. Quickly, he turned away, raised the book into the air, and with all his might, screamed out the ancient words on the page:

"In the darkness, your torches put out,
At the end of yourself,
When you've lost sight,
Whatever is hidden in darkness,
Will be brought to light!
Cres-phos. Cres-phos. Cres-phos!"

At that instant a peal of thunder clapped overhead, and the ground trembled and shook with a small earthquake. All of Fawn's smaller animals lost their footing and were hurled on their faces. When everyone came to from the jolt, suddenly, my attuned eye could not believe what it saw:

Standing like an angel between a dark row of trees, the Quiet Gardener appeared. His face beamed as radiant as the sun, and it almost hurt to look at it. Everyone's legs trembled and shook, and we could do nothing but gaze at him, except for Plume, who'd hissed and writhed and fell to the ground with his head inside his cloak, so he could not see him.

The rest of us couldn't speak. We shook and gazed at him, waiting to see why he'd come, for in the Garden he seemed gentle and meek, but now, he radiated ethereal power like a warrior, and authority like a great king or god. But he never spoke a word. Instead, he turned to us with his gentle, golden-brown eyes. No words were needed, for it seemed he saw into our fears and questions that we struggled and wrestled with inside the dark dead of night. And then, with sparkling eyes that danced, he smiled. We all stood very still; then with compassion beaming from his radiant face, he reached out his hand and touched our eyes, and when we opened them, he was gone. But immediately, we could see.

"Look! I see something!" screamed Harmon. "Professor! Get up! Look!"

And looking straight ahead, we saw a faint speck of *light*, far off and small, dangling in the air like a distant firefly. You had to squint to see it. It was the smallest beacon of light, a tiny speck flashing gold against a great dark horizon. It was then we all knew for certain we had just received a gift of grace from the Quiet Gardener. But it was up to us whether to take it or not.

"A glimmer!" Harmon shouted. "What the—what is it?"

Fawn's animals raised up. Their tails shot straight out behind them. The indigos hissed wildly and stared at the sky with their round purple eyes.

"Wait. They see it too. They know!" said Fawn. The strays' eyes looked straight at the speck of light, flashing far, far away.

"It's her!" I shouted. "It's Mistress! It's the Golden Key! It's lighting up in the dark!"

"Wha . . . wha . . . how? But it's flickering up so high. Out of reach," said Harmon, squinting into the wide-open sky.

"The Gardener knew! One of those vultures must have her in its clutches," Fawn shouted, patting her strays.

"It's not a vulture. It's even more deadly. Oh, not that . . . not that!" said Plume gravely, his eyes still half rolling from the moment before. "Tread carefully. This thing that carries Sunbeam across the sky is like nothing you have ever seen. We haven't much time. RUN! RUN!"

And in the next moment, we ran fast and hard toward the tiny glimmer of light in the sky.

❧ ❧

We ran for miles. The humans panted and sweated and could barely keep running. Suddenly, that supernatural strength began to surge through my legs. I knew what I needed to do.

"Listen everyone," I said. "I can carry you the rest of the way. Get on!"

I thought I'd be more labored with all the humans on my back, but the mysterious strength powered me forward. I'd been galloping like lightning through low hanging branches and rocky ground that stuck out in sharp points. Hard as it was, I never took my eyes off the tiny gold fleck in the sky. Finally, after a great stretch and many miles of rough terrain, we got closer. We came upon one of the enemy's hidden fortresses where the Key had brought us: to another high place.

No one ever would have found it. Wedged between cavern rock and outlined by a ring of shrubs lay a hideous dark crevice inside a cave, a cave within a cave. It was a secret fortress, small, but filled with powerful wickedness. Quickly, we crouched behind a clump of boulders and hid. We looked into the cave, trying to decide when and how to make our move. For there stood a procession of dark figures: Goglums. Their grey skin was barely lit in places where flickers of firelight fell. They all stood still as stones. All bearing that horrid mark: *the mark of the claw.*

In the center of all of it was a high table. Cloaked Golgums with altered faces slid in unison around the table, sprinkling red dust over it with their grey, wrinkled hands. Others lit torches along the stone walls of the cave. Smoke rose and filled the air. It smelled of dank must. Following the strange ritual, the horned prince emerged and took his seat on a throne, high on a mound.

"Dirty, filthy, little sycophants!" boomed the prince's voice down from his lofty throne. Slowly, they all raised their sunken eyes, and stared at him like they were dead.

The prince scolded, "Should I have had to run after this pathetic prophecy myself? If not for the great wandering scavenger, she might have got away!"

"Sly snake," whispered Plume. "The great scavenger. That's the wretched beast that snatched her."

The prince's cool, blue eyes gleamed in the firelight, his chin high and lifted up. Then he shouted, "I should come down and run ten of you through at a time with one thrust into your worthless, cold bodies for your lack of skill!"

The Golgums then crawled down on all fours and raised their faces like dogs to look up at him and chanted:

"O Prince, may you be lifted high, though we are destroyed.

To hear is to obey. To hear is to obey."

The prince continued, "You dare let a weak girl destroy my work?" he hissed. "You are all fools! Turn your dogged faces aside! And when I give the order, only then shall you turn back and bear witness to this high matter!" He stabbed his claw at the air. "Bring me this . . . One Called!"

And then came the worst. Everything after that was like a nightmare we all wanted to wake from. In the next moment, the great wandering scavenger descended from the sky, cawing out in terrorizing bellows that sounded like battle-horns. It swooped its mighty wings through the opening of the cave, circling upward, ascending to the very top in horrific splendor. The scavenger was an air show of haunting pride as it opened its black feathers, displaying a wing span that spread across the entire stone fortress. With each dip from the ceiling, its black marble eyes reflected the fire burning below.

As the scavenger paraded its prize in the air—Sunbeam in its hooks—the prince screamed out: "Servile buffoons! Even this mindless scavenger is swifter than all of you!"

"Let me go!" Sunbeam screamed. She flailed and twisted in mid-air, trying to break free.

"Bring her before me." The prince slammed his claw down on his throne.

Upon his command, the great scavenger dove down, opened its beak wide and let out another caw that rang out like a siren; it shook the whole cave. Once the scavenger reached the prince, the large bird gracefully swished its wings and floated in mid-air, dangling Sunbeam directly in front of the prince so that only a small space was between her and him.

"Feeble girl," said the prince. "Did you think you could complete the task?"

"I've come only for Gilda," demanded Sunbeam. "What have you done with her?"

"Do not bother me with trifles, Child," he smirked. "Only bow down and serve me, and you will again see your precious Gilda."

"Set her free; then you can have me," Sunbeam said.

"Ahhh. You think I bargain with children? What you long for comes only *after* you consent to serve." He began sharpening his claw. "First I make the incision, then Gilda goes free." He smiled and ran his cold claw along Sunbeam's cheek.

At the touch of his claw, Sunbeam's adrenaline rushed hot through her veins. For a moment, she didn't know how to answer. Her chest heaved with a mix of fear and rage. She began to tremble. Then suddenly, before she could think, she stared the prince square in his blue eyes and smirked, "Your doom is near. I'll have you crawling on your belly just before I crush your head!"

The prince's eyes glazed over, and he leapt up wildly, turned and yelled out in a great roar, "Bind her! Behold! You will see and know that I, Lord Wolford, will live forever!"

The great scavenger obediently turned wing and dropped Sunbeam onto the high table.

"Great wandering scavenger go forth! Wait and watch," ordered the prince. The mighty vulture squawked in obedience. Then it swished downward and flew out, disappearing into the black sky. The prince turned to Sunbeam who now lay on the high table. "Neither you, nor your precious Gilda will be alive before the next sun rises."

"Let Gilda go!" screamed Sunbeam. "Why would you kill an innocent girl? Take me!"

The prince raised his shoulders and sneered, "I care about nothing in life except for the glory of my throne."

The Golgums chanted:

"O Master, pleasure of my soul,

To hear is to obey. To hear is to obey."

As Sunbeam lay on the table, beasts wearing masks in the shape of smiling, wide-mouthed demons ran in. They hissed and danced excitedly, setting fire to the outer edges to form a flamed ring around the high table, while others beat drums. And as we stared speechless at the horrors before us, suddenly Harmon blurted in a whispered panic, "We've got to get down there. For heaven's sake, they'll kill her!"

"Wait, Boy. Use your head. See if the situation might change before rushing headlong into a pack of wolves," ordered Plume. "Wait, Boy!"

It was the longest wait of our lives. Those seconds seemed like an eternity as we waited for the next moment. We needed a chance to act. Our hearts seemed to beat terribly behind those rocks, hoping and hoping that we'd get the chance to save Mistress.

Sunbeam now lay bound and roped. She was wiggling in the rope. Her eyes flitted like a scared cat, and her face was completely drained of color, and they'd written across her forehead in blood:

"CALLED."

"Now," panted Harmon. "We have to get down there!"

"No, Boy. You cannot go in among them. You will die! Wait!" said Plume, holding him by the collar. Meanwhile, Fawn stared wide-eyed. She was too shocked to move or cry.

"What do we . . . I can't . . . how do we—?" she muttered in a very low voice, grasping for answers to the point of despair at the sight of her friend squirming on a table of fire.

The prince now loomed over Sunbeam. A mix of hisses and chants and fire and drums beat rapidly. Then, looking down at her body bound on the high table, the prince's claw went high into the air. It flashed in the firelight as he waved it above his head and cried out in a great voice:

"Here I stand, Lord Wolford, your Prince, to prove with my hand that the God of Light and anything called by him is weak and deserving of death!" Then he turned and stared at his hollow-eyed servants. "My loyal subjects, you are the true Ozmandians. For you chose to serve and live rather than have your master kill you for the hope of some weak light already put out!"

"O Master, you are the pleasure of our soul.

To hear is to obey. To hear is to obey."

Then the prince, through the eyeholes of his horned mask, stared hard at Sunbeam with his icy, blue eyes.

"Poor weak, little child. Why doesn't your great God of Light fight himself instead of sending you to be killed? Do you ever think you'll relight those lamps? Put out and dead as they are?" he hissed at Sunbeam.

Sunbeam, afraid and trembling as she was, lay silent on the burning table, thinking how on earth she would ever escape this death. Suddenly, she remembered the potion: *Use it for the battle that will take your life.* Then her voice burst out from the table of flames:

"Come here and fight me with your hands, not your tongue!" She was sweating and wiggling to break free.

"Child, use your sense. If you choose death, your sacrifice will be the life that saves all of Ozmandia. *Your* life for *all.*"

"My life—to save the whole island? Even—Gilda?" she panted.

"Yes. But, why die when you can live? Live here freely, and *serve*? There is no need to kill you. Little girl, give me your allegiance. Serve me," hissed the prince.

"No!" sneered Sunbeam. "Give me what I came for and I will go! I'll leave the Depths forever!"

Judging by the tone of her voice, you never would have thought my mistress was giving up hope. But I saw she was on the verge. I knew her. Her face was pale and terrified under the firelight. And at this point, if she didn't get Gilda back, I knew she'd rather die than continue on. And in this moment, surrounded by those flames on the table burning hot as a furnace, I saw it wasn't the ropes that bound her, it was her own guilt. And I assumed she'd already made up her mind she'd rather die right there than go forward without her other half.

"Where is Gilda? Tell me!" Sunbeam yelled.

"How far will you go to save your flesh and blood? The one you betrayed. Tricked! Your sweet, precious Gilda?" the prince taunted her. He accused her. He broke her down. As much as Sunbeam hated to face it, there was some truth in what he accused her of. Then he raised his claw high, "Choose death for the ransom. Or serve me and you two will again, be as one," he hissed violently now like a snake just before striking. "Serve me! Do you consent? Do you consent? SERVE! SERVE! SERVE!" he bellowed and shook wildly with his claw lifted, seething for a desperate "Yes" from Mistress, to cut and alter her forever.

"I . . . I . . ." Sunbeam stuttered and trembled and cried, feeling guilty as charged, blaming herself over and over for Gilda's disappearance on the burning table. Our hearts seemed to beat wildly in our chests, hoping and hoping she would not consent, but yet dreading what would happen if she did not! It was then we began devising our move.

"Listen, I'd rather die than see my mistress fall," I cried.

"Wait, Horse. He is sly. Wait to see if the situation changes first!" ordered Plume.

"He's going to tear her to shreds!" said Harmon! "We have to—!"

What stopped all this was a sudden scream that came out of the prince so deep it sounded like it rose from the very bottom of the earth. Then he snarled, showed his teeth and seethed, "Raise the flames! Grate the horns!"

The next moment, a few Golgums leapt out of the procession and heightened the fire while others raised twisted horns and blew high-pitched deafening noises. It was a sound worse than scratching a hundred rocks over a sheet of metal. The noise pierced into the top of your skull. It felt like it was shaking the wits right out of your head.

"Ahhh!" screamed Sunbeam at the deafening sound that shook her brain while the burning flames roared closer to her skin. In gut-wrenching pain, she arched her back on the table and wailed out in loud cries.

"Blow!" shouted the prince. Again, they blew the twisted horns—again and again. Sunbeam convulsed time after time under the repeated blows. Then all at once her head went back. She writhed so badly that her legs turned in and looked as if the bottom of her legs had been cut below the knees.

"You have one day, Child. One day. SERVE OR DIE!" hissed the prince. And he traced the point of his claw over the place where her heart beat. Then he whipped around so that we saw only the back of his horned head. He then marched his bewitched procession out until they faded behind him in the dark.

I knew we had less than minutes. For he'd left Sunbeam alone, surrounded by fire to contemplate her fate. It was for certain they'd be back. But in the mix of the heat and maddening sounds, it was too much for Mistress. She couldn't hold on. She was lying sideways, as if twisted dead on the table.

Quickly, we rushed down, but it was too late. She had fought and fought to break herself free, but she had lost. The heat had taken her air. Her face looked drained and completely white. Then, with my warhorse second sight, I sensed her cross over into some other place. And I saw her whole body relax and go limp, until she drew one last breath, and saw nothing but a blinding blue light.

౷ ໑

Suddenly Sunbeam, inside the blinding light, felt the world and everything in it melt away, except for a face . . . the face of the Quiet Gardener. He was there in the furnace, closer than ever. His gentle face beamed like a humble lamb that had been slain, surrounded by flames as red as blood, as red as the potion he'd given to save her life. Then he raised his golden-god face and turned to her. He set his eyes deep into hers. Then, the flames and embers suddenly began melting into one red stream of blood that trickled down his glowing cheek. In the mix of this there came a loud thunderclap, followed by a gentle voice:

"You do not owe the debt. You are not the sacrifice. It has already been paid. I prepared the ransom for the great sacrifice. I swallowed up death to wipe tears from all faces. And I did not come to be served, but to serve and give my life for many. When you have found the lost one, all will be complete, and you will receive joy for your pains. It is for those for whom my Father prepared it.

"Now, receive breath."

౷ ໑

In the next moment, Sunbeam was shaking on the table in a pool of sweat, panting and gasping for air. She tried to focus. She swept her hair out of her face and as she came to, she saw Harmon leaning over her.

"Sunbeam! Sunbeam! No! Sunbeam!" Tears had welled up in his eyes.

Suddenly, my mistress coughed and spattered, drawing in quick rapid breaths. Sunbeam pushed herself up from the table and felt an electric force flow through every limb, and she drew in a great breath of air.

"Wha—what happened?" Sunbeam muttered, barely able to talk.

"They almost killed you!" Fawn cried. "We thought they killed you," she trembled.

"The Gardener . . . he . . . he . . ." muttered Sunbeam. "How did you all find me?" Regaining herself, Sunbeam slowly got off the table, then leaned against me. "Whitewing, where . . . they have Gilda. We'll get her back, right?" she muttered in a low voice, securing the blood-red potion in her pocket. With each second, Sunbeam felt a tingling strength slowly seep through her body. It felt like the Gardener's water, reviving and refreshing her as good as new.

"I don't know, Mistress." I nudged her. I knew I had to carry her out of there before they came back.

By now, color returned to Sunbeam's cheeks, and she began to sort of glow. "Listen, you all should not have followed me here." Her voice was gaining strength back. "I could've escaped on my own. I will save Gilda from that devil's clutches, but I can't afford to lose any of you." She glared at the prince's throne.

"Get back up on the horse, Sunbeam," said Plume, speaking low, but authoritatively at the same time. "He's coming back expecting to have won. When he finds you escaped, all hell is going to fling wide open."

CHAPTER 12

MYTHS AND LEGENDS

We'd made it a good stretch away from the prince's high place. No one spoke or said a word for a long time. After a far distance, we decided it was safe to stop and eat. We'd found a bushel of holly and settled in behind it to hide. The children ate the fruit in the satchel. After eating, the color in Sunbeam's face had completely returned. And despite the bluish-red bruises on her ribs, she had fully regained energy at a supernatural rate. Sunbeam took out the letter she'd found the day before.

"We have one day. One day and this monster is going to have all of Ozmandia," Sunbeam said.

"It's crucial you unearth the lamps by sundown tomorrow," Plume ordered. His beady eyes seemed to grow more hollow. He pulled out the map. "We have to reach the Valley of Dry Bones, and the only way is *through* it. The lamp is hidden somewhere in the Valley."

"I'll go. But only for saving Gilda from that beast. Without her, this is—this is all for—where is the locket?" she asked.

"Here," said Fawn. "I picked it up where you were sleeping after they took you."

Sunbeam reached for it, but Fawn jerked it backwards teasingly, and wouldn't give it to her.

"Give me the locket!" Sunbeam raised her eyebrows.

"I'll carry it the rest of the way," said Fawn half-teasing, half-serious.

"Give me the locket, Fawn!" Before thinking, Sunbeam pushed her to the ground. Fawn jumped to her feet, wiping dirt from her chin. Fawn still gripped the locket in her hand.

"See? I knew it," said Fawn. She threw the locket on the ground. "There it is. Take it."

"Knew what?" Sunbeam asked. "Don't talk about things you don't understand."

"Oh, I understand plenty," said Fawn.

"Fawn, watch it. Do not say something you'll regret," said Harmon, uneasy.

"No, Harmon," Fawn said. "Sunbeam, you almost died back there. You're here with us now. Yet you're never really *here*. You're always off somewhere lost in a memory you cannot delete. I mean, we care about you and . . . that locket . . . it's . . . I mean we all care . . . but . . . Gilda's locket is not going to erase the hurtful past. You have to move forward. We have only till tomorrow—sundown!"

I sensed Mistress's distress. Her heart began to pound. Her throat tightened. Anger and rage pulsed through her veins, and she began to shake: shake because Fawn was right, but also because Fawn would never understand. Then she stood on her feet and fought back a rainstorm of emotions. "It will never be right. It will never be the same without her." She forced herself to speak in a low voice. She turned her face to the side.

"*You* are what mattered at the moment," said Fawn. "You should be thankful we found you!"

"Sunbeam, your mother, she's waiting for you to come home," said Plume. "Your lovely mother. She is not exempt from Wolford's destruction."

"Yes! And I'd rather . . . rather . . . I will return to Mother, but not without Gilda. Gilda was the good one. I don't deserve to . . ."

"No Sunbeam," Fawn said. "A healed memory is not a forgotten one. You have to move ahead. It doesn't mean you've forgotten about Gilda, it just means you've . . ."

"Forgiven. Forgiven yourself," Harmon said. By now he was standing behind Sunbeam who still had her face turned. "It's not your fault." Then suddenly, he took her hand and swirled her around to face him. "You build too many barriers," he said.

"Barriers. What do you know about barriers? None of you understand," said Sunbeam.

Harmon squeezed her hand gently. "I know that barriers are built. But we will jump, leap, and climb walls to break them down," said Harmon. With his glasses off, Sunbeam thought his face looked refined, yet chiseled and handsome. His dark, brown hair shined under a streak of moonlight. A piece of it loosened into a wave on his forehead.

What stopped all this, suddenly, was a terrible sound that came out of the sky. And then, an even more horrible sight: everyone looked up to find the great wandering scavenger blowing in like a storm, howling as it opened its beak wide and glared at Sunbeam. Before I could think, it had already swooped down upon Mistress, a skilled hunter of the night with its marble eyes; then swiftly sank its hooks into Sunbeam's collar, circled and snatched her straight up into the black horizon.

"Cunning snake!" shouted Plume.

In a second, Sunbeam was in view, but completely out of reach. She was a silhouette—dangling like a rag doll against the moon from the hooks of the large-winged beast.

"Black-hearted viper!" shouted Plume toward the hideous scavenger. "Think, children. You haven't time. I cannot run any further." He looked ill and pale.

"There's no way we can catch her!" shouted Harmon.

"Not up there we can't. Let's bring this thing down to size a bit, shall we?" said Fawn, who looked shaken, but yet confident and brave in her newfound powers. She raised her hands to the sky.

"Oh feathered ones,
Who flock the skies,
Bring this scavenger,
Down to size!"

With that, the multitude of bright-winged eagles shot across the Eastern Sky. They descended in high-pitched battle shrieks that rang out like a cavalry. They formed a close-knit flock, a winged battalion, and hovered over the large, evil scavenger. A roar of anger and rage came out of the scavenger so loud it sounded like it rose up from the pits of the earth. Then came screeches from its gaping mouth as the eagles forced it lower.

"It's working, Child! It's working! Bring the beast low!" shouted Plume, who'd opened his book and was flipping through it.

By now, the scavenger was swooping very low, for the eagles had brought him level with the tree tops. The bright eagles hovered over the vulture like an angelic, feathered blanket so it couldn't fly high. It was a war zone of wings.

The scavenger retreated lower and lower until it flapped below the trees, very close, almost in reach. But then, it suddenly pulled its slick wings back in a streamline point against its body. And its black marble eyes glinted, then became full of devilish cunning, like an obedient soldier sent to carry out the enemy's plan.

"Whitewing!" shouted Sunbeam.

By now, the thing was so low my mistress's voice was in ear-shot. She squirmed in mid-air, locked inside the great scavenger's hooks. If she'd been on ground, she could have taken it. But it had the advantage of being in flight. Then suddenly, in an instant, to our horror, the vulture let out a piercing scream, and the hideous thing shot further away at extreme speed through the trees.

"It's getting away!" screamed Harmon while Fawn was busy keeping it low, commanding the eagles from letting it ascend to greater heights.

"Get on, Son!" I shouted to Harmon. "We're going after it!"

If we didn't get Sunbeam soon, this thing would tear her to shreds. Or worse, take her to the prince, who certainly would.

"You know I can't ride!" shouted Harmon.

"Take your chance, Boy! Get on!" ordered Plume, hunching over, ill.

He'd have to ride. Because see, we hadn't any other choice. I had the speed, and he had the arms to catch her. And I'd rather die in battle than turn back. And if he rode well enough to defeat this vulture, it would be a great miracle. For now, he didn't have the luxury of practice falling. He'd have to stay on!

A determined fire ignited in his eyes. He jumped up on the saddle. He was feeling very brave climbing up, but when I set off at top speed, all that bravery left him. "Whitewing," said Harmon in a whisper. "I need to tell you that I—I—"

"Oh, you're OK, Son. You can ride," I said with my eye straight ahead at the great scavenger. Meanwhile, Sunbeam thrashed and shouted, trying to break loose. But it was no use. The vulture's talons set into her collar. I was running hard after it with skill. I dodged cypress and leaped over holes. I ran so hard it felt as if the ground pulled out from under my feet. And everything was shaking.

"I feel like I'm going to be sick," said Harmon. I'm going to fall!" He clutched my reins.

"Don't talk like that!" I screamed. "For heaven's sake!"

"But what'll happen if this thing kills us?"

"Well I guess . . . we'll be dead then."

Suddenly, Sunbeam let out a great scream: "Harmon! Harmon!" she writhed as the scavenger whisked her through the air.

As soon as Harmon heard her scream, suddenly, he set his feet firmly in the stirrups. And as terrified as he was to fall, he lifted up, jolted my reins, and fell into the rhythm of the race.

"That's it, Son! Ride! Ride!"

The boy had shocked me. Now up in the stirrups, his knees were bent, and his torso leaned into the motion of each gallop.

There was nothing but all-out galloping for miles. We splashed across a wide stream. It was there the boy almost lost his grip, but somehow, he shifted his weight and latched on. Although a little shaky in the jumps, he rode hard, his focus fixed straight ahead. By now, we were almost at the tail of the scavenger. Sunbeam was within reach.

"Listen, Son. I'm about to widen my gallop. This will burst us forward. And you're going to grab Mistress!"

"I don't—I don't—"

"Whatever you're going to say, don't say it. Just do it! Or Sunbeam will be smashed up by this thing! Ready?"

"R-r-r-READY!"

When we got upon the scavenger's feathered tail, I shot forth like a blast of wind. While all this was happening, the winged-beast was cawing and shrieking so loud I just knew my ears would burst at any second.

"Now, Son! Now!"

Harmon rode straight forward; his fears pushed to the back of his mind. His knees were steady into the ride. He rose up, and swiped into the air below at Sunbeam's feet, as if trying to catch a butterfly in a net.

"Whitewing! Harmon!" Sunbeam screamed in the mix of branches, sky, and moonlight.

I knew for him to successfully grab her, I must make a giant leap between the gap of air between his hands and her feet. But at the same moment, which was the worst thing I'd seen, was the look in the scavenger's eyes. Sunbeam was fighting for her life, but I knew then, the scavenger was getting ready to take it. And when Harmon swiped to grab her a third time, the winged beast shot upward, above the tree tops.

"Whitewing!" my mistress screamed. Sunbeam's face turned all shades of red. I burst forth on my hind legs harder than ever.

Then, something felt as if it shattered inside of me, and to my great astonishment and horror, great white wings materialized, shimmered and burst forth from each side of my shoulder points. Then the ground came out from under my feet—and to my shock, I was soaring through the air with tremendous speed.

"Wh . . . Wh . . .Whitewing! Are we . . . we . . . I DON'T BELIEVE IT!" Harmon shouted. If Harmon was shocked, I was even more astonished. But I knew that I only had to keep my wits.

"Look up! Not down! Hold on, Son!" My wing span fully opened and seemed to spread across the darkness for miles, glimmering white like seraphs in the night.

"Well in the name of—beautiful, Whitewing! They're Beautiful!" Harmon screamed against blasts of wind in his face.

"Now, hold on, Son! I'm going to ascend, and you grab Mistress!"

"I'm holding!" Harmon braced himself as we circled upward. I was just under the scavenger now, who bellowed in devilish fury.

You could hear Harmon's arms cut through the wind as he reached out. With one arm on the rein, and the other in mid-air, he snatched the back of Mistress's heel.

"Pull, Son! Pull!"

Awestruck in the rush, Sunbeam's fears pushed aside, eyes opened wide in astonishment to see me soaring at such a height. "Whitewing! Look at your dazzling wings! Dazzling! They're beautiful!"

Harmon now had her by the heel. But the scavenger's claws dug tight.

And then came the worst part. In a second, Harmon squeezed both of his knees as hard as he could on each side of my saddle. He held on with only both of his knees. One hand was latched onto Sunbeam's leg, which was still jostling in mid-air. And the other hand, which he used to hold my reins, came completely off.

Harmon reached into his belt loop, gripped his flute, and struck the vulture with tremendous force on its left wing. But this only angered the beast. It jolted upward, and to my horror, Harmon completely airlifted off the saddle and dangled in mid hair: one hand clutching onto Sunbeam's heel, and the other striking the vulture in repeated blows with his flute.

I flew steadily underneath Harmon. His legs swung wildly just above my saddle. There was nothing but squawking, twisting, and screaming in the half-light of the moon for some time. The beast jabbed his head downward in sharp, pecking motions to peck Harmon's eyes out, but Harmon dodged, ducked, and continued to strike it, blow after blow, swiveling in the air.

"The wing, Son! Break its wing!" I shouted, knowing this was the vulture's source of strength. With that, the creature raised its head and wildly set its marble eyes on Harmon. It was then I knew it aimed to kill him, too.

"Now, Son! Now!" I flew under his legs in the tempo of the flight. With the beast's sharpened beak seconds from thrusting into Harmon's eye or neck, Sunbeam whirled out her leg and blocked the bird's murderous attempt by kicking it in its flank. The beast bellowed deeply and curled its back in pain. Its mouth spread wide open in furious pain and bared razor sharp teeth. In this second, Harmon pulled with all his might in a downward motion on its wing, which unsteadied the bird. Then Harmon raised his arm, targeting the wing, and struck the beast with one strong, heavy blow.

The scavenger bellowed, wavering for a second. And this was the second Sunbeam needed to break loose.

"I'm coming down!" screamed Sunbeam.

THUD!—Sunbeam and Harmon came crashing down from the air and landed hard on my saddle. The bird wobbled and curled in pain.

"Hold on!" I said. With Harmon and Sunbeam now back on the saddle, I shot to the left over another row of cypress.

"Whitewing—they're the most beautiful things I've ever seen!" shouted Sunbeam, gazing at my great white shimmering wings.

If I thought I ever ran fast on the ground, in the air, I moved at triple the speed. I was flying fast. Suddenly, the beast's furious black eyes turned and glared—opening spiked feathers that stood straight off its skin—ready for a fight. The thing was determined, steady. And in the next moment, I could hardly believe my eyes. Sounds of whizzing, like sharp arrows, filled the rushing air around us. The scavenger flew upon me, thrusting its beak at my hind-legs like a deadly archer.

"Listen, I have to get this thing off of us, or else. When I descend, drop fast and roll!"

In a second, I dropped height and slowed. This sudden stop surprised the winged beast, and it whizzed over me, a black streak of lightning. Sunbeam and Harmon jumped and rolled in a fog of leaves and dust.

In the next second, the scavenger had reinforced. It dipped down and charged at Sunbeam's face. She raised both hands to protect her eyes. But before Sunbeam could get up to fight, in a flash, I swooped down on the enemy like a brigade of rushing cavalry. The beast was skilled in matters of flight. But I, having just found my wings, would try my best to defend Mistress from the cunning aerialist. Not having much time, I raised my wings— and put faith in the old tale that no creature or thing, except for the mighty sea or a gleaming spear, can match a flying warhorse.

The vulture circled and pecked to kill Sunbeam. Before its next strike, I shot upward and slammed into its undercarriage, sending it headlong into the sky like an arrow. It was flailing now and far from Sunbeam. I went up after it.

When the beast turned back, we were among the winds of the sky, face to face, wing to wing. Then in a flash, it darted into my face. The thing flew well, streaking shiny and black. It circled, zipped, and pecked at my eyes, trying to blind me with its sharp wings.

"Whitewing! Look!" Sunbeam shouted, which I faintly heard below, for Fawn's bright-winged eagles swooshed overhead like thunderous warriors, as if forming an enemy line, watching from the stands. Every eye above and below was now locked on me and the great wandering scavenger.

Its red beak aimed, pointed, and shot at me again like a serpent of the air. And there was nothing but wings, hoofs, and teeth for some time. Then it let out a cry and darted up toward the moon. Its marble eyes smiled with devilish cunning, then swooped down in graceful acrobatics, with wide strokes like a sword-show upon my flanks. I dodged and slashed my wings out sideways in repeated blows against its body. Each plunge of my wing filled the air like a zipping bow and arrow. But in the next second, the wicked aerialist did a mid-air somersault.

I looked up to find his beak upon me, wide open—his hooks tearing into my shoulder points from the place my wings began. I was dizzy and twirling along the horizon as he ground himself into my back. He dug his talons and scratched deep into my flesh, trying to sever both of my wings. And there was nothing but flapping, flipping, and tossing mane between wind and clouds. I had to get him off my back.

The next second, I had an idea. With all the strength I had left, I took a chance and shot across the horizon like a white blaze of lightning. He was still on my back. So at top speed, fighting dizziness, I sailed both wings outward to catch air. This brought me to a mid-air whiplash, which shot the bird forward like a black dart. I levitated for a second until the scavenger gained its bearings, turned and zipped back toward me. With his beak charging my throat, oozing red with venom, I raised my front hoofs. In less than a second, I brought down my wing in the strike of a thunderous sword on top of its squawking head.

"Vulture of darkness! Away with you!" I bellowed into the skies. Then I raised my glimmering pinions again and struck with such force that it completely snapped its great dark wing.

The thing widened its marble eyes, bellowing, while the nape of its neck coiled backward toward its broken wing. And jerking its beak around in mid-air, with a cracked wing, it dropped and flew headlong into the bark of a cypress tree. Its head splattered red against it—and it never moved again.

All fell silent. And for a moment, nothing was heard except the hollow scattering of the four winds.

Then came sounds out of the sky. "Well done! Well done! Four-legged warrior!" It was the bright-winged eagles, spread above like a heavenly blanket. They peered down on me with their sharp eyes. And everyone knows, eagles have the keenest sight of all. They were nodding like I'd just been knighted as one of their own. Then they turned wing in unity, and I watched until they vanished in a v-shaped flock across the vault of the sky.

☙ ❧

In a few moments, I was back on the ground.

Sunbeam ran up to me with Harmon behind her. "Whitewing! Valiant! A real flying warhorse! How did you . . . how did . . .?" They both stared wide-eyed touching my great pearlescent wings.

Before I could answer, suddenly, and just as surprisingly, something felt as if it burst inside of me. With that, my great wings flickered and gleamed like pearls; then just as quickly as they appeared, they vanished in a cloud of sheen.

Then Sunbeam and Harmon hugged me. "Beautiful! Gallant! Magnificent! Beautiful!" intermixed with bows and pats.

"So, it is true. I knew better than to change your name, Whitewing. If the stablemen could see you now! The Tale of the Flying Warhorses!" she gleamed.

Not having time to explain this miracle, I knew I needed to urge them onward. "Get on, you two. We should get back to the river," I said. They hopped on. This time, I carried my mistress by horseback, walking the regular way, to find Fawn and the professor—because at the end of the day, I was only a horse, and that was all.

❧ ❧

We'd been walking for some time. Everyone was quiet, taking in the excitements of the night. Harmon, still somewhat in the height of the moment and looking brave, seemed proud and his heart swelled. He had proven himself a great rider. He was holding onto Sunbeam's waist as they rode. It seemed to be all too much for him. As gentle winds whisked through the trees, golden strands of her hair brushed against his nose and cheeks.

"This could have been our last night on earth to ever see the stars again," Harmon said. "And I wanted to be with no one else." In the mix of branches and trees he stared dreamily at the moon then leaned in toward her lips, and without warning, Sunbeam pushed his face and screamed:

"Harmon! Watch out!" because he wasn't paying attention.

This put a stop to his wistful emotions and catapulted him back to reality. Because suddenly, he conked his head on a branch sticking straight out.

"Are you OK?" Sunbeam asked, trying to conceal her laughter over Harmon's clumsiness.

"I . . . I'm great. We . . . we better find Fawn and the professor," Harmon said, trying to mask his embarrassment, along with his throbbing head.

"Back to the riverbank," said Sunbeam. "That's where we left them. Hopefully they're waiting for us there."

We continued toward the grey river, to pick up where we'd left off, to keep following the ground plan Plume read us from the ancient book. And though I didn't say it aloud, I hoped everyone would be at the riverbank—together—and alive.

CHAPTER 13
THE RIVER

After a long stretch, we'd finally reached the river. To our relief, Fawn stood on the edge of the ghostly, grey current. Immediately, she ran to me and patted my mane. "This is no ordinary horse! This is a fine horse—this horse is!" said Fawn. "I watched you in the sky! A real flying warhorse! Indeed!"

What stopped all this excitement was suspicion of Plume's whereabouts.

"Where is the professor?" Sunbeam asked.

"He ran after you when the scavenger snatched you up," said Fawn.

"Should we wait for him?" Harmon asked.

"Let's rest nearby and see if he turns up," said Sunbeam. "I saw a cave on the way back for hiding, a little stretch down the bank. We could all use some sleep."

"And food. I'm starving," said Fawn.

It didn't take long to reach the cave. They looked inside.

"It looks safe in here," Sunbeam said. Harmon had already pulled food from the satchel, and to conserve what was left, they ate a small amount of dried beef and fruit leftover from the garden. Everyone felt exhausted, and they took in the quietness of the night. As everyone lay down, Sunbeam pulled the locket out again, staring at it.

"What is it?" asked Fawn. "When you look at your reflection in that locket, there is something chilling about your face."

"Go to sleep," said Sunbeam. She turned away.

"It's this. This is what it is," said Fawn and grabbed the locket.

"Not now Fawn," said Harmon.

"Here!" she replied and threw the locket back at Sunbeam. "What are you to do with it, Sunbeam? What are you to do?" And she rolled over and went to sleep. And shortly after lying in the dark, with many questions about the light, the Valley, and Ozmandia running through their minds, everyone else drifted off to sleep, too.

☙ ❧

We awoke the next morning with the dim sun breaking through the opening of the cave. The children finished off what was left of the dried beef and some figs. While they ate, I had water and grass. After eating, we knew we'd better get an early start.

Professor Plume still had not returned. Where could he be? Especially knowing we hadn't much time.

"Should we wait for the Professor?" asked Harmon.

"No," said Fawn. "He gave instructions. He said not to waste time . . . that the enemy will be on us again. He directed us to cross that . . . that river." Fawn swallowed. She gazed at the ghostly waters.

The thought of crossing the river seemed to make everyone's stomach churn like a thousand butterflies flitting around inside of it. It looked like everyone tried to muster up courage to step foot in it.

"Well, I guess we better get going," Sunbeam said.

After some time, we reached the edge of the river.

"You two go first. I'll keep watch." Harmon gripped his flute.

"Let's go, Whitewing," said Sunbeam. She had me by the reins at the edge of the water. Fawn stood on a little rock and looked at the water. She stared at its spooky, grey ripples.

"Those two dazzling wings would be nice about now," said Sunbeam, patting me.

"Do we have to cross this?" Fawn said.

"Of course, we do," said Sunbeam. I stayed close to her. We had no other choice but to go through.

"There could be snakes ... who knows what's down deep," said Fawn. Her hands started to shake a little.

"Just hop into it," said Sunbeam.

"Hop into it?"

"Well how are we going to get across if you don't?" Sunbeam said.

With that, Fawn set one foot closer to the edge of the water, but didn't go in. Then she stopped, quivering and looking back. "Well, wouldn't it be better if you two go first?" Fawn said, her eyes wide as saucers. "I mean, it's because of *you* we're in this mess, Sunbeam," she said, smiling politely.

"Really? Fawn!" snapped Sunbeam.

"What? What did I say?" Fawn said sweetly, side-eyeing the murky shallows. Her indigos swarmed around her. Their greyish-white tails fanned out, and their eyes changed to a deeper purple as they stared at the river.

"OK, I'll go first," said Sunbeam.

"I'm coming in too," said Harmon. "We should hurry. They could be just beyond the trees."

As soon as Sunbeam's feet hit the water, the grey waters drifted through the channel with a noise that sounded like ghostly hums. Sunbeam clutched the Key still dangling from her neck, and in the other hand, Gilda's locket. It was no game wading into that dreary river. And Sunbeam stood and thought for a long moment before she convinced herself to go farther.

Fawn called out from the edge of the bank and said, "I'm doing this with you." Then Fawn went in. Her strays went in with her. "I'm up to my ankles!" she called to Sunbeam who was slightly ahead of her. Sunbeam was now knee deep in the current that seemed to hum louder with every step.

"I'm coming in, too," said Harmon. And in a second, he was knee deep in the river, holding his flute above water. "This isn't so bad," he said.

Then, bending their knees, they all dove straight ahead into the river—and splashed in all together. When their heads came above water, they found the river had become a gentle current. But in the next second, the soft ebb and flow seemed to pull them under like quicksand: they were floating, but subtly sinking at the same time. They had to kick harder and faster to stay above as the hums of the current began to sound like ghostly chants. I was right next to Mistress, kicking my legs to stay above.

"What's happening?" Fawn yelled.

"I don't know, but something just touched my foot," yelled Harmon.

"Don't think about what's down there. Just keep swimming," said Sunbeam.

The soft, grey current became smooth, but the hum of it expanded into deafening murmurs and whispers until it filled their ears. Their faces began to soften with unusual delight and look absent; it caused them to become very still and weary, gazing at the sky dreamily. They all seemed entranced now, floating in its whispering warmness. I...I was immune to whatever was happening, and so were Fawn's strays.

Then, each one of them looked into the water and two things happened: First, they gazed at the river and watched it mirror their own faces from its reflective, grey beams. And the second thing that happened, the ripples changed in size, and their reflections began to change. And the reflection that came after was still their face, but a different version:

Harmon's reflection morphed into an exaggerated version of what he looked like back home: shy, with glasses and shoulders that sunk inward while mocking fingertips pointed and laughed at his face. His real face turned away, dropping tears into the river, adding more droplets to its ghostly estuary. Then his reflection leaned closer and began whispering to him as if telling a secret. *Bumbling awkward fool. No one talks to you. Talent? You have nothing. Look, and see yourself.* The reflection began to cry and cower down until it glared back at him in severe, terrified expressions.

Fawn's reflection had also distorted: it showed her reflection tending lovingly to animals while fingertips of kids pointed and mocked her. *Loner. Outcast. You have to go to the animals because real people don't care about you. Powers? It is a lie. Look and see, weird girl.* The reflection's smile turned into a long frown, and one tearful eye looked down at its scowling mouth while it whimpered and executed horrific grimaces of dark melancholy.

Sunbeam's reflection was different from the others. Hers, instead, showed the face of Gilda. And she gazed and gripped the locket harder and harder until she couldn't tell who was who. *Lost. You have ruined your sister and yourself alike. You will both be destroyed together. Called? Look and see what you will never find.* The reflection wailed out in loud cries as the face of Gilda morphed into tight features of severe punishment and disapproval at Sunbeam.

As all this went on, entranced and brooding at their own distorted reflections, they began to sink in sadness. The warm waters mocked and swallowed them like slow, sorcerous quicksand. Fawn's indigos paddled and whined and pawed Fawn's shoulder as if trying to help her. Being animals, they were immune to the hex.

Then to my horror, the whispers of the haunting river began to chant like a slow steady current:

"Reflection. Reflection.
See and bow.
Accept and drown. Accept and drown."

And to my shock, Mistress and the others chanted back.

"River of Reflection. To thee we bow.
Ourselves we see. Brooding Deep
Accept and drown. We Drown. We Drown."

"No Mistress! No! Harmon! Fawn!" I yelled and kicked. But they were sinking in deep waters of wizardry. I, being an animal, was immune to its stream of sorcery. Then suddenly, the Golden Key began flashing.
"Mistress! The Key! The Golden Key!" I shouted.
In the next moment, a voice thundered loudly from the riverbank:
"Study long,
In the River of Death,
You Study wrong!
Down paths to spirits of the Dead,
Dark Be gone!"
It was Professor Plume, holding up his book and reading from the ancient pages. He looked sickly, pale as a ghost. And I initially questioned, was he casting this spell, or breaking it?
Immediately, Sunbeam gripped the Golden Key hanging from her neck. And a light broke through from the river and shone out brightly into a great, golden blaze of ripples. Their dark reflections started whimpering and shrinking until they faded away in the Key's golden beams. This began snapping them out of the trance.
Suddenly, they started kicking and spattering water, for they had almost been submerged in the wicked river. As the golden ripples continued to expand, they slowly broke free from

their deep brooding and altered reflections and returned unto themselves—all except for Sunbeam.

"Waste no time! Swim across! The river is deceitful!" shouted Plume. He was still standing on the riverbank.

"Sunbeam! Wake up!" shouted Fawn. Her strays' fur was matted wet and their eyes were deep purple saucers. They paddled hard to stay alongside Fawn.

"Mistress hold on to my mane," I yelled.

But it was no use. She was not coming out of the trance.

I looked for the professor to see if he could help, but just as I turned around, he was fading into the woods.

Then, to my utter horror, the river began pulling Sunbeam down till it sucked her underneath.

"Where is she?" yelled Harmon. "I can't see well!" He secured his flute by gripping it between his teeth. The water stung our eyes. Everyone fought to see, swallowed in a croon of hums and sucking undertow.

"Go on you two! I will stay with Mistress!" I shouted and kicked in the water.

Harmon used both hands and worked hard to stay above. Meanwhile, Fawn screamed, "Keep swimming! Or we'll drown! I'm losing strength!"

"Not without Sunbeam!" shouted Harmon. His words came out muffled behind a mouthful of flute.

"We have to swim across! We're going to drown!" yelled Fawn, panting for air and spattering up water. She fought, kicked, and swam with her strays in the river until she ended up, by miracle, on the other side, exhausted and shaking on the bank. And by her feet, her indigos scuttled around her, shaking their fur like wet dogs.

However, Harmon dove and dove into the grey water, over and over again, barely coming up each time to search for Sunbeam.

The water was growing deeper and darker and treacherous, and then it began whirling into a ghostly torrent. Harmon's arms flailed. His legs kicked in the plunging current until he could barely breathe. He couldn't hold on any longer. If he didn't make for the bank, he knew he'd drown for sure. And with every stroke across, his heart ripped at the thought of leaving Sunbeam behind to drown. And I, I was braying and crying and kicking, but made up my mind I'd go down in that river with my mistress. I was only a horse. And my sole purpose was to give Mistress smiles.

"Swim Whitewing!" Fawn cried. "You're drowning! Swim to me, Whitewing!" Her face was a red streak of tears.

Harmon, by this time, after a great deal of swim-strokes, kicking and coughing finally managed to reach land. He lay on the edge of the bank soaking wet, quivering pale with his fists balled up in frustrated griefs and screams.

Meanwhile, I was still fighting the haunting river.

"Swim, Whitewing! Swim across!" yelled Fawn. But suddenly, just as she yelled *"swim"* Sunbeam burst out of the water like a gleaming silver splash. Her face looked blue. She spat out water and coughed and gasped in violent breaths. The crown of her blonde head bobbled in the grey cascade.

"I can't . . . can't . . ." Sunbeam muttered. She was now talking, but talking in a different way: monotone, lifeless. She looked alarmingly glazed, lost in the eyes. In her hand, she gripped Gilda's locket.

"Mistress! Hold on to me!" I yelled, trying to paddle forward. But as much as I hated to admit, I was losing strength. The water was swallowing us like a phantom's wrath.

"Whitewing. Go away. Go away," Sunbeam said in a cold, placid voice. It was clear to me the river spared all of us, all except Sunbeam.

In the roar of the shadowy torrent, I stuck out my neck for her to hold on, but my legs grew weaker and weaker by the second. We needed to cross at that moment, or it would be all over.

"No," Sunbeam muttered. "Go away. Go away."

In the height of the current, and with everything in me, I would not cross without her. And I began drowning inside the roll of the ghostly water. I let out a horse's cry.

"Go away. Swim away," Sunbeam barely spoke again between gasps of air. My mistress's face was blank. Her eyes still looked absent. I knew something was terribly wrong. I wouldn't leave Mistress.

"Her face looks chilling again! Lost! Look at her face! What is it?" shouted Fawn. She shivered on the bank.

My eyes gleaned the waters and Mistress's hands and the Key and the locket all at the same time.

"It's that locket! That's what it is!" shouted Fawn.

Then to my horror, I knew Fawn was right. That locket was weighing her down in the river like a heavy anchor. The river, it seized the opportunity to swallow her up in her weakness. It was as though the river gushed into her broken places—it smiled at her heaviness to sink her. The further she sunk, the more the river laughed.

"Mistress! Let go of the locket!" I shouted and paddled with all my might.

Harmon looked upon us from the bank. Then he looked at Sunbeam, and he too, understood. "Sunbeam! Let go of the locket!" Harmon shouted. "Let go so you can swim!"

"No. Gilda. No. Gilda." Sunbeam chanted through mouthfuls of water. We barely stayed above the phantom's hums that led down to watery paths of the dead.

"Mistress, let go! You're drowning," I shouted.

"Let go!" screamed Harmon.

Meanwhile, Fawn was still shivering in a ball against a rock.

Then without warning, another current snatched Sunbeam below. She needed *both* hands to swim, but she clutched the locket in the other. It flung her down, and each plunge was more grueling and longer than the last. All the while, her face looked blue, and her eyes looked more and more absent and hollow.

"Let go! Mistress!" I brayed. But she would not. Instead she rolled and tumbled with the locket . . . until her head bobbed once more and disappeared for good. Looking into the river, my warhorse second sight was strong, and I knew her thoughts and feelings.

⌒⌒

At the bottom of the river, Sunbeam's heart leaped when she saw bones at the bottom, skeletons anchored down in heaps, all dead, but each one still held onto what had anchored them down inside their bony fingers, lying there, drowned.

Then she saw the Gardener's eyes, like deep golden springs of peace against the haunting grey. His eyes gleamed from the bottom of the river, sparkling from a deeper spring. Seeing his gaze, she felt like she'd been snapped out of a dream, one of those dreams where you can't move. It struck her heart.

Ahead. Always straight ahead.

And instantly, she was launched back to the top.

⌒⌒

"She's back up!" shouted Fawn. "Let go, Sunbeam!"

Sunbeam floundered in the water a moment. And before she could release the locket, in a flash, a stick cut through the wind and wisped by my ears. It was Fawn. Impatient, she hurled a big stick. It struck Sunbeam's arm hard, knocking the locket clean into the air.

"It is that! That's what it is!" shouted Fawn.

The locket soared like a glimmering beam against the sky until it landed in the center of the ghostly torrent and was swallowed up. And everyone knew that even the strongest of all men would never be able to retrieve it. And with that, Sunbeam burst forth from the water like a splash of dazzling sunlight, for the weight of the locket had been flung from her. Sunbeam screamed out:

"No! Gilda! No!" Sunbeam yelled in foam and tears. But this time she spoke in her regular voice.

"Get yourself across!" yelled Fawn. "Gilda's not back, only *through!*"

"Grab on, Mistress!" I reached out my neck and Sunbeam grabbed on. And with a loud warhorse cry, I cut through across the current. And with every paddle forward, my horse's heart tore in two. For it was more than enough punishment that our lives had been uprooted, but now in the current, I was made a helpless slave under the mighty river. And I could never live this down if I did not make it across.

Harmon, Fawn, and the strays all watched helplessly as I swam with Mistress hanging onto my neck. It felt like the final hour: that moment when you've worked your heart out for the greater good and lie beat down on the battlefield—helpless—but not wanting to surrender. And even though Sunbeam's limbs ached terribly, weak and gasping, she finally released my mane and began to swim alongside me. Over and over, Sunbeam set one arm over her head, and then the other, until we finally reached the bank, together. Sunbeam fell down shivering on the dirt.

And as she lay there, Fawn blurted, "Your face, Sunbeam. Look at her face, it doesn't look so chilling anymore!"

CHAPTER 14

UNEARTHED

It had been a long time of shivering and silence before we had to pick up and move on. Ironically, ever since roped and tied on the table, the fire that meant to burn Sunbeam, instead, ignited a sense of urgency. Like wild fire, it quickened her steps all the more. She had only one day to unearth the Sacred Lamp. That was the truth that burned inside us all.

Otherwise, every person down to the last child in Ozmandia would be altered. Sunbeam secured the Golden Key and the red potion. Touching the potion, she remembered the Gardener's red streak of blood trickling down his cheek while she lay half-dead on that hellish furnace. Recalling his kingly features, she drew strength:

> *I have prepared the sacrifice. I swallowed up death to wipe tears from all faces.*

As cold, wet, and broken as Sunbeam was, she got back in the saddle. She continued down the road she'd chosen. Plume had instructed us to cross the river, and we'd done that, but we hadn't the slightest idea which direction led to the Valley of Dry Bones. Every so often, I looked at the Key for a sign, but nothing.

Plume was the one with the map, the ground plan in his old book. And we hadn't seen him since he'd vanished at the river bank. After a long stretch of silence, Harmon said, "This road has to get us somewhere."

"Yea, well somewhere could be no telling where." Fawn rolled her eyes.

The heavy winds kept blowing the fog past us, but yet, the fog never actually went away. It became so thick and cold.

"I'm hungry." Fawn plopped down under a tree. Her strays gathered around her feet. Sunbeam looked at her, and in a moment, thought of what Fawn said earlier in the river: *It's because of you we're in this mess.* And she darted her eyes away.

"I didn't think you'd say a thing like that . . . back at the river . . . after all we've been through."

"What? I practically died back there. I didn't mean what I said. I just meant . . . you're hard to handle. Look, I'm sorry, Sunbeam. I didn't mean it. But you—"

"No," Sunbeam said. "For one day—see what I see—and feel what I feel. Then maybe you'll get why I do what I do. Till then, don't criticize what you can't understand." Her eyes were a green storm. There was a long awkward pause of silence.

"Hungry, anyone?" Harmon bumbled, but they ignored him. He shrugged and started playing his flute.

Then Fawn continued sharply, "I'm trying. But of course! I'd rather be somewhere else! If I said I didn't, I'd be lying. But maybe a real friend is someone who sticks by you when she could be somewhere else. I'm here. Isn't that saying something?"

Seeing Fawn's defeated eyes, Sunbeam dropped it. She knew how Fawn was. And she also knew she didn't mean half the things she said when hungry or tired. Meanwhile, Harmon continued playing his flute. Suddenly, in the mix of all this, Sunbeam realized she needed to be alone. The strain of the day was breaking over her. And she didn't want to take it out on the only friends who tried their best to see her the whole way through.

"I'm going for a walk. I'll be back," Sunbeam said.

Suddenly, Fawn turned her face toward her and raised an eyebrow. "You're not leaving, Sunbeam. We don't need you lost again. And speaking of lost, where is the professor?"

"I'm sure he'll catch up." Harmon leaned against a large rock and continued a light melody.

"He's been acting—funny," Sunbeam said. "Or maybe it's his eyes. They're looking different. And I'm not sure why I'm feeling—uneasy around him."

Sunbeam was right. I did not trust him. However, I had noticed his growing paleness and dark-watching eyes long before they had. I couldn't pin him as either evil or good. Just—strange.

Fawn continued, "I don't know. You know how he was at Thornridge. He's always been—peculiar, but a good teacher."

"Harmon's right. I'm sure he'll catch up. I'm off for a walk. Not far." And with Fawn staring at her and Harmon on the rock lost in his music, Sunbeam faded away into the woods alone, with only me at her side.

⮞ ⮜

As soon as she was away, I sensed her doubts. Sunbeam thought of the mission entrusted to her: Wolford, the lamp, her mother, and the lost one.

When the lost one is found, the circle will be complete, and you will receive joy for your pains.

She wondered how on earth all this fell into her lap. She was just a regular girl—either struggling in school or in trouble. To think of herself as *Called* was beyond her. Her eyes stared at the ground. She twiddled the Golden Key inside her fingers. She knew her mother must be worried to death. And she knew she had one more day, or her mother would be cut and altered forever. And clutching the Key, afraid as she was at the possibility of failure, she knew what she had to do.

Suddenly, Harmon came shambling through the woods. With his hands in his pockets, he approached her casually. "You want something to keep you warm?" he asked. "You're still cold and shaking."

Sunbeam was lost in thought, and Harmon startled her. She seemed a little annoyed by his interruption. However, he had just risked his life to save her. She thought the least she could do was put up with his annoyingly handsome grin.

"No. I'm OK."

"You're shivering," he said. "Here."

He took off his jacket and laid it around her shoulders. Every now and then, the breeze blew strands of her golden hair against his face. "Your hair smells like . . . like rain and flowers," he said. It seemed that the fragrance of her hair transported him. He stared dreamily at the sky.

"Thanks, I guess . . ." Sunbeam studied his profile. For the first time she noticed how long his eyelashes looked, and the way his lips curved into a slight grin.

"Remember last night?" he said. "When we flew through the trees under the stars? I keep thinking about it." Suddenly, he looked away. He heard a noise and seemed to not want anyone to know that he was covering her with his jacket.

"What is it?" Sunbeam said.

"I thought I heard something." Suddenly, Harmon started looking around. Musician's ears are very sensitive. "Did you hear that?" he asked.

"What?"

"That." Harmon whispered. "Shh—listen."

"I don't hear anything, Harmon," Sunbeam said. Just before he encroached upon her solitude, she was focusing on important matters. And here he was, warming her with the same persistence that pulled her from the strong grip of the enemy. "Thanks, Harmon," Sunbeam said sharply. "But I just want to be alone."

"Look, I'm here to help. That's it," he said.

In that moment, Sunbeam barely recognized him as the bumbling boy in music class. That boy back home was fading away. His dark brown hair swept over his eyes. Quickly, she stood up and walked away. She was almost gone until he grasped her hand to stop her.

"Shh. Listen," he warned her. "There's something close." He looked alarmed.

Suddenly, leaning her ear into the same direction, Sunbeam heard it too. And looking down, the Key began lighting.

"The Key. It's warming," Sunbeam whispered, alert. She grasped it. This immediately put a stop to her and Harmon's carrying on.

They hid behind a clump of trees. I stayed near Mistress. It was a shock. The noise sounded like desperate sighs mixed with secretive mumbles. And it was heard behind a cluster of pointy branches, all dead and broken. They crawled beyond a heap of sharp timbers, and the closer they got, the heavier the deep sighs grew. They crouched to see.

Just then Fawn came walking through the brush and called, "Sunbeam! Harmon! It's misty out here and—!"

"Shh!" Sunbeam snapped. "Get down!"

"What is it now?" Fawn said.

"We don't know."

We peered through the cypress until we came upon that which we heard. Sticking out of the thicket of dead leaves and thorns, a hem of a cloak was on the ground.

"It's a black cloak. Is it a Golgum?" said Fawn.

"Whoever it is—whatever it is—has its face turned," said Harmon.

We could only see the back of its head. No one moved a muscle. We stared in silence until the figure raised its hands in the air like it pled for mercy to some foreign god. Then its head went back down in bowing motions, up and down—up and down—in some kind of rhythmic ritual. Deep, sad groans rose out of its mouth that sounded like cries and pleadings in hushed mumbles. It had knelt down on its knees. And then, upon raising its hands, the arm of its cloak-sleeve rolled down and bared a deep slash wound, scarred over: *the mark of the claw.*

Our hearts froze. We dared not move to disturb the Golgum's quiet, sad ritual. We didn't feel the strength for another fight. And as we were slowly backing out of dodge, the thing froze, then stood on its feet. It became still. Very silent. We could hear nothing but our hearts beating. I stayed close by Mistress.

"Don't move," whispered Sunbeam.

If this thing turned around, it would be all over. Now that the thing was on its feet, my eye recognized it as familiar. But even though I recognized its posture, it was different: in an altered state. But what came next was worse: Heaving its shoulders up and down in deep wails, it twisted the back of its head around, and there, hunched over against a heap of dead rubble, with its teeth slightly bared, its forehead scrunched, and eyes sunk down into their sockets, bearing that horrid mark of the claw across its forearm—stood Professor Plume—completely disfigured— bearing a face of sheer horror that sent a bone-deep chill all the way up the back of Sunbeam's neck.

He lifted his face completely and his eyes met with Sunbeam's. We stood frozen: shocked in that moment where you're on the verge of running, but still trying to decide the least harmful thing to do. Then in a voice very deep and low, like a ghost, Plume's eyes turned from black to grey, and he wailed:

"It's in the book. It's in the book."

And with sharp teeth, he stooped and crawled on the ground toward Sunbeam.

"Get on, children!" I said quickly. This immediately snapped them out of the horrific shock that their teacher hadn't *really* been their teacher all along, but something hideous. And with a great deal of hustle, they mounted. But Plume still had his eyes set on Sunbeam—crawling toward her. In a second, I reared back on my hind legs and carried them at a great speed further into the woods—until Plume's face melted into a hideous cloud of dust behind us.

∾ ∾

After a far stretch, we'd lost him. No one could speak a word. Everyone was in shock: they pictured their professor's face twisted on the ground, snake-like and slithering toward them. It felt like a nightmare, like the end of the world was coming.

We'd finally found a nook between some trees—a good hiding spot to sleep for the night. Just as we nestled in, Fawn's indigos showed up and ran to Fawn. They always managed to track and find her if time called for her to run away. Everyone sat down to rest, but held their gifts close by in case of danger: Sunbeam's warrior strength, Harmon's flute, and Fawn's strays lay ready to spring if needed. It was colder and foggier than ever. Sunbeam had only till the next day—sundown. And now, between the shock of her professor's betrayal and without his ground plan, she was tempted to despair.

"Sometimes I feel like we'll never see Ozmandia again," said Fawn in a low voice. Her face looked mournful as a person's could be. "And what the heck was that? Our teacher—a demon—a Golgum?"

"The bigger question is why? What does he want?" Sunbeam stared at the Key.

"Our . . . our teacher is some kind of ugly demon . . ." Fawn murmured in shock the more it sunk into her head.

"Who'd have thought?" Harmon said shaking his head in disbelief. "The professor. Our enemy all along. I can hardly believe it."

"He's probably reporting to Wolford right now, making plans for the next attack and rounding up the whole force. We've got to find the Valley of Dry Bones. He'll come back strengthened by his friends," Fawn said.

"And to think he was setting us up; leading the enemy right to us," Sunbeam said. After a long silent moment, Sunbeam stood up. "Look, we thought he was on our side, but we have to try—try and finish this without him." My mistress's blood ran as cold as that misty night, mulling over Plume's betrayal. Even though she tried to sound brave, the fear of failure pounded through her veins. Her heart quailed. She wrestled with the truth that the God of Light had called her . . . had given her power, and yet she felt a little unsure how to use it. If she failed, slipped up even once, she'd never see Gilda again, and Ozmandia would be dead forever.

"The first thing we must do is find the lamp in the Valley," Sunbeam said. "If I succeed, we'll open the doors of the portico, and relight the lamp."

"How do you know this is the ground plan now?" said Fawn.

"I just know. The Gardener spoke it to me . . . in a dream."

With that, all three of them agreed that the very first thing they must do was find the Valley of Dry Bones. And everyone seemed to wonder if Sunbeam would make it out alive, but no one spoke their doubts out loud. Against all hope—they clung to hope—because hope was the only thing that kept them moving—to restore what Lord Wolford had stolen from their forefathers long ago.

"Let's try to put these worries out of our minds," Sunbeam said. After much talk, they all lay on their backs and stared at the night sky, and then slowly drifted asleep in the cold night. Meanwhile, I was keeping watch, not even talking or moving, but standing near them.

It was in the dead hours of night by now, and they'd been asleep for several hours. However, it seemed only a little time had passed when Mistress awoke but knew by the feel of things that something was not exactly right. Her head was wedged on the ground against Fawn's shoulder. The other two still slept as soundly as if they were in their own beds.

Sunbeam got up, secured the potion and clutched the Golden Key. A breeze blew, and the climate changed slightly. I felt something uneasy settle in the air. The woods were very quiet—in fact, they were too quiet. Sunbeam could faintly make out the trees in spite of the mist. She almost shook the other two awake, but because she was listening so hard, she felt to wait. I stood near Mistress, guarding her.

"Whitewing," she faintly whispered. "The Key, it's . . ." But before she could finish her sentence, she saw something quick and black darting into a row of trees. She stopped dead still. She looked into the night, very quietly, as though waiting for it to reveal a mystery to her. Then she saw the black shape slink down on the ground and vanish without a sound. I lowered my head and said in the lowest whisper a horse could make, "Get down, Mistress. Wait here till I come back." I edged out of the foliage to go see.

Barely breathing, Sunbeam did not order against my going. So I walked out boldly in full view of whatever was roaming around the trees. While I stood and waited to see if anything would happen, Sunbeam shook the other two awake. They looked pale under the moonlight as they awoke, with a great deal of yawning and stretching.

Then suddenly, a deep, hellish voice came out of the trees and echoed in a hushed whisper: "Well, Horse, aren't you a hero. May you reign forever among all these wild demons of the Depths," said the voice. And before we knew what was happening, out stepped Plume, barely visible in a haze of mist and darkness.

Suddenly, little sharp squeals broke out from Fawn's strays. Then, very slowly, barely breathing, Sunbeam made her way up on her feet. The other two, when they laid eyes upon him, started jumping to their feet to assist, until Sunbeam said: "No. Stay here."

Then trembling on her legs, she stepped out to face him. The closer she got to her betrayer, the higher her shoulders raised.

Her walk became smooth and light, and her eyes narrowed—transforming for combat. Then she lifted her chin and said, "Why are you here?" She stood trembling, not because she was afraid, but because there was something deeply familiar about Plume. And the thought of killing him . . . the one who'd helped her, but betrayed her at the same time, made her shake.

"Now . . . Sunbeam . . . let me explain," said Plume. He stood tall and strong, how he looked in his teacher form at Thornridge. He stood with his book in hand—in his normal state. I watched him closely, ready to engage. Sunbeam took one slow step toward him, looked straight into his beady eyes and said, "Tell me why you're here?" The closer she got the more grey-faced Plume became. Indeed, Plume shuddered seeing the change come over her face, and the power that radiated from her eyes.

"Wait, Sunbeam!" he thundered. In a second, he stuck out his hand as a sign of peace. However, recalling his altered face, his teeth, and the way he'd crawled toward her to ravage her, Sunbeam did not take her eyes off him for a second. Sunbeam moved slow and steadily toward him, like a warrior without a shred of mercy. And Plume, fearing his very life, was trembling so bad he could barely move.

"Sunbeam, wait. You must trust me!" he yelled.

However, Sunbeam didn't trust him at all. The truth was out now: he was her enemy. And she advanced toward him. Plume nervously pulled a dagger from his cloak.

In a flash, Sunbeam struck him hard with a side-stroke that sent him on his knees. Then her arm went down like lightning, and she seized the dagger from his hand, and before Plume could react, she had it pressed against his throat.

"One move and you're dead," Sunbeam said. Plume was down on his knees, with his arms pinned around his back and the dagger's blade against his throat. With this, his face began contorting and he shook violently while his eyes rolled in the back of his head.

"Stop! No! No!" he shouted. In a moment, Sunbeam could sense the same devilish charms welling up in Plume, the same dark powers she'd felt in the Golgums who, only a day before, tried to kill her with blinding magic.

"It's in the book! It's in the book!" Plume wailed and moaned. Then contorting and twisting, he began transforming. With his arms pinned, Sunbeam felt the wizardly strength pulsate and charge down his arms as she struggled to keep them restrained behind his back. Suddenly, he broke loose and flailed his arms madly into the air with great strength. His strong arms seized her and held her in a tight embrace like a bear with both arms, so she couldn't escape. She was flailing to break free while the Golden Key, still dangling around her neck, flashed and burned hot. Before she could think, and not knowing why, Sunbeam grasped the Key and pressed it firmly against his skin, right over the *mark of the claw*. The scar sizzled and pulsed red on his arm. "Agh!" shouted the professor and drew back in pain. This stopped his ghoulish transformation.

And with that, Sunbeam's movement quickened so that before she could think, she had him on his backside. And in a blaze, she raised the dagger into the air, and just before she drove it down into the center of his cloak, Plume put up both hands to defend himself and cried out, "Sunbeam no! I am your father! I am your father!" And he wailed, twisted, and put his hands over his eyes and let out sharp breaths—then uncovered his eyes and lay there on the dirt squirming and pleading for his life while a tear rolled down his grey, pitiful face.

And in that second, just before killing him, she felt the fight go out of him, and she dropped the dagger.

⮞ ⮜

Plume lay on the ground. No one spoke or uttered a word. With the dagger in the dirt, and looking at Plume's pitiful face, Sunbeam's stomach began to ache. Her face went white. She felt she'd collapse on the ground at any minute. She grabbed a hold of my mane. I held her up. She staggered and stammered but could find no words. This was the very first time, that she could remember, she had laid eyes on her father. And to think, not only was it hard enough taking in her father for the first time, but to learn he was a wretched Golgum, too?

After a moment, Plume rose from the dirt, and uttered softly: "Sunbeam, you must never think, even secretly in your heart, that I am a stone-hearted father."

"I don't understand," Sunbeam said. She felt ill and dizzy.

"This was never the plan," Plume continued. "My plans to take care of you, Gilda, and your mother are what I wanted, but turned instead, into thwarting the Dark Prince's mission from killing my wife and daughters. There is much—much you don't understand," he said.

"Tell me," Sunbeam barely uttered. She drew in slow breaths, listening intently to every word that poured out of his mouth. That familiar feeling resonated all around her, and now she knew why. They carried the same blood. He was the father she'd never seen, yet never forgot. And now all she wanted was truth—some rock of solidity on her unstable, trembling knees. Meanwhile, Harmon and Fawn never budged. They stared upon Plume, just as speechless as Sunbeam, listening.

"My dear Sunbeam, there are reasons why. And it all started with the tyranny of desire. I desired more—more than what I could give you and Gilda and your mother. I worked . . . slaved day after day. But that fiend, Wolford, took everything. No one could get ahead. I did not want you and your sister deprived of the advantages I knew I could give, so in hopes to give you a better life, I joined the Guild. I joined because hopeless as I was . . . I hoped there'd be advantages. I did it for you, not for doing evil, but in hopes that out of that evil, I could bring something good back to my family. But little did I know, it was a lie."

"What was a lie?" Sunbeam muttered.

"Wolford's promises. In my desperation to provide for my family, he held up silver and gold in his wretched hands, and with a gleam in his hateful eye, he said, 'Serve me and you and your family will never be in want,' with those calm, blue eyes. And even though everything inside me told me to turn and run, I was lured by the desire of the silver he poured out like rain. And with my whole heart screaming no, I lay on that wretched stone table, thinking of all the good I could do for you and Gilda and your mother. And I lay there, squirming with terror under his dark wizardry, but also squirming under the shame of returning back home, empty-handed. And so I closed my terrified eyes, and consented. Then he cut and altered me. But by the time I realized what I'd done, it was too late. I couldn't go back because I was a different person then. How can you return home when you don't remember what home is? And yes, that wretched liar is right, I was never in want for anything again, because he took half my soul. And without your soul, you are left without desire. You become like a dead person, a soulless corpse. So much that even if a thousand trumpets blew in your ear, you would never hear them. That is how it feels without a soul.

"After he altered me, I was not conscience of my state, and not moved to ask for anything in life. I did not suffer anymore because I was like dead. And the idea of asking to return to my previous life did not enter my head because I lost all memory of it. My body was alive, but its will was dead, and my freedom disappeared. I was slave to the one who had purchased my soul: The Dark Prince."

"But how . . . how then did you find me?"

"Gilda," Plume said.

"Gilda—you saw Gilda?" Sunbeam said, wide-eyed and dizzy.

"Yes."

"Is she—alive?"

"I don't know," he responded solemnly. His face hardened, but his eyes looked sunken with deep regret.

"They brought her in, eight years old, a child, roped and bound. Mind you, I'd been gone for years, lost of all memory until my eyes fell upon my own flesh and blood, and something inside me awakened. I didn't know at first what was happening, but each day, it grew and grew until that small piece of soul I did have left, sparked the truth and memory I'd lost. My dead life started slowly resurrecting. For reasons I couldn't understand, I longed to gaze upon the child's face, but I didn't know why. Every night I would sneak into the hiding place where she lay. I'd watch her sleep. And something in me wanted to protect her—save her. And staring at her angelic face, night after night, it finally awakened me totally into the realization of the memory I'd lost many years before: she was my daughter. And not only her, but you. It began pouring through me: I had two daughters.

"Immediately, I was jolted out of the Dark Prince's spell. And I flung open the barred, iron doors and fled with Gilda into the night to save her and return home. She stared up at me, afraid under the moonlight, so fragile and pale. But I kept telling her over and over, 'I love you. I'm your father. I'm here to protect you.' And running in the dead of night, my soul wrestled against the Prince's dark stronghold he had over me: whether to take her back and serve or flee forward to freedom. Because when that hellish Prince owns half your soul, you are torn: wanting to do good, but fighting his evil right there beside you, luring you back as his slave. With everything in me, I ran and ran with Gilda in my arms.

"I thought certainly I'd make it out of the Depths. But those hounds broke out, found and beat me almost to death. Then, with me screaming and kicking on the dirt for the memory I longed to keep alive, they ripped Gilda from my arms and threw me into a dark cell, where I awaited my execution for disobedience against the master.

"I did not know where they took Gilda. Call it grace, one night a guard left the iron door unlocked, and I escaped and searched the Prince's hellish ranks, the whole time struggling between good and evil, between serving and freedom, for he owned half my soul, and he always will . . . *until* we unearth the lamp's light and awaken those in darkness.

"Without any hope of finding Gilda, and with my life at stake, I did what I knew to do: find my other daughter. I would not let him take both of you. So I set out of the Depths until I found you. I took the book, the book Wolford seized from our forefathers and wants to hide from the world, the one here, I hold in my hand, that reveals the truth about his wiles. And I studied it and was able to fight against his evil with these tiring rituals. I must do these long, tiring rituals—day after day, night after night— to avoid serving and obeying him, to break the spell over me. Every night, his dark sorcery roams to latch on and draw me back under his arm.

"In studying the book, it was then I knew *you* were Called, and that's why he'd brought in Gilda, but after careful study, knew he took the wrong one. So I followed you, to protect you. You are the One Called, Sunbeam. You must do what I could not. Let your love and strength remain in the heat of this struggle. For a great wrong would be done to all those like me, who walk around in darkness, if they were not given the chance to strive . . . and live again. Sunbeam, beyond this fire, you must be all light."

"How?" Sunbeam barely uttered.

"Your spirit," Plume replied, looking withered and grey. "It is there that the fire of intense love must burn, with the help of a superior power that lifts you up, with the outflow of his passion . . . to become all fire, all light."

"What about Gilda?" she asked, a tear escaped her eye.

"We must run forward to truth," Plume said. "And in that light, we must *believe* all these broken pieces will come together."

CHAPTER 15

THE VALLEY OF DRY BONES

Despite the shocks and horrors from the previous night, everyone slept soundly until dawn, which was lucky for Mistress because she needed strength. She had only till sundown.

The dawn broke over the trees. And what came next alarmed us: a haunting echo of horns blowing over the Depths. "That's him," said Plume sharply. "He's blowing the horns. That wretch is ordering the gates to be opened."

"Gates?" asked Fawn, yawning to wake up.

"The Gates. The gates where he locks behind the most hellish creatures you've ever seen. Up! To the Valley." Plume stood tall, his book in hand. He flung open the pages. "Here!" He pointed to the map. "The Valley of Dry Bones lay in this region—it is in this maze of sorcery Sunbeam must find the Sacred Lamp. We are very close. But just beyond the Valley is the Holy Mountain. And there—on that Holy Mountain beside the sea—we set the lamp upon its sconce, and light it up."

Our eyes followed the tracing of his finger over the tattered map where the section of the Valley looked like a wasteland of decayed bones: ancient heroes who'd never made it through. But just beyond, it looked like a lush mountain at the end of the island by the sea; then large trees that shaded the top of white stone columns.

"What is that?" asked Harmon. He pointed to the white columns.

"The portico," said Plume. "The place Wolford first showed his cunning face, until he closed the doors of the portico and put out all the lamps. This is where our fathers met—where the God of Light once shone in the Good Council of Oran. It's there we will meet. But first, Sunbeam must make it through the Valley, find the lamp, and come out on the other side alive."

Sunbeam's heart seemed to stop, but she squinted her eyes and said, "Let's go."

"No. I'm fighting with Sunbeam . . . I'm going through the Valley with her," Harmon said. He put his hand on her shoulder.

"Me too," said Fawn. Her strays gathered around as if they also agreed to cross the Valley.

"It's not possible. You'll both be swallowed up in one wave of a sorcerous ambush. You haven't the anointing to cross. Sunbeam must walk it alone," Plume said. "She is the One Called. It's in the book."

"How do the rest of us get to the Mountain then?" asked Fawn.

"We take the route *around* the Valley, but Sunbeam will go *through*—it's the only way to take back the lamp the Prince has stolen," Plume said.

"So that's it? She goes alone?" Harmon threw his flute on the ground.

"Sometimes, it is in walking alone that we find our strength . . . and our soul," said Plume, standing tall, his coattail flowing in the wind.

Before Plume could finish, another sound of horns echoed over the Depths like dark magic calling up graves and doom. And knowing she was close to the Valley, to the bones and dead rottenness, Sunbeam's face went a little pale. The others seemed to be quietly wondering if the things lurking in the Valley looked as bad as those horns sounded—and they wondered if she'd make it through. Because if she didn't get through, they wouldn't, and neither would Ozmandia.

"It takes just *one* to spare the entire island," said Plume. "Now try to compose yourself. Don't slouch your shoulders, raise them up, try to at least look like the warriors you are." Plume turned to Sunbeam. "Ozmandia would all stand in honor and salute me if they knew I was your father." His dark eyes gleamed proudly at her. He tried to spur her on, but this time, it was a bit more endearing, in a fatherly way, not in a teacher way.

After a short silence, Sunbeam muttered, "But—what if— what if—"

"Don't say it. For I now commit you to the Father, God of Heavenly Lights," said Plume. And as the sun rose slowly to the top of the sky, he gazed upward, reached out his hand to Sunbeam and said, "Come. It will soon be dark. We don't have another night." With that, they saddled up and went out, shuddering in the truth that Sunbeam would step into that wide-open Valley that stretched out for miles.

❧ ❧

After a long stretch—rounding miles of trees, dirt, rocky terrain and barren slopes—we finally reached it: The Valley of Dry Bones. When we came upon it, the first thing everyone seemed to feel was excitement—great relief for making it to the edge. But after stopping and taking a good hard look, the second thing everyone seemed to feel was dread. For Sunbeam stood on the edge of witchcraft and bones that stretched out as far as the eye could see. It was like standing at the end of the world.

There was a large iron gate at the threshold that seemed to stretch straight up to the sky.

Our eyes fell upon the High Gate, and the Golden Key flashed, pointing us straight into, what looked to be, the Gates of Hell.

And plastered on top of its iron frame, a set of large horns stuck out on each side, like Wolford's mask, hideous. Then Sunbeam's eyes scanned the door, and underneath the horns, words had been scratched deep into the Gate with a claw—and read:

Those who Enter
So do by Consent
Where every Vile thing
Is banished, bound, and Sent.

"It's Wolford. This must be his reign." Sunbeam studied the words clawed across the Gate.

"Yes. We've come to the opening of Hades," Plume said.

My mistress's blood ran cold. Just looking at it, you felt an empty wind seep through your limbs. And it was here that it felt like the journey had just begun. And Sunbeam thought of a hundred deaths she'd rather die—than to die like this.

"I feel deep inside that we all should pass through this Valley together," said Harmon. His eyes stared at the gate of sin.

"No. Only the One Called can enter. And though *each* of you is crucial to this journey, each must run their own race. This one is hers. She must go alone. Except of course, for Whitewing. He is only a horse," said Plume.

Only a horse? I thought to myself. The squabbling professor was eager to make boasts was he? He could be like those humans who talked to horses but was too hard-headed to *listen* to them. But I had bigger matters to address. I dismissed his remark.

Sunbeam's hands trembled as she clutched my reins. Her pulse beat rapidly. With sweaty palms, she swallowed hard at the Gate that joined to look like a door opening into eternal death. Then Plume, as if sensing her fear, spoke softly: "Run on, Warrior."

My mistress was all pale. The sun was in the middle of the sky but would soon be falling behind the crest. I knew I'd better speak lest she turn and run. And knowing I would walk this hellish Valley at my mistress's side, I said, "Take hold of my bridle, Mistress. We're going through."

"Why naturally you are, Horse!" said Plume, patting my head. "You're loyal. That's the bloodline in you. True stock! Now, hold your head up a little more and raise your neck and try to look more like a warhorse," he said. Plume tried to sound like a tough sergeant. For Sunbeam's sake, I sensed he wouldn't let on about the fears running through his mind. There was a short silence. I assumed many different ideas other than this one went through their heads.

"Is—is there any other way?" asked Harmon. "Is there any way *around* this?"

"There is no way around, or back, only *through*," said Plume gravely. "It's in the book." He touched Sunbeam's shoulder gently, knowing that this was the worst path of all, but the only one laid out.

"Let's get on with it then," said Sunbeam. With her heart hammering, she stepped forward. Harmon leaned toward her and uttered, "I may lose this last chance to tell you—that I—I . . ."

"Don't say it," Fawn cut in. "It's not time to say goodbye. Goodbyes are sad." She walked quickly to Sunbeam and took her hand, as if trying with everything in her not to break. Then Fawn lifted her face, "I won't say goodbye. But I will say what an experience this has been." Then she looked at the ground, otherwise I assumed her weeping heart would have gotten the better of her.

In the mix of this, Harmon swallowed and seemed to push his emotions down to the bottom of his chest, and said, "We'll meet you on the other side, at the place of high kings."

And because it appeared their hearts were churning in their chests, I presumed they all knew this might be the last time they'd ever see her, but no one would dare say or show it. No words were needed. Sunbeam closed her eyes.

With everything in her, she tore herself away from her friends and stepped toward the open-mouthed gate. The only thing she could focus on was the Golden Key, and the keyhole to the gate, which waited patiently for her to twist and unlock. Sunbeam's heart pounded violently. "This must be where he's taken Gilda." Her terrified eyes scrunched in determination.

In that second, the thought of finding Gilda rushed a sense of bravery through her. And before she could think, she inserted the Golden Key, twisted the lock, and drove me through it.

∽ ∽

After having entered all that bravery left, because to our horror, the minute we crossed the threshold, the gate slammed shut behind us, echoing through ghostly winds. We were in darkness. Her heart sank. Quickly, she turned back, but a pillar of ash blinded her. There was no sight of her friends. They'd vanished.

What little sunlight there was in the Depths was now completely cut off in the underworld of the valley. Everything sloped into unending darkness, down to deep bottomless pits of secret sorcery.

"Harmon? Fawn?" said Sunbeam. She looked around the infernal valley. A mix of fire and ash filled the cleft all the way up to a dark sky. The heat caused her to gasp and choke.

"They're gone."

"Mistress, breathe," I said. Although I helped Mistress, my horse knees trembled as much as her chest pounded.

"What if I—I can't—" Sunbeam gasped. She became very sick, for gigantic rocks and bones were everywhere. When you looked at them, they were shaped like evil, black-gowned monks with grimacing smiles, taking pleasure in fleshly torture. Sunbeam shuddered at the grotesque figures and bones. And knowing there would be no help from anyone, a feeling of faintness and nausea came over her. She doubled-over at the delirious horrors. Suddenly dizzy, she fell to the ground—for there was no doubt, we'd been thrust into the underworld of the gravest of all evils.

Sick, Sunbeam heaved onto the ground, an expression of horror in her eyes. But we had only till sundown. We had no choice but to move.

"Mistress, get on," I said. I knew my mistress. I knew she'd get back up. Our hearts and hoofbeats had run together, one and the same, to the rhythm of one drum. And if I died, at least I'd been loved by my best friend, and to any good horse, that would make it worth it. In a moment, Sunbeam took a breath and stood on her feet.

"Let's go. We've come to get the lamp," she said. She pushed all fear to the back of her mind. We set forward.

She led me straight down the Valley. The rocky ground was hot sulfur. My hoofs heated like fire rings around my legs. The dry air smelled of decaying fungus, which wafted from a stream of murky green runoff dripping down one of the clefts. It flowed into crevices along the ground. Along the floor of the Valley, we stepped over skulls of rotted bones. I didn't know how much longer I could keep walking, until suddenly, the entire ravine went dark—pitch-black. Then it became still, very still.

The black of darkness spread. There was nothing but eerie quiet and stillness. But suddenly, in the next second, the large stone-figured monks lit up with heads of fire. And in the flickers of the flame, we saw there was a way.

"There," said Mistress. A path leading down into a vault materialized between the large, gowned monks whose smiling grimaces began contorting to wild scowls. We stepped on the path of stone masonry and followed it with caution. Then after many paces, the silhouettes of the gowned monks melted mystically before us, and their heads of fire snuffed out into emptiness, and to our horror, the ground opened and—we began falling.

As we fell down—down—down—all of Sunbeam's sensations seemed completely engulfed in a rushing drop, as we fell into the bottom of the underworld.

∂ ∽

The fall seemed to go on forever. In the rush of the long drop down, Sunbeam was on the verge of passing out, but fought and held on to the last bit of consciousness she had left.

We hit the floor of a black pit. And Sunbeam lay swooning. My second sight was extremely strong, sensing Mistress. At the very bottom, she felt her mind had lapsed into an empty listlessness. There was an unnatural stillness and sense we were among many forbidden evils.

"Mistress?" I asked, I was up on my hoofs, but not yet steady. Sunbeam did not answer. "Mistress?" I asked again, worried she had fallen into shock. For the darkness of eternal night swallowed us. I could not see her, but I could hear her fighting for breath. The severity of the pitch-black hole smothered us. This feeling of faintness went on a while, and Mistress lay on her back until she began breathing more easily. Then all at once, that supernatural strength slowly pulsated through her body, restoring all her senses.

"Whitewing? There has to be a way out of this dungeon," she spoke very low. Then she reached out in the darkness to stand, and her hand fell on something hard and cold.

"Whitewing?" she whispered. Her heart was hammering. She could hear it pound at the bottom of the pit. "Where are you?"

"Here," I replied.

And by the sound of my voice, she knew the thing she had her hand upon was not me because my voice came from the opposite direction. And she ached in still silence, dreading what it could be. Then she slowly removed her hand. She cringed to get a glimpse at the things lurking in the hole.

"We're surrounded by the walls of a grave," Sunbeam whispered. Then very suddenly, there was a slight motion across the pit. Quiet motion—then a pause. Then goosebumps hit the back of Sunbeam's neck. In absolute darkness, she shut her eyes. Then very suddenly—overcome by desperation, she opened her eyes, and in a flash across the dark—Wolford's blue eyes— and trembling terror flashed through her. Her most dreadful suspicions were confirmed. Then in a second, she blinked again— and he was gone.

Both of us saw it, yet neither spoke a word. And we remained still for a long moment. Regaining her senses, she remembered time was running out and tried to stand to her feet. "We have to move," she muttered. The misery of suspense was unbearable. She attempted to move forward, dreading every step. She'd walked about six paces. Her eyes squinted ahead, desperately trying to find some little trace of light. And as she groped in the dark, suddenly, after about twenty more paces, her hand fell upon another thing, dry and jagged. Then another—then another— then another, until she dare not take another step, for we sensed we'd been surrounded by many more evils. Then all at once, the Key grew warm and faintly lit. And what came next sent a chill down her legs. We heard furious whispers:

"The master wants to meet you at the place of reason.

The place of reason!

The place of reason!"

Then suddenly, we turned to find we'd met with the most hideous sight: our eyes beheld four things withered completely down to the bone. And slashed dead in the center of their chest bone, was a claw mark where their hearts used to be. They stood still, and flickering in the light of the Key, we could see their hollow sockets all looking at us with wild, hungry expressions. The next moment, they flung their boned arms in the air and taunted:

"The master's orders.

The place of reason!

Reason! Reason! Reason!"

Sunbeam could do nothing but stare speechless. One of them was feasting on a leg-bone, one of his own kind. The leg-bone stuck out the corner of its mouth, for he'd been gnawing on it while he gazed quietly at us. Another one had a head that was knocked crooked. It had a hump on its shoulder. And though the head was turned upside-down, we could still see his hungry face and teeth peering out from it. All of them were staring at Sunbeam and then one said sharply, "What are you doing here?" They waited for her reply.

"I need to pass through," Sunbeam muttered. I watched closely and so did she, for they looked calm, yet ready to feed upon us with any wrong move.

Then after a moment of silence, one stepped forward and sneered, "What's the password?"

"The password's right *here*," said Sunbeam, and she raised up a fist. "Now be gone. I've come to set a fire ablaze." Her eyes narrowed, and she began to transform. Her chin raised, and her shoulders lifted.

"Look, a little girl!" taunted one.

Suddenly all the bony carcasses burst forth in sneers and mumbles and growls. Then the one in charge said, "Surely you will die in this Valley! And you will be the cause of the people's destruction," the carcass grinned, its big head full of wickedness. "See, it's all been a lie. Your light does not exist. You've been fooled."

"Liars! Let me pass," she said. All her fears pushed down.

"Here you are, a wretched sinner, to take the place of your fallen fathers! If your God of Light lives, why would he send a weak child?" they snarled.

"No, the light is near, and your lies destroyed!" said Sunbeam. She was totally transformed now. Fully alive among the dead.

"Well," mocked the carcass. "I don't know about you all, but I've heard about as much of this stupid light as I want to."

"Uh huh! That's right, that's right," snarled the others behind him, clenching their jaws down tight.

In the middle of their sneers and growls, Sunbeam thought about her dreams and the Quiet Gardener: his golden eyes in the fire where she lay between life and death. And she burst out, "There is a light. You refuse to see it."

"Yea right! Who? Where is it? Show it to us!" said several of them. They mocked and snarled.

"Who are you to argue with such a high power? And who am I to make it come to sight at my demand?" Sunbeam said.

"You seem to think we're gullible in the head," one jeered, and knocked on his hard skull. "We have no use for stories about lamps or light. An old made up tale for fools!"

"Why do you mock the light? I have seen it." She thought of her dreams. And there she was, in the pit of Hades, speaking before she actually knew what she said. For her deep sensitivities were talking now, not her head. Suddenly, they all burst out laughing and growled: "Uh huh! That's right, that's right!" They hissed and laughed. It was then I had enough of their squabbling, and I broke forth and said, "Would you call my mistress a liar?"

"Now you best tame your mouth, Horse!" replied one of them. "Unless you want to be muzzled! We want nothing to do with the God of Light. We see after ourselves . . . on our own! No more simple tales about setting fires ablaze!" They sneered, baring that horrid mark of the claw slashed across the center of their chest bones.

Then suddenly, the laughter fell away. In a moment, there was a foreboding silence, and their sneering grins turned to deep gloom. They stared at Sunbeam with sad, hungry expressions. Then after a moment, one spoke in a low deep hiss. His bones rattled as it slipped forward: "Look at it. Look at it. The Called!" It pointed its bony finger at Sunbeam. Then all at once, the others hurtled forward. They formed a hideous chant of angry whispers: "Look at it! Look at it! The One Called!" they mocked. Then all together, they broke forth in quick sharp snips, trying to lurch and tear her flesh.

"To the bone! To the bone! The One Called!
Bring her to the master. Torn to bone!"

Abruptly, their large teeth started snipping and biting wildly
inside the dungeon walls. And Sunbeam found herself leaping
and dodging their bony fingers and vicious jaws. We could
hear nothing but grinding teeth and hungry sighs. In a second,
I bolted forward and brought my hoofs down in great force on
top of one. In one stroke, its bones shattered into a heap on
the ground, immediately drawing a hideous swarm of stinking,
green-glowing flies.

"What on earth are those things?" blurted Sunbeam in disgust
at the glowflies.

"I don't know Mistress! But we don't have time to guess!
Look out!"

For there were three more bony creatures. And they weren't
giving up. They quickened their speed.

Suddenly, in a flash, as if bursting forth from a slingshot,
Sunbeam shot straight up, then landed on her feet. The Key
was flashing wildly, and she could see just enough to slay these
hideous fiends. She had no weapons. She'd have to use her own
strength. Once up, her eyes transformed—she narrowed her
gaze on them. All fear vanished from her face as she raised her
shoulders upright. She moved quickly, with agility and accuracy.

Then, "Ahh!" Sunbeam screamed. For one of their jaws had
nipped her. Pain rushed to her forearm; she began bleeding a
little. And she knew she'd better finish it quick, or she'd be torn
to bone. All three creatures leaned forward, turned and set their
teeth at Sunbeam. Then together, they snarled:

"You will die in this Valley!"

"Devilish lies, be gone!" Sunbeam shouted. She turned and
kicked one in the ribs. And to her surprise, in one wild kick, the
monster shattered to pieces and lay dead at her feet.

However, the other two looked at one another with solemn faces. They circled around her at rapid speed. Their bones shuffled against the dungeon. "Uh huh! That's right, that's right," they scoffed. "You will die in this Valley. The master's orders. The master's orders." They circled and circled, faster and faster. They shuffled their bones and snapped their jaws so fast you could barely see them. They looked like streaks of white ghosts. Then coming at her on each side, they leapt together head first, their jaws stuck out toward her. Sunbeam knew she better strike fast and not miss. And with tremendous power, she flew upon one of them, and grabbed its big head and twisted it so that there was a loud crack. And instantly, the thing fell, and didn't move again.

But when she looked up, she found the other one latched onto her leg, sinking its big-headed jaw into her flesh like a dog. She shook and rolled and kicked the thing, but its jaws were like steel. And on top of it, to her shock, the stinking, green glowflies began swarming around us like contamination, glowing green like septic poison. They were the same color as the water we saw earlier that dripped green and smelled of fungus. We swatted at them, but they radiated a severe, steamy heat that scorched.

Her face was deathly pale, and in a second, I rushed upon the carcass, and slammed down on it with my hoofs, which cracked it in two. But Sunbeam could not believe what she saw next: while the skeleton's body lay shattered on the floor, the head of the thing was still latched on her leg, tearing at her flesh.

"Beast!" shouted Sunbeam, gritting her teeth in pain. Like lightning, she reached her arm and grabbed a sharp bone off the ground from the heap. "Get from me!" she screamed, then drew it up like a sword, and with the pointy side face-down, rammed it straight through the top of its big bony head. Suddenly, the skull stopped moving, and rolled and rolled until it stopped, face up and open-mouthed—dead. And to our shock, the green glowflies all buzzed in a line and swarmed into its open mouth, lighting the skull up green against the dark.

"Big mouth beasts!" Sunbeam gasped. She stood to her feet. Her arm and leg were bleeding, but to her relief, not enough to cause any great harm. After she caught her breath from the scuffle, she looked at the bones and figured they had once been men in the world. "I wonder how many other people might end up the same way as them? We have to hope the light exists—and find it."

With that thought, Sunbeam's adrenaline rushed through her veins. Her powers awakened like never before in the soul of the Valley. It was in that moment, I saw her for the first time, not as my mistress, but Called. I saw what she was capable of. For those who keep the most inside of them, at the proper time, usually bring the biggest change. As she stood pondering over what happened, startled, she heard a loud clamor of bones rushing up from somewhere in the pit. She stopped and listened. Sure enough, more were rattling behind them.

"They're coming for us," she said. And with the Key in hand, giving us light, the arrow began pointing left. "This way," she said, "before those beasts fall into their wicked regimes and drag us back to wherever they came from."

We veered left into another chamber of the pit. With Gilda on her mind, Sunbeam felt that even in the hellish tomb, not all was lost. At times she wanted to believe she was fighting her way through the web of some nightmare. But in truth knew her realization was no dream at all. If the evils of the first stage were not bad enough, as we entered the second stage, things got even worse.

∾ ∾

We moved forward and entered into the second phase. And she drew back, aghast at what she saw next: among the dungeon was black magic—things too hideous to say out loud. There, it became even hotter. It was a strange place: burning coals mixed with bones that glowed out from the walls. We witnessed many sad visions. There were fires along the ground, and bogwallows crawled out from holes in the stone wall to drop coals in the firepits. In the firelight, we saw shadows groveling like slaves against the walls of the tomb: Golgums and other vile things with plagues on their drawn-up bodies. And more glowflies flickered green against the stone walls, feeding upon their sores and the death. But the Golgums down in the Valley looked different. They moved slower, their eyes, more hollow. These Golgums didn't have anything to do with life and living things at all. These were shriveled to bone, like the dead among the dead. These Golgums seemed like ancients who had served Wolford the longest; therefore, the more they had altered themselves. Sunbeam dreaded to look.

"Whitewing," Sunbeam said. "We have to get out of this dungeon soon, or we'll wither away."

The walls felt like rough stone on her fingertips—jagged, grimy, but hot. Very quietly, she followed a slim narrow path, not to be seen, stepping cautiously. Then she stood still. She touched the red potion secured in her pocket and entered another chamber. Treading forward, she suddenly heard screams from the shadows on the wall: victims, chained and bound. She hesitated to move another step.

"Quiet," she whispered. "We cannot be seen."

She continued to crawl forward while I stooped as low as a horse could get—and then—she decided to cross the entire chamber. She took a breath of courage and began to crawl precisely, trying to cross as discreetly through it as she could. She went about twenty paces until she found herself in a very disturbing situation. Groping about the stone, we suddenly saw plainly the ruin prepared for those who could never escape: the victims of Lord Wolford. They were starved men, all withered and chained, screaming of thirst in the torture prepared for them. Then we looked, and to our horror, was a man in an iron cage. Guarding the door of it was a hideous beast with a large round belly, stone grey flesh and deep pits like a toad all over his husky face. The man inside the cage shook the bars, and his forehead was bathed in clammy sweat, for his soul was in the place of the underworld. And he screamed out to the beast, "Have mercy on me! Just a dip of water to cool my tongue! I am tortured in this flame!"

The beast sternly replied, "A deep division has been set in place, so that those who want to pass from here to you cannot. In your lifetime, you received your good things. All given by the master!"

The man answered, "Then I beg you, warn my family. I have children, brothers and sisters. Warn them, so they will not also be tricked into this place of torment."

Then the beast snarled, "They have their own minds! Let them use them!" And he slammed the iron cage with his staff.

Upon seeing this, awareness of evil spirits kept Sunbeam fully on guard. Under the horrible circumstances, Sunbeam continued on quietly, lest she be seen. Creeping in the chamber, a quiet sound drew her attention, and a large rat was roaming on the floor. It scurried off. Then what came next was worse: an enormous, slimy, green glowfly buzzed down with famished eyes, enticed by the smell of the fresh cut on Sunbeam's forearm. It took much work and swatting to frighten it off.

After a little while it scatted off, and she resumed her cautious steps. After about fifty more feet, feeling her way through many angles of crooked walls, she looked downward and found herself standing atop an iron-barred ceiling of a prison. She fixed her eyes on the horrible objects down below in the cell. And there, she could never again deny the tragic fate for those who followed the Dark Prince. For below, sitting perched on a throne was Lord Wolford. His mask was off. There he reigned, completely uncovered in all his hideousness. And his skeleton legion crowded around him and praised him. It looked like a secret meeting in the dark hour of night. And the vibrations of the cell shook every time Wolford spoke.

"How many more might turn and serve the same way as you loyal ones?" Wolford said from his throne. His legion stopped and listened.

"We are on your side, Master," they wailed and whined. And looking to the left of the cell was a Golgum who'd been beaten and lashed.

Then Wolford boomed, "Look and see what your master does to those who don't obey. Let that be a lesson to you all!"

And the pitiful Golgums whimpered and moaned and said, "It shall, it shall."

Then one of them, whining, stepped forward and got down on his knees, then lifted his face to the prince and whispered, "Master, somebody's coming for us, we've heard," the creature moaned.

Then it grew very still. After a moment of silence, Sunbeam did not move a muscle. She could barely breathe. She looked down, and knew that if she failed, she might be hurled into the same abyss below. In complete silence, Wolford slowly raised his eyes from the depths. He peered a gleaming, blue eye up through the circular ceiling of the cell and fixed his gaze straight at Sunbeam. And in an instant, the fires below went out, and everything went completely dark.

In the next moment, Sunbeam plunged forward into the dark abyss. She moved on in silence, suffocated by the raging pressure and in disgust at Wolford's secret arts. Anger swelled in her chest against Wolford, who'd tricked many souls. She wanted the struggle to be over. She groped forward in the dark. The mystery of the chamber swallowed her. The walls started to look blurred. For many seconds she felt vibrations along the walls, followed by echoes of wailing laughter.

"Who's there?" she demanded.

Then suddenly, there creaked a noise like the quick opening and closing of a door while a red slither of light flashed through the dark, and then quickly away. And in the next second, there moved a quick slithering motion across the chamber—then another flash—Wolford's blue eyes—then they were gone as quick as they came.

"Show yourself," said Sunbeam. There were great evils masquerading.

In the mix of it, the Key suddenly lit. A faint glow spilled a pool of light just beyond our feet enough to see. Then there came a very foul smell. The same murky green runoff we saw earlier was dripping down the chamber into filthy water on each side of our walkway. It became clear that the stone walkway had narrowed between deep, contaminated water, which was now on each side of us. One wrong step, and we'd fall into the stinking trench.

"Phew!" said Sunbeam. "It smells like something dead."

"Watch out Mistress! Look!" I said.

A look of disgust came over her face. For she'd just about stepped on a dead rat and then another rat feasting on some old, shriveled crumbs. Then suddenly, the walls of the tomb began rumbling—incessantly—vibrating the polluted waters beside us. Sunbeam kept steady on her feet. She gasped and struggled with each loud blow until she fell and lay struggling to her feet. I was still on my hoofs—the walls shaking—I ran to Mistress. And the quaking caused a small drop of blood from her cut to splatter into the trench of water. When we finally raised our eyes, what we saw next was unspeakable.

"Watch out, Boy!" yelled Sunbeam against the vibrations that felt like they shook the wits inside her head. To our shock, the murky water in the chamber began glowing in colors of green around the red drop of blood. Then we looked down and it was swarming with sharp wings sticking out from the water—like fins. The wing-fins rushed down in armies through the water and circled madly.

"Watch out! Something's down in there," said Sunbeam.

Then in the next moment, the wing-fins kept circling underwater, but exuding greener radiance.

"What on earth?" gasped Sunbeam.

Then, abruptly the things began swarming out of the water like one big army. To our horror, it was the filthy glowflies, or whatever these things were. They were daring, brazen, ferocious—their large round eyes fixated on Sunbeam as they swarmed in packs to make her their food.

"What are these things used to eating down here?" she gasped.

"I think we both know that answer," I shot back. I watched their shiny, black eyes pin-point her fresh cut. Then suddenly, the filthy things stuck out their sharp wing-fins, glowing greener and hotter, staring ravenously at her blood. In the mix of all this, the walls still trembled, shaking the tomb in steady blows.

"Horrid devils. Get!" snapped Sunbeam. But they were not easily scared away. Among the shaking vibrations, Sunbeam jumped to her feet. She tried to steady herself. Instantly, the flies were startled by the suddenness of Sunbeam's movement, and they retreated back alarmed. But this didn't last long. Because then suddenly, a couple of the most daring flies latched onto her neck, and this appeared to be a sign for a regular ambush. And coming forth from the murky water trench in the tomb swarmed a whole legion of them. All wild. They covered and stuck all over Sunbeam's skin in clusters. Once on her flesh, they contorted and turned into something different, like leeches that sucked and scorched the skin raw.

"Filthy bugs!" yelled Sunbeam. She began kicking and swatting at them. At this point, I quickly reared and beat my hoofs, but it was all in vain. They were too small and too quick. Violently they glowed, stinging and scalding the skin to suck out her life. Sunbeam's eyes rolled anxiously around. She was completely hemmed in by hundreds of them leeching hard on her. Their filthy, green bodies began to lengthen and contract on her skin, fastening their slimy suckers at the place where she'd been cut. They piled upon her arms, throat, and legs—and Sunbeam was stifled in complete disgust and pain.

"Get! Get!" She yelled and kicked and screamed at the venomous creatures. Then suddenly, in a flash, there came a light that illuminated the whole chamber. And in an instant, startled by the flash, the wild flies all fled down holes, water, and the deep crevices of the tomb—vanishing rapidly in steamy trails of green.

And although shaken, Sunbeam stood and went on with her walk toward the mysterious source of light, which came from a crack inside the chamber.

"Hurry, Whitewing!" screamed Sunbeam, running toward the lit opening.

"Careful, Mistress," I warned. And just as I said it, suddenly, a red vapor of heat filled the dungeon and there appeared Wolford's blue devil eyes, glowing with wild and hungry excitement, glaring upon Sunbeam in a hundred directions. And gasping for breath, Sunbeam looked down at the Key which pointed her to the cracked opening, and she screamed out: "To the door! No more carrying on with these demons! Hurry!"

As we approached the lit opening in the chamber, there suddenly came a sound of tortured voices weeping bitterly, and Wolford's blue eyes became like fire from all directions still glaring at us. The heat was rapidly increasing.

"Hurry, Boy! The walls are closing in! To the door!" screamed Sunbeam, trying to steady herself in the walls' vibrations. The closing walls pressed us onward until we'd finally reached the threshold of the third change of the Valley, and we crossed into it.

"We're at the end, Whitewing. I feel we're near the end. The lamp must be near!" said Sunbeam, relieved from the escape. For we were now in a lit part of the Valley, up out of the tombs and into a wide-open barren wasteland.

"Get on, Mistress!" I said. The sun was slowly setting. "We haven't much time!" With that, Sunbeam saddled and grabbed the reins. "Run, Boy! Run!" she commanded. And just as we set forward, there came a low rumbling, moaning sound. "Death!" it screamed. "Death! You fools!" And then quickly, an outstretched arm caught the back of Sunbeam's collar and yanked her to the ground. And when she looked up, it was two hideous Valley Golgums, the bony ones—one holding a set of glaring knives—and the other—holding Gilda.

"Sunbeam!" shouted Gilda. "I've waited so long!" she cried and writhed to break free from the creature's arms. When Sunbeam laid eyes upon her, her heart began pounding as it had never done before in any other fight.

Sunbeam gasped. She couldn't speak. At first, she thought her sister looked a little different, but then didn't, and she couldn't make up her mind at this point. And she couldn't speak for many minutes but thought something looked a little changed about her. After a long silence, Sunbeam uttered, "Gilda?" A tear escaped her eye. And just as she said it, the Golden Key began flashing in glorious golden hues, baring Sunbeam's fingerprint on the round of the Key.

Then in an instant, the one beast holding the knives, flipped them up, and turned them upon Sunbeam. And the other Golgum held Gilda. Sunbeam's heart was a violent hurricane inside her chest, for the sun was setting behind the crest. And she knew in one instant she must save Gilda, and in the other—many lives of Ozmandia.

∾ ∿

"The Day of ransom is upon you. Your beloved sister will go free—and you will pay for it with *your* life," crooned the Golgums. The atmosphere was intolerable, overlaid with deep crimson skies. The Golden Key flashed Sunbeam's fingerprint vibrantly. The intensity of suspense grew. Meanwhile, Gilda had been brought in, bound in chains, squirming in the creature's left hand, and with the right hand, the creature had a dagger to her throat. Then the thing jerked Gilda and shouted, "I will knock off her head and give it to the birds!"

Sunbeam quickly thought of the best move to make. The sun was setting, and seeing the blade to Gilda's throat, fear suddenly drove the blood in rushing bursts through her heart. She'd have to be strategic. Beads of sweat broke out from every pore upon her chest and forehead. Then very suddenly, Mistress started to her feet. Once she moved on her feet, the Golgums flinched back.

"Hold the prisoner!" said the bony Golgum, pointing his knives at Sunbeam.

"Let her go free!" Sunbeam shouted. "On the vow that you can take me! Then it will be well. I will keep my word!"

"Do you think we've come to hear your negotiations? We'd rather plunge a sword through you than let you even dare debate with us. The master's orders." They moaned and whined. "We know you! You are the enemy of our gods!"

"If you won't hear my arrangements, you devils, you will learn who I am," Sunbeam said, raising her shoulders.

"No! You will hear *our* arrangements," they snarled. "Turn your back toward us; then we bind you! Your doom is coming!"

"You better not touch a hair on her head!" Sunbeam said. She turned around cautiously, and the bony golgum bound her wrists with the rope. It was then I knew I had to dash between the shocking horrors taking place between Sunbeam, Gilda, and the bony Golgums. But as I set to run, my legs were held firmly to the ground by a chain of bony, dead hands that reached from the ground.

"You will fall," said the bony Golgums. "Watch Ozmandia break! Watch flames and bloodshed consume the land! Know that we will never stop till we have dragged you to the master by your hair; then waste your whole house!" they hissed. "Weak girl. The hour has come." Then very abruptly, the one holding Gilda knocked her to the ground and stepped on her chains.

"Don't listen to them," cried Gilda. "Go back! They'll kill you!" And just as Gilda said it, the one with its knives on Sunbeam, very suddenly advanced. In an instant, its withered face stretched wide and bared teeth, and it started swinging the blade in a thousand different motions. In the mix of it, the Key was continuously flashing golden hues—Sunbeam's own fingerprint.

"You have no more power," said Sunbeam, and suddenly, a great strength rushed down her body. She broke free from the rope. In a second, Sunbeam was moving swiftly on her feet. Before she could think, his blade was closing in on her. However, without flinching, she ducked. The edge of it swiped overtop her head in a loud rush.

"Go back!" screamed Gilda. "Don't do this! Go back!"

In the next moment, the bony Golgum slid forward quickly like a serpent, and had ejected another blade—then it moaned, "Murder is a messy, bloody thing. Shame I will kill you in front of your own flesh and blood."

"Go back! Turn back!" Gilda squirmed, bound in chains on the floor of the Valley. Then in an instant, the moving dead glanced at Sunbeam's chest and leapt toward it, blade pointed out. Like lightning, Sunbeam dodged to the left, but the thing whacked her on the shoulder with the handle of it. The blow was hard, and Sunbeam felt a little dizzy, but only for a moment.

Quickly, she swept her foot out in a circular motion, and kicked the thing hard in the leg. This unsteadied the bony Golgum. Sunbeam kicked it again in the center of its chest—until it toppled over—and dropped its blade. With that, Sunbeam scooped the blade from the ground and drove it through his bony backside, so the thing lay face down in the dirt. The hideous Golgum writhed on the ground and wailed, "The master's orders," until it dissipated into sheer dust on the floor of the Valley, adding another number to its many dead.

In another instant, Sunbeam was back on her feet, wild-eyed, alert, unstoppable. She moved faster than ever before. And narrowing her eyes on Gilda, she set forward to save her, and slay the other bony thing. But before she reached it, the Golgum was already cowering down and shrinking back in horror because Sunbeam had soared the blade through the air in a direct line. The dagger stuck in the dead center of its chest—straight through the mark of the claw—and the thing fell—slain in dust and ash.

In the next moment, Sunbeam flew to Gilda to cut her chains. The sun was halfway behind the crest. She hadn't much time.

"Gilda!" Sunbeam said. She held her sister very tightly. Looking at her, Sunbeam could barely speak. She had dreamed of this moment for the last five years. And now standing up close, she thought Gilda looked changed, but could not pinpoint exactly how. After some minutes, tears streamed from her face.

"Gilda, I'm sorry. I—I—"

"No. Don't say it," cried Gilda. "I already know. The hour has struck. Unlock my chains."

With that, Sunbeam ached seeing Gilda in shackles, for she had been bound around the ankles, knees, waist and chest.

"Gilda, your chains will finally be unlocked," Sunbeam said. She knew there wasn't much time. The sun was falling. Then very quickly, she grabbed the Golden Key from around her neck, and with it still flashing her fingerprint, twisted and unlocked and unbound Gilda, lock by lock. And with each twist of each lock, she thought she'd make up for every wrong she'd ever done to her beloved sister. Then Sunbeam set her sister straight up and pulled her to her feet.

"Drop the Key, Sunbeam," Gilda said.

Reluctantly, Sunbeam looked around to see if anything might come out of the Valley, then very slowly and cautiously, she dropped the Golden Key on the ground. It was still flashing Sunbeam's fingerprint in golden hues. Gilda stood upright on her feet with her hands at her side, unbound.

"Gilda, we must go now," Sunbeam said. She picked up the Key and put it back around her neck. Then she grabbed Gilda by the hand and attempted to pull her toward my saddle to make way to the mountain. Oddly, my legs were still bound by the sorcerous, bony hands. Just as she pulled her, Gilda pulled back—then stood still.

"Gilda, it's OK. Come with me," Sunbeam whispered, watching the sun fall in the sky.

"No. You can avoid this, Sunbeam. Forget your pride and accept the mercy of the Prince. Go back."

"What do you mean?" Sunbeam stopped.

"I know of your quest. He will kill you. The Prince has ground the mountain to powder and broken its sacred lamp to pieces. There is no light. Forfeit this foolish work to relight it. Let's go back to Ozmandia and live," said Gilda. A tear rolled down her cheek. And in that moment, Sunbeam was very relieved to have Gilda and go back, but in the next moment, was very worried. She started feeling a little sick.

"Gilda, I have to go forward. We have to believe this light exists. You've been in the dark so long, it's hard to imagine. Come and see it," said Sunbeam gently.

"Follow you?" said Gilda. "Look," she cried and raised her hands, which had scars and bloody marks from the chains that had bound her. "Look at what became of me for the sake of following you. For that game you convinced me to play. Listen to me this time. Let us turn back." Gilda took a step forward. And Sunbeam thought her eyes looked changed. The Key very suddenly began flashing—faster and faster.

"Gilda. I won't do this without you. Trust me," Sunbeam said. A tear trickled down her cheek upon seeing the condition in which she found her beloved sister. And she vowed in her heart to make it right.

"Keep away from it. Keep away from the light," said Gilda. "Stay with me." She began squeezing Sunbeam's hand very tightly and pulling her back. Then all at once, Gilda began invading her slowly, steadily, and started pulling Sunbeam to the ground. Meanwhile, I watched and waited, but knew something was wrong. I couldn't figure out just what. I tried to intervene, but my legs were still bound by the bony chain of hands that had come out of the ground.

"You killed me, Sunbeam. And I prayed to the gods every night in this Valley that you'd come, and that I might find myself with my sister again. And here you are. Stay with me, Sunbeam. Turn back and stay," Gilda cried. Tears rolled and rolled down her face. "And now my beloved sister," cried Gilda, "shut your eyes and prepare for me to drive this dagger in your heart, like the one you drove into mine five years ago." She raised up a dagger that was on the ground from the fight earlier, and before Sunbeam could think, she looked up and jumped to her feet.

"Gilda!" cried Sunbeam. "What have they done to you? I'm here. My life is nothing without you."

"Destroy yourself, Sunbeam. Let the dead bury their own dead. Don't leave me," Gilda said and advanced toward her. Then very suddenly, Sunbeam found herself stooping low, trying to avoid her dagger.

"Gilda! Gilda! No!" Sunbeam screamed and cried, dodging and jumping. Sunbeam could see Gilda's terribly scarred hands extending toward her with the blade. Then Gilda lurched and seized upon and tore Sunbeam's shoulder. And Sunbeam was mad with horror.

"Gilda. You're sick, Gilda! What have they done to you? I'm so sorry!" Sunbeam cried in horror as she dodged her sister's jabs, for she could not bring herself to strike her beloved twin.

"Stay in the Valley so that we may together, live as one again," said Gilda.

Sunbeam looked and saw her beloved Gilda advancing again toward her, which she could hardly understand or even think about. In a second, Gilda crouched low and her eyes looked even more different. Sunbeam felt the change all in one moment. And in seconds, Gilda was streaking across the Valley like lightning, like Sunbeam looked when she fought. And now they were really going at it—Gilda with her blade and Sunbeam blocking Gilda's blows, but not striking her. And they moved as fast as two golden streaks of thunder against each other, fast and hard! I could barely tell who was who, or what was up or down.

"Gilda! No! Without you I'm lost!" Sunbeam yelled in between ducking and lunging and drawing back and whirling around— she hadn't time to feel sad over the tragedy happening before her. I tried desperately to run between them, but I still couldn't move. I was chained. I could only stand frozen, knowing I could do nothing for these two now—for they were mutually doomed.

Then vaguely amid the thunderous fight, Gilda lurched downward furiously like a gold streak, to drop down on the side of Sunbeam, and tried to knock Sunbeam's leg out from under her. But out of the corner of one eye, Sunbeam saw it and dodged the blow, and whipped her arm out quickly to the side. Then she grabbed Gilda and held her down firmly in the dirt. Gilda now lay on her backside, her eyes gleaming furiously. But Sunbeam's only thought was to keep Gilda alive and get her to the light. Amid the kicking and rolling, Sunbeam held her down as hard as she could, but the worst of it was, she could not keep Gilda in position, for she was, like Sunbeam, very strong and matched her strength as an equal. The only difference in the two, was Gilda fought for death, and Sunbeam, for life.

Then Gilda, like an enemy taking any opportunity she could get, wherever she saw her opponent's chest or face unguarded, would strike. And suddenly, Gilda saw an open weak spot, and quickly in one strong stroke, rammed the point of the blade into Sunbeam's arm. And in that moment, Sunbeam lay swooning and dizzy—and in the shock and horror of it, was unable to fight.

At this point, Sunbeam lay bleeding, exhausted and struggling for breath. And what made her swoon even more was the fact that Gilda was still fighting her as hard as she could, and in that moment, Sunbeam sank under the truth that her greatest enemy—was also her dearest love.

In the next second, Sunbeam saw an open spot to take Gilda. She knew in that second she could kill her—end it. She went to strike but held back. For the thought of the act sent a deadly nausea over her. And her mind grew bewildered like never before. She lay there exhausted and struggling in the shadow of a memory that held her down. And over her there came a sudden motionlessness as she thought about all her wrongs that led up to the fight. And in this guilt, Sunbeam began to despair and lay in sickness of the situation—and she desired to fade away and forget what was happening before her eyes.

She could not look upon this horrible thing—knowing she would die if she did not kill Gilda, but also knowing she could not bring herself to slay her beloved. And now, Gilda was over her, holding her down by the arms—furious and sad, crying, "The day of ransom is upon you. A life for a life. Yours for mine and mine for yours—two as one."

Hearing Gilda's words, Sunbeam's sickness elevated unto misery and death. Her heart grew faint. And all her warrior strength completely melted away. And she could do nothing but lie on the ground. Gilda was in such a terrible, hopeless condition. And now justice would be served: her twin sister, rightly so, was acting as her accuser—there to set it all right, by demanding Sunbeam give her life.

"I died in this Valley, Sunbeam. The Prince has ground the light to darkness. Turn back and let us live as one," cried Gilda over and over. And under Gilda's words, the sentence of death seized Sunbeam's ears as her twin's voice grew into one solemn cry. And as Sunbeam listened, the light became darkened in her heart, and she wept.

"Gilda . . . the light . . . the light . . ." Sunbeam uttered under her breath, drifting away.

Then another change came over Gilda's face—it was very stern. Gilda stood over her and pled, "How could you possibly light those lamps?" She wore a very hard expression.

"Gilda there is a light. Let us go to it," Sunbeam murmured. She was low and weak from the death sentence Gilda was issuing her. Then Gilda's expression grew in intensity and so did her expression of hardness. Then very slowly, Gilda reached down and picked up the blade lying on the ground.

"We belong together. You did not save me in time. In that knowledge—despair and die. We'll live forever in this Valley, in darkness, but as one—beloved twin."

"Gilda . . . please . . ." Sunbeam uttered. The deadly nausea was swallowing her soul. And she felt every fiber in her body lose feeling as she ran her fingers over the scars on Gilda's body. And everything started dimming and the light became meaningless. And Sunbeam began thinking of what peaceful, sweet rest could be in the grave with Gilda.

"I feel as though I'm falling into the deepest sleep," Sunbeam barely whispered, only minutes before being slain. And she lay there reaching for Gilda as though she'd never return to life.

"Mistress!" I shouted, still bound by the sorcerous, bony hands chained around my legs. "Get up! Get up!" But my words were futile. Gilda was putting her to death.

And moving slowly toward her with the dagger, Gilda hummed, "The day of ransom is upon you. Debt owed. Your life for mine. A life for a life."

Sunbeam was awfully hurt and completely winded, unlike any weakness she had ever felt before. She struggled for breath until she could no longer fight. And with Gilda's dagger in the air, Sunbeam drew in one last breath, and went completely limp.

☙ ❧

In the next moment, Sunbeam saw a golden gleam fall on her from the sky. It was so radiant she thought it was a rising, bright morning star. And she saw the Quiet Gardener as a High King above all kings kneel down toward her. He raised his face and their eyes locked. And in the glowing brightness, she recalled his words:

"*Take my potion upon you. Use it for the battle that will take your life.*"

"*I cannot do it. I haven't the strength. Without her I'm lost . . . dead,*" cried Sunbeam, *shaking on the line between life and death.*

A streak of red blood trickled down his glowing face in streaming glory against a blue sky.

"*The strength is in the blood,*" he said. *His eyes shined in a pale mist of golden starlight.*

∾ ∿

Suddenly a new kind of trembling swept over her, and Sunbeam opened her eyes. Weak and only moments before death, and with what little strength she had, she reached for the potion. And just before Gilda's blade drove into the center of her chest, Sunbeam spilled the red potion. It splashed and spattered all over herself. And before you could even think, a great Voice boomed very deep and low so that it shook the ground.

"*I am the ransom. I gave my life to wipe tears from all faces,*" thundered the voice as it shook the whole Valley.

Then all at once, everything became quite clear. Gilda's face began to change. Her ears grew thicker and pointed out at each end. Her eyes became beady and red—then glaring blue—then the nose shrunk down between her veiny eyeballs and there were hideous, hairy scales of husk all over her face. And her arms extended and rose upward until they were stabbing at the air with rage—only they weren't Gilda's arms, they were something else—an arm that at the end, bore that hideous claw. And what she thought had been Gilda was now, undeniably—Lord Wolford. And when Sunbeam realized the depths of his terrible sorcery, a relief and strength came over her, then she burst out, "It's not Gilda! For heaven's sake! It's not Gilda!" And with mighty warrior strength rushing through her body, she stood and picked up the blade, and with the Golden Key flashing wildly in a sheen of glory around her neck, she screamed:

"May the God of Light be the judge of all these dark spirits, and his gentle Son bring a new and shining light with his red blood that speaks louder than anything evil!"

Then with great force, she slammed the blade straight through the center of Wolford's chest. And there was a second change, as the Dark Prince writhed and shrank and hissed under the power of the red potion—a great pillar of dust swept in—and Wolford was gone, disintegrated in a swirl of dust and ash.

"Look! There!" Sunbeam said. And before our eyes, was the glorious Sacred Lamp of old, glinting from the ash heap.

And instantly, standing with her feet in the pool of red potion, Sunbeam felt unspeakable hope. And there was a light blue coolness about the air and joy in her heart.

Sunbeam looked at the sky, for the sun was almost completely set. And then she retrieved the lamp. She looked as though she just awakened from a refreshing sleep. And she saddled quickly and shouted, "To the mountain!"

CHAPTER 16
THE LAST HOUR

Time was almost out. With a loud beat of hoofs and Sunbeam's head tossing, we ran, charging up the mountain. Now out of the Valley, there was another change.

"Look—there!" I said, charging upward. It was beautiful. Rushing down high cliffs, refreshing water flecked like crystal from dazzling waterfalls the color of moonstone. The light blue water looked as refreshing as the Quiet Gardener's pools. Then suddenly, Sunbeam saw figures moving steadily up the hill, so small they looked like specks against the great waterfalls. A bit closer, she could barely make out the figures waving their arms wildly but couldn't tell if they were welcoming us or warning us. We ran on ahead until the waving figures were no longer specks, but Harmon, Fawn and Plume, waiting in great anticipation for us.

"Sunbeam! You're alive!" shrieked Fawn. Quickly, they all jumped to greet us. Sunbeam raised the Sacred Lamp into the air like a trophy. We were met with many embraces, kisses, and sighs of relief.

"My Child. Well done! Well done!" said Plume.

We all stood on the mountain, happy. Then Plume broke forth as he gazed at the sun, holding his book, "We must hurry. Up—up higher," he said. His cloak whipped madly in the fresh mountain air by the sea. "It's not over—the lamp! The lamp!"

"Gilda. I'm coming!" said Sunbeam. And we ran up higher and higher to a dreadful height, but no one had time to be afraid, but only triumphantly charged. And then finally we rounded into a lush green grassy hill.

"Keep running!" shouted Plume. "Run up—up higher!" His voice could barely be heard over the rushing waterfalls. Then suddenly we all wheeled around, and a wondrous sight met our eyes. And in all the earth you couldn't imagine what we saw: glorious pearl-white clouds swept across a rising crimson moon, where the sky and stars began. The sun was almost totally set behind the trees. And the stars grew brighter and spread out deeper and wider across the sky—to the ends of the earth—as if the God of Light was calling us home.

"Keep going! UP—UP HIGHER!" thundered Plume. We ran and ran. And at the peak, an old forgotten city towered high. Tall gates stood waiting to be opened. We now stood at the very top of the Holy Mountain over the sea, which looked to be an old, ancient boundary to a new world forgotten long ago. It looked unending, grassy, and free.

"Children! We have more work to do!" shouted Plume. "The portico!"

Sunbeam rushed to the door of the ancient boundary and everyone gathered close behind her. The Golden Key was glorious and golden, still showing her fingerprint. She took a deep breath, lifted her shoulders and said, "Night is coming. It is time! Fullness of time!" And she inserted the Key and the doors of the portico flung open.

"The lamp! The light! Hurry or it's all over!" yelled Plume. Sweat poured down his face for the sake of all the lives that depended on these last minutes. Now the sun was only a thin slice of orange. And the landscape would've looked black if not for the stars that cast pools of silver. And from the top of the ridge they could see mile after mile of Ozmandia underneath them.

"Look! There!" Sunbeam said. And before our eyes, a large bronze sconce shimmered and pulsed, as if calling to the glorious lamp of old, waiting to be set afire with a great new blaze. With that, Sunbeam placed the Sacred Lamp in the candle cup. The Golden Key warmed slowly at first, but then more and more rapidly until the Key burned hot as fire.

"Light it! Light it! With the Key! You must hurry!" urged Plume.

"It's burning my hand! I can barely hold on!"

"You must!" Plume said.

"It's scorching!" Her face looked red and her hands shook from the Key's heat. Sunbeam thought for sure she'd melt under the glowing spell of the Key that sizzled hotter than fire in her hand.

"Hold on! You must! Light it! Light!" shouted Plume.

"I'm going to drop it!" said Sunbeam.

"You can do it, Mistress." I nudged her.

Sunbeam shook, and holding on through her suffering, let out one last scream of despair till at last the Key was so hot the lamp's wick caught flame and flickered and shot out magnificent bronze sparks around her until it became one huge ball of fire. Sunbeam dropped the Key. And the smoke rose up.

"It's lit! It's lit!" thundered Plume. Everyone stared at the glorious light; it began to heighten. And a streak like morning dawn began to illuminate the horizon, as if the vault of heaven opened and spread till it outshined the moon and stars. Sunbeam looked and gave a nod, for we all knew it would be a changed world. And floodlit from above, the light swept over every living thing below, like shifting shadows; every flower and tree looked crisp and brilliant for miles and miles over Ozmandia.

Then we heard sounds come below from the island, sounds of weeping and howling and opening of prison doors as if souls were being set free in Ozmandia. And a cool, gentle wind rushed across the mountain that sounded like a choir of winged angels. It breezed closer and cooler and more refreshing. And looking down on the island, the people's eyes—thousands of them—turned upward and gazed toward the light.

Then very suddenly, with the Golden Key wild and flashing, Sunbeam looked into the lamplight, and there was Gilda's face, glorious inside the fire, but not consumed. And her heart began beating hard. And this time, Gilda didn't look different at all. She looked just how she remembered her. Gilda looked like a princess before us, with a crown on her head and in shimmering garments, pure and white. Sunbeam stared at her twin in astonishment, for she knew without a doubt, it was her. Gilda looked light and fresh; then in the vision of the fire, Gilda turned lovingly to Sunbeam and spoke, "Because the God of Light lives—I live," Gilda said gently. She gazed at Sunbeam with an overflow of love. "Those of evil meant harm for me, but he used it for my glory, and to save many lives," she said. "And now, my beloved Sunbeam, you must remain in the land of the living, for your time has not yet come."

"No. Gilda. But I'll . . . I'll never see you again." Sunbeam fell and wept bitterly for her. And after some minutes of weeping, Gilda broke the silence.

"Sunbeam, know that I LIVE. We *will* see each other again one day—nothing can take my love from you," said Gilda. She was glorious and golden in the light of the gods. And looking down at Sunbeam and the Key, the fingerprint gathered itself up in a golden swirl and disappeared, for the lost one had finally been found.

"Sometimes it's not until we find what we least expect, that we realize we were the ones lost all along," said Gilda, smiling.

"Gilda. You're free. You're so free," Sunbeam cried and cried. But for the first time in five years, Sunbeam felt unspeakable joy and could hear the birds singing.

"Yes, and now you are free too, Sunbeam—and many, many others," Gilda gleamed.

Then all at once, behind her entered the Quiet Gardener, the Father's Son. His hair flowed under his crown adorned in jewels. He wore a gold sash across his waist. His eyes were the brightest of golden brown, and he was more powerful than the sun in all its radiance. In splendor and loveliness, he surpassed anything on earth, and in his hand, he held the stars. Sunbeam fell down at his feet knowing surely he was worthy of honor. He looked at Sunbeam, full of compassion and said, "She is one of the God of Light's children, who embraced her on that day she came home."

Then slowly, he turned to Gilda, "My Child, I hold the keys to life and death, and here, grant you authority to return to the land of the living—if this be your desire."

Gilda looked down at Sunbeam, and with glowing joy pouring from her heart said, "Why should I return? Sunbeam, I have tasted and experienced fuller life in the City of God. It is here I wish to remain until we are together again in paradise, beloved sister."

Then Gilda vanished, fully *alive* and *free* inside the mist and glorious light of the higher world.

In the next moment, animals came running in droves, and a great crowd of people rushed up the Holy Mountain, so great a crowd they couldn't get through the portico, all drawn and gazing at the light. The eyes of their hearts began opening as they drew near under the brightness. Then Plume, standing nearby, suddenly didn't look as grey and hollow. And his shriveled flesh plumped out upon his bones—*the mark of the claw* vanished— and the emptiness was lifted from his eyes, as well as the rest of the Golgums like him on the island. Then he flung his book away, for he no longer needed to be burdened with the tiresome rituals day after day—because he too, had been freed. And joyfulness he hadn't known in many years seeped back into his whole soul; then his spirits lifted—for rushing up from the crowd, came Sunbeam's mother.

"Sunbeam!" she cried. Her mother's eyes no longer looked defeated, but bright. "All these years, I had to protect you.

And now it all seems worth it." She embraced her tightly. And succeeding her came Harmon's parents, then Fawn's. They rushed from the crowd among the people of the island scattered for miles and miles along the Holy Mountain—a line of brightness that glimmered under the light of the new fire.

Then Sunbeam stood and addressed the crowd, "Ozmandia! Hear me! Lord Wolford—this man is full of arrogant pride—a liar and enemy of the true God of Light! I was given the power to fight him, and I took my stand to slay this demon, and having cast him out, he shall never enter this door again—if we do not permit him!"

Then a movement came over the crowd, and the fire burned brighter, smelling of a fragrant incense. And one of the people lifted their voices and shouted, "By this, Ozmandia has again come into the light!"

And the crowd sat and talked and told stories and laughed among each other. Harmon played his flute, and many marveled and danced to his music. Fawn and her indigos played on the grass; her parents even agreed to take them home to live on the farm. A joyful hope replaced everyone's tears because they knew the old order of things had passed away. Each person had a story to tell. And there were miraculous transformations—so beautiful that words could not express them.

Then Sunbeam ran to the edge of the mountain and looked over the sea. I stood close beside her. And to our astonishment, far off in the sky, a great winged-horse soared across the stars, looked down and nodded at me in approval, until vanishing into the gleaming horizon. "Whitewing, you're the best warhorse to ever live." She hugged my neck.

The sea was rising and splashing and glittering under the stars. And seeing that the Key's flash was fading, and knowing what she sought, she had found, she threw the Golden Key into the sea. And it soared across the sky. And knowing she'd seen many peculiar things through those doorways, laughter filled her eyes as she watched it soar. And it was all because of the Golden Key she had begun her journey into the strange adventures that led her to unlock many mysteries. As she watched it fly into the sea, her heart heard the God of Light speak to her like a lamp into her soul:

Beloved, because you devoted your heart to seeking, you have found me. Though I was not very far off all along. For all those who seek, will find.

Then she turned around in a flurry of unspeakable joy, and the Golden Key was gone. For she left it behind, and since then, has often wondered who might be out there seeking—and who would be the next to find it.

EPILOGUE

Since those many years ago, it's been said the Golden Key turned up in a province along the Great Northern Moors. And whether it's been received by anyone or not, the Golden Key keeps drifting, moving, weaving in and around and out of the world, calling to those who have their own journey to cross.

So if you ever do find the Golden Key, take heart—for everyone has Doors that need to be opened, and Doors that need to be closed.

Your four-legged servant,

Whitewing